LIKE
LIONS

BRIAN PANOWICH is an award-winning author, a firefighter, a husband, and a father to four incredible children. His first novel, *Bull Mountain*, topped the best thriller list of 2015 on Apple iBooks, placed in the top twenty best books of 2015 on Amazon, and went on to win the International Thriller Writers Award (2016) for Best First Novel, as well as the Pat Conroy Award (formally the SIBA Award) (2016) for Best Mystery. The book was also nominated for the Barry Award, the Anthony Award, the Georgia Townsend Book Prize, and was a finalist for the 2016 *LA Times* Book Prize. *Like Lions* is the second novel set in the fictional McFalls County, Georgia.

ALSO BY BRIAN PANOWICH

Bull Mountain

LIKE
LIONS

BRIAN
PANOWICH

HEAD
ZEUS

First published in the UK in 2018 by Head of Zeus Ltd

9 7 5 3 1 2 4 6 8

A catalogue record for this book is available from the British Library.

ISBN (HB) 9781784082697
ISBN (XTPB) 9781784082703
ISBN (E) 9781784082680

Typeset by Adrian McLaughlin

Printed and bound in Germany by CPI Books GmbH

Head of Zeus Ltd
First Floor East
5–8 Hardwick Street
London ECIR 4RG

WWW.HEADOFZEUS.COM

For Neicy

For Mom

And for my cubs,
Talia, Ivy & Olivia

Strike a few matches
Laugh at the fire
Burn a few edges
Put them back in the pile
Swing from the pain I don't want to kill
It's time to go play in a minefield

—Travis Meadows

If you're going through hell, keep going.

—Winston Churchill

PROLOGUE

Bull Mountain, Georgia
1972

Annette memorized every board in the floor.

It had taken her months to get the pattern right. She knew which slats creaked and moaned when she stepped on them, so she was careful to keep her bare feet only on the few that were nailed down tight. Those particular strips of seasoned oak had become her partners in crime. She'd let them become her friends. She trusted them not to betray her. She couldn't say the same about anyone or anything else. Still, she was cautious, because this was her first attempt to navigate the route in the dark. She counted to ten every time she eased her weight down on each of them, and stepped in a slow-motion zigzag pattern down the main hall of the house. She passed the room shared by her two oldest boys. Maybe after tonight, the constant bickering between the two of them about who deserved the top bunk would finally stop. That thought was a small attempt at making herself feel better about what she was about to do. She paused at the boys' door and listened to the slightly broken snore brought on by her middle son's deviated septum. She remembered the day he earned that lump of mangled cartilage. His father was none too pleased when the boy spilled a can of paint in the barn. He was four. She leaned on the solid wood of the doorjamb—another tested accomplice in her crime—and allowed her son's nasal breathing to break her heart just enough to steal her own breath—but not enough for her to make any sounds of her own—or shed any tears. Her tears had dried up a long time ago. She placed two fingers on her lips and then gently placed the goodbye kiss on the door. She looked down and sought out the next board in the pattern and then the next. She moved as slow and fluid as molasses. Several minutes later, she arrived at the last door on her left. She paused, quiet as a thief, and felt as though she deserved the title. She gently tucked the dollar store gym shoes she'd been holding tight into her armpit. She'd fished them out of a dumpster down in Waymore a few weeks ago on one of her un-chaperoned trips to the valley and hidden them under the bridal chest in her closet. They were men's shoes and two sizes too big, but they would keep her feet safe outside from any thorns or bramble on the forest floor—safer than anything she'd been allowed to own. She let her hand rest on the tarnished brass of the bedroom's doorknob. Still moving at a snail's pace, she took nearly a full minute to turn the knob enough for the metal tooth of the lock to clear the latch. She had oiled the hinges early yesterday morning, so the door moved without so much as a whisper. That door had also become part of her crime, but she took her time inching it open.

The baby was sleeping. Annette crossed the moonlit room, still careful of each practiced footfall, and watched her youngest son's chest rise and fall in his crib. The sight of him was enough for her to find out she did still have the ability to cry. As she stood above the crib, her tears began to swell behind the dark pockets of skin that circled her eyes. She was sure they would come. She was also sure they would be the end of her. It would be her tears. The salt of them would blur her vision and cause her to misstep, or a small, involuntary sniffle would ring out like a siren in the dead quiet of the house. Her inability to quell her emotion would be what got her caught. It would be what got her killed. She closed her eyes and took a deep breath. She was thinking too much. She needed to move. Moonlight shone through some curtains she'd made from an old bed sheet, and the blue light turned the baby's rusty-red hair into shiny copper wire. She leaned in and used the back of her hand to smooth the thin strands over his fragile skull, and then quickly scooped him up in her arms and pulled him into her chest. Her movement was awkward and fast and she almost dropped one of the shoes she'd been carrying. In that moment, her heart pounded so hard it rippled through her every muscle. She stood with her eyes closed and squeezed down on the shoe between her elbow and her hip. She stayed frozen like that until she felt herself breathe again. She repositioned the shoe under her arm and held the baby tight to her as he stirred awake.

"Shhh," she whispered with a voice barely audible. "I've got you."

Comforted by the warmth and safety of his mother, the baby fell back into dream without so much as a coo. This was the only thing left to chance. It was the only thing she couldn't plan for. Her infant son's reaction to her could have ended it all right there, but her son, her perfect baby boy, would not be her downfall tonight. Two of her sons had already been lost to her, stolen from her. She'd watched over the years, helpless, as this place had laid claim to them. She thought that maybe when the boys got a little age on them, they would show some spark of her in them, but there was nothing. Nothing was growing inside their hearts but the same pitch-black void that had already taken her husband, his father, and so many of his family before him.

But not you. Annette cupped the infant's fuzzy copper head. *I can still save you. We can save each other.*

She eased back from the crib, and slipped out of the room as quietly as she'd entered, leaving the door open for moonlight to spill into the hall and light her way to the front door—to the woods—and on to a new life.

Annette had been stealing money from her husband over the past several months—just a few dollars here and there. Rolls of rubber-banded cash, and loose stacks of tens and twenty-dollar bills lay all over the house at all times, so she was certain the small amounts she'd slipped up her sleeve, or tucked down her bra while cleaning up would never be noticed. She'd wrapped her escape fund in a red hair-tie, and buried it in a jelly jar near a cluster of sweet gums out by the edge of the clearing. She'd also stashed a little bread and salted deer meat wrapped in plastic wrap, and a wool blanket for the baby in case the weather shifted, but it was dry and hot tonight. She wouldn't need it. That was good. It meant less to carry.

The front door opened with the same oiled ease as the baby's bedroom door. There were no locks for her to open. They were there, but they were never needed. No one dared come in this house. The house stayed sealed tight by fear, and that fear kept any intruders from entertaining the idea of coming in. It also kept Annette from ever thinking of leaving. She slowly pushed at the screen door. The normal loud click of the door's latch had been silenced by the small strip of duct tape. She'd put it there before going to bed. It was a risky move and could've been discovered, but she had no choice. That latch clicking open at this time of night might as well have been Gabriel's horn. She even heard the phantom echo of it in her head as she pressed on the wire mesh. She'd never be able to forget that sound, no matter how far away from it she got. That sound would always haunt her. It was the sound of a prison cell being shut each night. Locking her in with the very thing that kept everyone else out.

Once she was on the porch, in the pitch-black shadow of the overhang, she eased the door back into the frame, and then took two wide steps to the solid brick at the front of the steps. Just past the yard and the clearing in front of her was the life she'd been dreaming of for almost a decade. A life she had meticulously plotted into existence. It would be a life for her and her son somewhere far away from the blood and anger that was her world. She felt the cool air chill the sweat on her neck and she allowed herself another deep breath. When she caught the sweet smell of tobacco and corn whiskey mixed in with the night breeze, a sheet of ice instantly formed in the spaces between her skin and bone.

No.

She closed her eyes and listened. She heard nothing but crickets. There was nothing else, but she didn't have to hear him to know he was there. She just knew.

She squeezed her eyes shut and held the baby as tight as she could. Her body stayed still but her mind went frantic. She prayed for God to make it a trick of her imagination. She begged him.

God said *run.*

She couldn't move, and in that instant of hesitation, there was no more God to speak of, just the smooth click of the hammer on her husband's revolver.

"Is it another man?" she heard him say from the darkness behind her.

She still couldn't move, not even to flinch. She couldn't speak. The ice on her bones spread to her blood, turning it to a heavy slush. The pine trees on the other side of the clearing swayed in slow motion as the distance between them and her tripled. She couldn't even close her eyes to blink, despite their being dry and cold.

"I asked you a question, woman."

She knew he wouldn't prompt her a third time. She found her voice and spoke honestly.

"No."

"Is it because I hit you?"

"No."

"Then why?"

She wanted to lie but she knew it was pointless. She said nothing.

"You know it took you almost ten minutes to get down the hallway. I was falling asleep out here."

"I—"

"If you're thinking of opening that mouth with the intention of lying to me, 'Nette, then this shit is gonna get uglier than it already is. So I'm gonna ask you again. Where do you think you're going?"

Annette looked down at her son and accepted the reality of the moment. "Away."

"Away where?"

"Just away. Away from you."

"Turn your ass around." His voice was low and filled with the wet gravel.

Annette's body loosened and she did as she was told. Her husband sat in the pine rocker on the porch. He'd made it for her the first time she'd gotten pregnant. He was shrouded in the darkness of the overhang, completely invisible, until he was ready to be seen. When he stood, the first thing she saw was the flash of silver in his left hand. She'd already heard that Colt come to life a moment ago, and now she could see it hanging there by his hip like a steel glove—a natural extension of his hand. Annette knew that hand well—how hard and unforgiving it could be. She could make him out now. He was shirtless and barefoot. All he wore was a pair of work pants he'd grabbed from the bedroom floor.

"While you were creepin' the halls in there, I saw that tape you put on the screen door. Smart. You always were really fuckin' smart. I loved that about you. Sharp as a tack." He was already talking about her in the past tense. "I knew this shit was coming. Yesterday you had the whole house smellin' like WD-40, so I knew you were ready to make your move. You oiled every door in the house—every hinge. I'm guessing you put that shit on everything so I wouldn't be able to tell it was just to cover your way out. That was smart, too, but that's what fucked you."

She couldn't see his face but she knew he was smiling. He spoke so casually that it made her feel sick.

"See, if you hadn't greased up the back door along with all the rest of them, then you might'a heard me comin' through it after you got out the bed." He stepped forward and backed Annette completely off the porch. "That way you could'a run."

"Just wait," she said, putting up an open palm to ward off the oncoming slap, but Gareth didn't raise a hand to her. He just grinned at her and stepped off the porch. She could see all of him now in the moonlight. His pale skin lit up and she could see every cut line of muscle in his chest and every vein in his arms. The light was so bright she could read her name tattooed over his left nipple—*over where his heart was*, he told her once. She remembered that same night he beat her with a rolled-up magazine for not wanting to get one to match. That was the night she decided to leave him. That was almost ten years ago.

"You lookin' to be free of me, Annette?"

"Yes," she said.

"'Cause you don't love me no more? Is that it?"

"No, Gareth. I don't." She was surprised that it was so easy to say, and could tell it stung him to hear it, the way his upper lip curled. Anger was always his response to pain. She regretted saying it, so she tried to soften it. "Just let us go, Gareth, please. I'll disappear and never bother you again."

Gareth's lip curl loosened and became that half-smile she'd learned to hate. "I am gonna let you go, Annette. That's a promise." He looked down at the silver Colt.

"Don't do this, Gareth. Find some mercy in your heart. I'm your wife. You loved me once, didn't you? You can just walk away. You can let us walk away."

"My wife?" Gareth chewed on the word. "That means 'til death do us part, 'Nette. Right? That was a promise we made. Wasn't it? You remember that?"

Thin tears had begun to streak Annette's face. "Yes."

Gareth lifted the gun and trained it on his wife.

"Gareth, wait."

"Shut up." He took another step and held the Colt just a few inches from her face.

"Wait," she said again.

"I said shut up. I don't want to hear one more word. Did you really think I would ever allow this to happen? Are you really that stupid? You thought you could just take my son, and I would let you do it?"

"He's our son," she said. She almost sounded ashamed. She looked down at her bare feet in the wet grass as Gareth pushed the silver Colt even closer into her face.

"Get on your knees."

"Gareth, please."

"Now." The wet gravel returned to his throat.

This is how it ends, she thought. *He's going to kill me right here, right now.* She would be rolled into a canvas tarp, tossed into a truck bed, and hauled off to some remote human landfill out by the Southern Ridge.

"Do what you have to do, Gareth, just please don't hurt our son."

"Hurt our son?" Gareth laughed and it was genuine. He made a show of looking around the property. "You're the one who just took him out of the safest place on this mountain. You're the one that was about to take him into those woods with nothing but a blanket and, oh, wait..."— Gareth dug into his pocket and tossed a wad of money on the ground—"... a blanket and $340 that you stole from me." The cash wasn't in the jelly jar anymore but it was still wrapped in the red hair-tie Annette put around it before she buried it. Gareth let that revelation sink in, as Annette's eyes turned to dull glass. The reality of what that fold of money meant broke any spirit she had left.

He knew. He'd always known. She'd never had a chance.

Her legs went weak and she fell to her knees without being told again, but the fall jarred the baby. He woke and struggled against her, but she didn't loosen her hold. She stared down at his tiny round face, a face that would someday look just like the man standing in front of her with a gun, and felt a bittersweet rush of peace that at least she would not be alive to see the transformation. She took strength from that and looked up at her husband. She wanted to tell him how the flames of hell were waiting to roast his bones, but she didn't. She couldn't. Not once she saw her middle son, Buckley, standing just a few feet behind his father. He was wearing one of his father's T-shirts. It hung past his knees, and draped over one pale, boney shoulder. He was almost seven, and showed no sign of fear out there in the dark—just curiosity. Annette wiped at the river of salt and tears pouring down her face and tried to sound like the boy's mother, and not a broken mess.

"Buckley, baby. Go back inside. Everything is okay."

The boy scratched at his hip, but didn't move.

"Okay, baby? You listen to Mommy now, and go back inside."

"Deddy?" the boy said, and looked up at his father. Even in the presence of his older son, Gareth never lowered the gun.

"Buckley, go over there and fetch your baby brother. Go put him back in the crib."

"No," Annette pleaded. "Just let us go."

Gareth stepped in close enough to rub the cold steel barrel of the revolver across her cheek. "You hear that, Buck? Your bitch mama don't care nothin' about you or Halford. She just wants to take Clayton, and run away. Damn the rest of us. She don't love us no more, son. Whatcha' think about that?"

Buckley didn't answer. He just walked over to his mama and held out his arms to her like his deddy asked. It was pointless for her to refuse. Deddy said it, so the boy would do it. What she said, what she wanted, meant nothing. It never did. She kissed the infant's forehead, and handed him over to his brother. The baby began to cry once he was in Buckley's arms and the bony little boy struggled to right him. He was small but strong, and kept a firm hold until the baby settled, and then finally he spoke. He looked directly in his mother's eyes.

"Bye-bye, Bitch Mama."

Four words, barely loud enough to be heard by anyone, were thunder in Annette's ears. She felt as old and hollow as the hickory stump out back that she and Gareth would sit by together and plan their life before they even built this house. None of that mattered anymore. Nothing mattered beyond this. Nothing. She prayed that Gareth would at least wait until her children got back inside before he did it. She dropped her chin to her chest. She had nothing left. Not a single emotion left to spend. Gareth pressed the barrel hard into the bush of her thick brown hair and he pulled the trigger.

The hammer slammed against the pin with a muffled

click. Annette flinched, and then slowly raised her eyes to Gareth. His eyes had dissolved into black slits, but they were different. They were wet. She'd never seen that before. She watched him lower the gun and pick up the fold of money from the grass. Annette held her breath as he tucked it down the front of her blouse. He was rough about it, and it hurt, but she didn't care. He wasn't going to kill her.

"I loved you," he said.

Annette said nothing.

"The best I knew how." He wiped at his face with the back of his hand. "So just take that money you stole from me and get off my mountain. Don't come back. If you ever come around here again, or if you ever come near my children again, then this?"—he held up the Colt—"This won't be empty the next time."

She stayed on her knees, unsure of what to do.

"You understand me?"

She nodded her head, even though she didn't understand. She felt a magnetic pull in her chest toward this man—toward this monster—but she didn't move.

"Then go on. Git." He tucked the Colt into his waistband and turned his back to her. She watched as he walked up the steps to the house and peeled the tape from the latch on the screen door. She listened to the horrible clicking sound it made as it shut behind him. It sounded different to her from the outside.

Buckley watched from the front-room window as his mother scrambled in the dark to pick up her shoes, and then watched her disappear like a shadow into the woods. He held a tiny hand to the glass and pressed it flat. He'd never see her again.

Bye-bye, Bitch Mama.

Gareth walked into the kitchen and picked up the baby from the cold stone-tile floor, where Buckley had left him, and held him until he stopped crying. He laid the boy back in his crib and sat down in the rocker by the window. He pulled a walkie-talkie from the pocket of his pants, adjusted the volume down low, and keyed the mic.

"Val, you there?"

"Yeah, boss. I'm right where you told me to be. She's comin' right at me."

Gareth held the walkie loose in his lap and stared at it.

"Boss, you there? How you want me to handle this? She knows a lot."

"I don't care about any of that."

There was a long silence. "She's your wife, Gareth."

"I don't care about that either."

He didn't wait for an answer. He switched the two-way radio off and set it on the floor. He stayed awake for the next few hours hoping to hear that screen door open again. He was sure it would, but it never did.

1

"THE CHUTE"

SOMEWHERE OFF THE GRID IN THE WOODS
OF NORTH GEORGIA
PRESENT DAY

The initial blast turned the front door of the infamous mountainside barn-turned-pool hall into an explosion of splinters and kindling, but the jam-packed, sweaty crowd inside didn't seem to notice above the music. It was the second roar of buckshot that peppered the ceiling and shattered the disco ball that got their attention. The music scratched to a halt, and shards of mirrored glass, acoustic tiles, and plugs of pink cotton insulation rained down all over the dance floor. Gun smoke and drywall dust filled the bar with a dense blue fog, thick with the smell of cordite. Within seconds, the main lights popped on. A man decked out in black tactical clothing, with an over-stretched leg of tan pantyhose pulled over his face, racked the shotgun in his hands for a third time.

"All y'all sons of bitches get yer peckers on the floor, or I swear to God somebody's liable to get one blowed off."

A room full of statues gave him a collective blank stare, but the man appeared at ease, pleased to finally be the center of attention.

"I'm not fuckin' around here, people. The last one of you queer-baits left standing is gonna have a real bad day. Now stop staring at me all slack-jawed and drop." The gunman made a sweeping motion with the barrel of his Mossberg toward the cement slab at his feet. The floor was slick with freshly spilled Jägermeister and stank of stale beer, but the patrons of the late-night hideaway began to understand what was happening, and as the smoke cleared, they started to drop, one by one, to their knees. The bar was a ramshackle building that used to be an old marijuana dry-house. It was built on a cement slab, a simple stick-frame made of two-by-fours, sheet-rock and plaster, and it made its reputation in the Blue Ridge Foothills for its complete disregard for the moral majority. In this region of North Georgia, the joint was a rare breed. The place also made buckets of cash on a nightly basis. The clientele of Tuten's Chute, or just The Chute, as the locals knew it, were mostly a mixed bag of vagrants, deviants, curious college students, and fetish chasers from other parts of the state. They were the kind of folks that didn't fit in at the more traditional whiskey bars found around Helen and Rabun County. They were the kind of folks most people didn't care to know. The man with the gun moved further into the club, as three more men with stocking-smeared faces, dressed in similar paramilitary clothing, filed into the bar behind him. All three of them moved in a practiced pattern as they flanked the crowd, and spread over the wide-open dance floor, taking inventory of the club's layout and its occupants. The main gunman bounced his stare from one set of eyes to another, waiting for a pair that would hold his own, until he found some.

"That one, right there," the gunman said, pointing to a big hoss with an oversized shaved head. He was the only one who hadn't dropped to his knees. Another gunman came up behind him and brought the butt of a rifle down hard between the man's shoulder blades. The blow knocked the big boy to his knees. "The man said get down, ya fuckin' retard."

The big man grunted like an animal as he fell, but quickly shook off the pain and began to get back up. A second hit from the man with the rifle stopped him, and this time he sprawled out across the floor on his belly. Everyone in the bar cringed in disbelief as the man with the large head began to get up a second time. The main gunman pressed the barrel of his Mossberg hard into the doughy flesh of the man's neck and pushed his head back down flush to the floor.

"Stay down, Corky, or you're gonna lose that big-ass melon."

The man on the ground said something into the cement that no one could understand.

"Stay down, Nails." There was a new voice in the room, and everyone's heads turned toward the bar. Freddy Tuten, another tree-trunk of a man, had emerged from a small office behind the bar. "Just do what the man says."

"I'd listen to your girlfriend, Nails."

The man on the floor did listen. He stopped moving and lay face down on the cement. The man holding the shotgun lifted it from Nails' neck, and gave his attention to the man he'd come to see. Freddy Tuten was every bit of sixty years old, but he was built like a heavyweight boxer. The gunman only knew Freddy by reputation, but the rumors were true. He'd always heard Freddy was rarely seen wearing anything other than a pink taffeta bathrobe with a cursive letter *T* embroidered on it. The man with the shotgun didn't believe any grown man in these mountains would be able to get away with dressing like that until now, because tonight was no exception. Freddy was dressed as described right down to the letter on his lapel. He even wore a light-blue shade of eye shadow and bright bubblegum-pink lipstick. But as crazy as the old man might've looked, the gunman still knew he was a man not to be underestimated. The rumors also talked of Freddy's weapon of choice—an aluminum baseball bat—and the things he'd been known to do to a man with it weren't pretty. Freddy stood behind the bar holding that bat loosely with both hands. The three-foot tube of metal looked like it had seen just as many years as its owner, and by the dents and dings, they'd been hard years.

"Well, well, well," the gunman said. "You must be the famous Freddy Tuten."

"That's right, and you must be the dumbest shit-bird this side of Bear Creek."

Despite the flattened nose and the distorted swirl that the pantyhose made of the gunman's face, it was clear to see he was smiling. Shotgun versus baseball bat inspired confidence. Rumors be damned. He lifted the Mossberg and pointed it square at Freddy. Tuten took one hand off the bat and pushed his shoulder-length salt-and-pepper hair back behind one ear. "I'd lower that scattergun if I was you, son."

"That's some big talk from a fella in a pink bathrobe. What if I just pull the trigger instead? You reckon that bat is gonna stop a load of buckshot?"

Tuten shook his head. "No, I suppose it won't." He tossed the bat onto the bar and it rolled off the outer edge, landing on the floor with an unremarkable thin *tink*. "I don't think anything could save me, if that's what you decide to do, but I can promise you this, pulling that trigger is the only option you got if you plan on leaving here alive."

The man with the gun laughed, but it sounded forced and hollow. He was done talking to this old buzzard. They came there for a reason and he needed to get to it. He knew better than to waste time talking. That's what the old man wanted. The gunman turned, raised his voice and addressed his men. "Curtis, you and Hutch zip-tie everyone on the floor like I told you. JoJo, you stand over there and watch this old fairy while he opens the safe. If he does anything other than what I tell him to do, blow his fucking head off."

"Hell, yeah, I will," JoJo said and trained his rifle on Tuten from the end of the bar. The man in charge reached into his pocket and pulled out a thick fold of black plastic. A few of the people being hogtied on the floor flinched when he shook open the trash bag and laid it on the bar in front of Tuten. The old man looked more like a disappointed grandfather, than an aging drag queen being robbed at gunpoint. He picked up the trash bag and shook his head again. "Stupid," he said softly, and turned toward the back counter.

"How's that, old man? What'd you say?"

"I said you're stupid, boy. Stupid. I mean, you do realize that you just told everyone in here the names of all your buddies—Hutch, JoJo, Curtis. I mean, damn, son. How hard do you think I'm gonna have to work to hunt you fellas down now after all this nonsense is over?"

"Well, maybe that tells you how fuckin' concerned we are about you and that pink robe of yours knowing who we are." The gunman tried to sound hard, but Tuten knew he'd just put a little fear in him. He could smell it on him. His voice was shaky around the edges.

"It ain't my robe you need to be concerned about, dip-shit. It's who the money in that safe belongs to you need to worry about. Who do you think you're robbin' here, anyway?"

"It looks like I'm robbing the tooth fairy."

Tuten shook his head a third time, and walked over to the safe. "You keep it up with the gay jokes, son. Keep thinking this little smash-and-grab you and your boys cooked up is gonna pay off for you. I can promise you it ain't."

"Just give me the money, bitch."

Tuten's temper was being tested now. There was only so much of that shit-talk he could take, but he kept himself in check and did as he was told. He moved aside a few bottles of Valentine's famous pecan whiskey, and then picked up a framed eight-by-ten photo that he used to obscure the front of the combination safe built into the wall. He paused for moment and stared at the picture. It was a photo of himself and another man dressed in army fatigues that had been taken over forty years ago. The sepia-tinged photo didn't even look real. It looked more like a prop from a World War II movie, or a fabricated piece of nostalgia that you'd see hanging in a Cracker Barrel restaurant.

"Chop, chop, fucker." The gunman tapped the barrel of his shotgun on the bar. Tuten set the picture down carefully in front of a row of plastic liquor bottles and went to work on the lock.

"You know," he said as he twisted the dial. "I guess it's better that you're stupid. I mean, I'd hate to find out you're really smart, with a job, and a family—kids maybe—you know, with people back home depending on you."

"Just shut up and keep spinning that thing."

"Because that would be a shame. Being stupid makes being dead a whole lot easier on everybody."

"Hurry the fuck up."

"Oh, and JoJo, Hutch, and Curtis over there? Man, I really hope they're stupid, too." Tuten looked back over his shoulder. "Aw, hell. I reckon they'd have to be since they followed you in here." All three men stared at Tuten and he flashed them a wide, toothy smile.

"Relax, boys. He's just flapping his gums. Trying to throw us off our game. It's like I told you before. Everyone knows this place ain't got no juice behind it anymore. JoJo was right. There's no big bad wolf waiting in these woods anymore. It's just this old bitch now, raking in cash from these other bitches." He turned to Tuten. "So you can cut the act. We all know there ain't another living soul on this mountain that gives a shit if you live or die. So shut your mouth, open the safe and fill the damn bag. I'm done telling you." The gunman used the barrel of the shotgun to slide the trash bag across the bar closer to Tuten, and looked around. "I'm getting sick just standing in here. This place smells like a water-treatment plant. I don't know how you pillow-biters can stand it."

Tuten didn't say anything else. He was tired of the banter as well. He stared at the picture on the counter as he worked the lock. It was his brother, Jacob, in the picture with him. That photo had been taken three days before a Korean soldier shot him in the face. It was the only thing in the entire bar he cared about, and he was sick of listening to this homophobic piece of shit talking the way he was—disrespecting it. Tuten spun the combination lock without taking his eyes off the photo—left, right, and left again. The gunman didn't notice the picture at all, but he did notice the old man's gnarled-up knuckles. Lumps of scar tissue crisscrossed all of them. The gunman wondered what the old bastard had done in his life to earn those scars. He must've been a brawler, but that was a long time ago. Now he was just an old man wearing lipstick and eye shadow. The gunman tapped the bar again.

"Five seconds, old man."

When the safe clicked, everyone in the room could feel the tension ease. Tuten pulled the steel door open and made sure he reached inside slow enough to not get anyone too excited.

"That's it. Now let's go. Fill the bag."

"You want the dope, too?"

"Hell, yeah, we want the dope, too," JoJo yelled across the bar as if he was the one being asked.

Tuten filled the trash bag with fist-sized rolls of cash, and two Ziploc sandwich bags packed with muddy-yellow bathtub crank. The man with the shotgun was beginning to get jittery at the sight of the money. They'd already taken too long. He looked back and surveyed the room. His boys had zip-tied the hands of everyone bellied down on the floor with little to no resistance, but Curtis was still having trouble with the same bald guy who didn't want to stay down a few minutes ago.

"What's the problem, Curtis? Tie that asshole up."

"I'm trying, Clyde, but goddamn. Look at this one's hand." Curtis pulled up on Nails' left arm. The man's hand was twice the size of a normal man's hand, and swollen into an oval shape. The stubby fingers spread out across it were barely one knuckle long and were mostly overgrown by thick, yellowed fingernails that curved over and hid his fingertips. The man's hand looked like a rubber glove that had been blown up and tied at the wrist—but with claws.

"What the fuck?" Clyde said. "Just tie it up, for Christ's sake."

Curtis struggled with the thin strip of clear plastic. "I can't get the damn zip around it."

"Fuck it, then. We're done here anyway. Just shoot him."

Curtis let go of Nails' arm and stood up straight. He started to pull a small-caliber handgun from his belt. "Hold, up," Clyde said. "That peashooter ain't gonna do it. Move. Let me do it."

"Just wait a minute." Tuten tossed the bag of cash and dope on the bar. "Why don't you just take what you came for—Clyde. Just take it, and leave that man be. He ain't gonna cause you no trouble. You got my word."

Clyde cocked his head and stared at Tuten. "Oh, shit. What's up with the sudden change of tune, Tuten? You got a soft spot for the retard, here?"

Tuten just pushed the bag of money closer to Clyde.

"No way." Clyde laughed. "Is this water-head motherfucker your boyfriend?"

"Nah," Tuten said. "It's nothing like that. Nails ain't gay. I just don't want him to kill you before I get a chance to find out who your people are."

"Him—kill us?" Clyde laughed even louder and this time it was genuine. He turned back to the bar and put the shotgun on Nails, but by then it was too late. Nails swung the mangled fist that Curtis couldn't get tied across the floor like a wrecking ball. He caught both Clyde and Curtis in the ankles and took their legs out with one swipe. They both fell backwards to the floor, and Clyde's shotgun went spinning toward the door. Within seconds, Nails had grabbed the aluminum bat that Tuten had clearly given him a few minutes ago, and used his good hand to bring it down full force into Clyde's left shinbone. The crunching sound and snap of the bone echoed through the room.

"Damn," Tuten said, stretching out the word. Clyde screamed in an almost inaudible pitch, and a dog barked from somewhere outside in the woods. Nails slid Clyde across the debris-covered floor by the foot connected to his shattered leg and pulled him into reach. Clyde passed out.

Nails looked at the skinny man with the wrecked leg, with no sign of mercy in his odd, oversized eyes. "I'm sorry, Fred. I gotta kill him. I ain't no retard. He called me a retard—twice."

"I heard him, Nails. Do what you gotta do, but leave me at least two of the others alive."

"Hold up!" Curtis shouted. He'd dropped his .22

when he fell but managed to scamper toward the door and got to Clyde's shotgun. He aimed the long gun at Nails. "Now who's the mother-fuckin' man?" he said, and racked the Mossberg like he'd seen Clyde do. The unspent round Clyde already had in the chamber ejected from the side of the weapon and spun like a top on the cement. Everyone in the room looked at the little red pinwheel—hypnotized by it.

After a long moment, Curtis pulled the trigger. There was only an empty click. Nails and Tuten looked confused, before Tuten let out a belly laugh that hit him so hard it turned into a smoker's cough. JoJo and Hutch, who had been frozen silent until now, bolted for the door. Curtis threw the useless long gun at Nails—who caught it—and slid further back toward the ruined door, leaving Clyde passed out on the floor.

Nails sat up holding the gun. He was still confused. "Did that just happen?"

"Yep," Tuten said, as he came around the bar and used a paring knife to start cutting the zip-ties off his friends.

Curtis finally got to his feet and hustled toward the waiting El Camino outside. JoJo had already gotten into the driver's seat and had it cranked and waiting. Curtis hopped over the tailgate into the bed of the shiny black muscle car as Hutch jumped into the passenger seat.

"Go!" Curtis yelled. "Go!"

"What about Clyde?"

"Fuck Clyde, JoJo. Just go!"

JoJo stomped on the gas and the car roared. The

car-truck hybrid kicked up a dust storm in its wake as it began to peel away from the aborted robbery. It went a little less than twenty feet down the pig-path before the engine revved on its own and the chassis jerked, slamming Curtis into the back window. The car jumped another few feet down the dirt road, and then finally sputtered to a dead stop.

"What the fuck, JoJo?"

JoJo twisted the key in the ignition, but heard nothing but a low-pitched winding sound. "It's flooded," he said.

"Flooded?" Hutch barked. "How the hell can it be flooded? We were already moving. Try it again."

JoJo turned the key again to nothing but a clicking sound, barely louder than the crickets outside.

"Did you get gas like we told you to?" Hutch said, looking back through the window toward the men who were now crowding the front door of the bar.

JoJo looked indignant. "Of course I got gas. I filled her up right before we got here. The tank's full, man."

Curtis banged a fist down on the roof above them and hollered through the back glass.

"Goddammit, JoJo. Did you put diesel in her again?"

Now JoJo looked both offended and ashamed. "Hell, no, man. I used the green handle. You said to use the green handle."

Curtis banged both fists down on the roof. "No, no, no, you idiot. I said *don't* use the green handle. I said—"

It didn't matter anymore what Curtis had to say. The left side of his face and most of his shoulder disappeared into a fine pink mist that covered the glass of the back window that Hutch had been looking through. He immediately sprayed the inside of the window with vomit.

Nails stood on the porch of The Chute, covered in Clyde's blood, balancing Clyde's shotgun in the crook of his elbow. This time no one paid any attention to the red shell casing that flew into the bushes.

"Don't kill any more of them, Nails. I need some of them alive."

Nails lowered the gun and tossed it into the bushes. "I can't do it anyway. Not with that. They only left me the one shell."

Tuten pulled his robe closed in the cool night breeze and cinched the fuzzy belt tight around his waist. He hoisted the rifle JoJo had dropped in the club when he ran out over his shoulder and started walking toward the car. "The tag says Boneville."

Nails put a hand over his eyes and squinted. "Yes, it does."

"Where the hell is Boneville?"

"Who cares?" Nails wiped his hands across the fronts of his blue jeans. "You want me to call Scabby Mike?"

"Nah, it's the middle of the night. Let's give him something to work with first. You take that one." He pointed the rifle at Hutch who had already gotten out of the dead car and taken to the woods. "I'm too old for that running shit. I'll have a chat with the driver."

Nails took off after him.

JoJo was still sitting behind the steering wheel, gripping

it with both hands, when Tuten walked over to the driver's door. The boy was mumbling. He was still trying to remember if he'd used the green handle or not.

2

WAYMORE VALLEY TOWNSHIP, GEORGIA

Clayton Burroughs listened to the message from Scabby Mike for a second time, and then tucked the cell phone back in his pocket. He had been standing in the last aisle of Pollard's Corner Gas 'n' Go long enough now to forget what he was even doing there. The Percocet did that sometimes. It made him foggy. With his hands tucked deep in his pockets, he fiddled with his phone and wallet, waiting for his head to clear, and then looked around aimlessly at the length of dusty aluminum shelves. Jars of Duke's Mayonnaise, and pull-top cans of Vienna Sausages, and Dinty Moore Potted Meat were lined up in neatly kept rows in the often forgotten grocery section of the small outpost. Clayton doubted that any of it had been bought or restocked in years. No one was going to overpay old man Pollard for out-of-date pickled eggs, or dented cans of baby formula, when there was an IGA just a few miles up the road.

Wait a minute… baby formula. Finally, a bell went off.

Clayton's eyes settled on a stack of Carolina-blue travel-packs of baby wipes, and the fog finally lifted.

Diapers—right. That's what he'd written on the note. *But was it Huggies or Pampers?*

He could never remember. He was pretty sure Kate preferred Huggies. He recognized the red plastic bag they were packaged in from somewhere in his travels around the baby's room, but he wouldn't bet his life on it. The drugs made him forget shit from minute to minute. That's why he'd written himself a note, but now he couldn't find the note either.

Jesus, Clayton, if you're going to use diapers as an excuse to leave the house early, you should at least remember the brand.

He dug around in his pockets again, pulling out the same wallet and cell phone he'd already taken inventory of three times. "Goddammit," he mumbled, and then walked over to the baby-supply section, bent down and snatched up the red plastic brick with a huff. He tucked it firmly under his arm like a football, and decided not to spend another second of his day worrying over it. He had a fifty-fifty shot at getting it right. Maybe for once he'd get lucky.

Yeah, right, considering my recent streak of good fortune, he thought. *It's more likely I'll find out the kid don't even use diapers anymore.*

Kate probably used a box of his old sheriff's department T-shirts. It would make sense. After all, he was a shit magnet. He almost smiled at the absurd extent of his own negativity, until he tried to straighten himself upright, and lightning shot down his left side from armpit to kneecap. Every time he got cocky, or the pills made him forget it was there, the pain hammered him back into reality. It was always there—always—and it would never let him forget. It was particularly nasty today. It was penance for being shitty to Kate the night before. She wanted to talk. He didn't. He just wasn't up for conversation. Then again, he never was anymore. He remembered a time when his silence wasn't a personal assault on her emotions, but an attractive strong, silent-type quality that she used to love. He curled his lip into another almost-smile. He knew that was total bullshit, but he'd become a master at rationalizing his bullshit lately. He tried to stand again, and another lightning bolt burst down his leg. That half-ass smile on his face morphed quickly into a tight grimace. He might be able to rationalize his bullshit, but there was nothing to ration away the fire that lived in his bones. He closed his eyes, steeled himself, and straightened out his back the rest of the way. The pills normally got him over the hump in the morning, but he reckoned not even twenty milligrams of Oxy could counteract karma. He pictured his wife from the night before, swaying back and forth in the swing on their front porch.

"*You should feel thankful you're alive,*" she said. "*You could've died out there in the woods, and then where would we be?*" She said shit like that constantly—but she just didn't get it. When every time you take a step the wrong way, or take a seat too fast, or do something stupid like bending over to grab some fuckin' diapers, and you feel your bones scrape together and cut grooves into each other, it's pretty damn difficult to feel thankful for anything. He pictured Kate again sitting in that same swing right now at that very moment, stabbing a sewing needle over and over again into a tiny voodoo doll with a red beard and a silver star on its chest. He shook his head.

Jesus, Clayton? That woman is your best friend. What's wrong with you?

His crazy was getting out of hand this morning.

Clayton walked up to the counter where old man Pollard was stationed on his stool in front of an ancient push-button register. Cardboard displays and spin-racks filled with fishing lures and cigarette lighters cluttered up the counter. The elderly purveyor of beer, bait, and corn-nuts leaned down hard on the counter—his neck stretched to the limit. He peered over his wire-rimmed glasses at a group of kids in the back of the store by the soft-drink coolers. Clayton followed the old man's stare to the swarm of kids. He only recognized one of them. A kid named Reggie Cole. He was a good kid, but he was being raised and ruined by a shit-bird of a father. Clayton could relate. The whole pack of them were decked out from head to toe in camouflage hunting gear with orange-shock trim. Kids spent more time buying gear from Ace Hardware in order to look the part these days than they did actually walking down any real game. He doubted a one of them could even shoot worth a shit.

"Punks," he mumbled. They were heisting beer. He was immediately reminded of how his brother Halford had been caught doing exactly the same thing by the same old man perched behind the same counter over twenty years ago. Their deddy had whupped his ass for it, too. Not for the stealing, but for the getting caught. Halford took that beating without a single tear. Clayton had listened from the other room and cried for him. He remembered his brother coming in his bedroom later that night, and telling him not to ever let nobody see him cry. He said it made him weak. He said he deserved the whuppin' and if things had been reversed, he wouldn't be all curled up in the bed boo-hooin' for him. Clayton didn't believe it back then, but knew it for the truth now. Clayton shook off the memory, and dumped the diapers on the counter. He grabbed a couple of Slim Jims, and a copy of the *McFalls County News-Times*, and slid the goods over to the old man.

"Dammit, Clayton. Good morning."

"Morning, Tom."

The old man adjusted his glasses. "Now, dammit, I know them kids are robbing me blind back 'ere."

Clayton didn't bother to look back at them again, and Pollard pulled Clayton's groceries toward him and held the diapers up for inspection like he'd never seen anything like them in his store before. He did the same thing with everything else.

"I got me one of those big funny mirrors put up a couple months back, but dammit, I still can't see a thing in it. Don't know what the hell good it does."

"Well, if you can't see that mirror from twenty feet away, Tom, I'd say you're already blind, without any help from them dumb-ass kids."

Pollard gave Clayton a blank stare over his glasses, grunted, and then rang up each item using one finger to tap on the ancient cash-resister's keys. While he waited, Clayton turned and looked into the circular fisheye mirror hanging in the back corner. It was obvious these kids had pulled this caper off before, but not enough times to perfect it. They were runnin' it slow. They stood in a mass configuration, directly in front of the mirror to block the view of the beer cooler, while the smallest one in the bunch—Reggie—came up through the blind spot. In a minute or two they'd all provide the little runt cover, while he toted a couple of twelve packs out the door. They'd leave one in the group behind to buy a Coke or something as the rest of them filed out. That part was key. It made the visit legit, in case anyone tried to question their intentions. They had the heist down, but their timing was off, and normally that would cost them, but due to the pain being so bad in his leg this morning, and the fact that Clayton liked the little runt, Reggie— hell, just because they had the balls to make the run with him in the store, Clayton kept what he knew to himself, and turned back to Pollard.

"What I owe you, Tom?"

"Can you make out what's going on back there, Clayton?"

"Nah, I can't see a thing."

The old man yelled over Clayton's shoulder, "Ya'll need to buy something or get the hell on. Don't think I can't see what you little shits are up to."

A few of the kids laughed.

"Goddammit, Clayton, I got me a .22 under here, and I ain't too old yet to show these little bastards what's what."

"They're just kids, Tom. Leave the gun where it is."

"Just kids, my ass. Kids should be in damn school, not fiddley-fartin' around the back of my place of business."

"I hear you, Tom."

"I'll comp you all this stuff, if you go back 'ere and cap one in the foot. Don't care which."

"Which foot, or which kid?"

"Dammit, Clayton, I'm serious."

"No, you're not, Tom. Now, c'mon, what do I owe you?"

"This gonna do it for ya?"

Clayton hadn't planned on diving down any rabbit holes today, but his answer came fast and automatic, without a single thought of debate.

"How 'bout two pints of Evan Williams and a pack of Camel Lights."

And that, ladies and gentlemen, is how fast the devil can leap up on your shoulder and dictate the downfall of your afternoon.

The old man got all toothy again, as if he had just recognized Clayton for the first time since he came in. "Well, all right, then."

While the old man fished the squat brown bottles out from under the counter, Clayton spun a rack of generic Zippo-type lighters and looked at the different designs. Some of them had some real insightful representation of southern culture on them, phrases like *Get 'er Done*, or *The South Will Rise Again* painted in red, white, and blue letters. Another one read *Liquor in the front, Poker in the back*—real top-shelf wit. He wondered who the asshole was that got paid to come up with that garbage. Clayton would like to punch that asshole in the mouth. A few others had pictures of fish, tractors, and Confederate flags, because that's clearly the entirety of what made up the mentality here in Clayton's home state—fish, tractors, and Confederate flags. That shit irritated him. He wondered why it didn't irritate everyone.

The whole world thinks we're fuckin' Duck Dynasty. And hell, they're just a bunch'a Ivy League pussies, getting richer than they already were by making the South look like a goddamn joke. Ten minutes alone on this mountain and every one of those peckerwoods would be shittin' in their Under Armour.

He chewed his lip, snuck a peek back at the kids, and stopped spinning the rack of lighters. He pulled one from the plastic clip. It was just brushed silver—no pictures, no ridiculous idioms, no bigoted stereotypes. He slid it across the counter next to bottles of bourbon. "I'll take that, too."

"All right, then," Pollard repeated. He inspected it on both sides, and tossed it in the bag. "That'll be twenty-six bucks." The register said $38.32.

Clayton gave the man two twenties. "Keep the change, Tom."

Pollard took the bills and inspected them, too—on both sides. Neither man said goodbye as Clayton headed out the door. He got in his Bronco, cranked up the engine, and fished through the paper bag for one of the bottles of whiskey. He unscrewed the cap and took a hefty nip to fight off the cold morning air. He adjusted the heater vent to hit him straight in the face, and watched as Reggie Cole hoofed it out of the store with a couple of twelve packs of High Life. The rest of the crew followed, all of them laughing it up. Clayton smiled, and thought about his brother again. At least Reggie wouldn't be toting an ass-whuppin' tonight for getting caught. Clayton took another sip and let the whiskey burn the sides of his tongue before he swallowed. He missed his brothers, and the whiskey only made the guilt of them being gone that much worse. He almost took out his phone to tell Scabby Mike to meet him somewhere else. Mike's message had said to meet him at Burnt Hickory Pond. Normally, Clayton would've gone out of his way to avoid that graveyard. It was too soon. But maybe it was time. Maybe he was overdue for a visit with the family.

3

Burnt Hickory Pond

Clayton had arrived at the pond first. He'd already drained the first half pint of bourbon on the drive over, and now stood in the tall, overgrown saw grass that half-covered the three headstones set in a clearing between the pond and the woods. Clayton understood why Halford and Buckley would want to be buried here. The place had meaning to them. As kids the three of them spent more time here than anywhere else on the mountain, but it never made much sense to Clayton why Halford made the decision to bury their father here, too. Outside of stopping the forest fire that Buckley started once trying to flush out a hornet's nest that burned out a patch of hardwoods near the rim of the forest—the same patch of petrified trees that gave this place its name—to Clayton's knowledge, his father had never even stepped foot on this chunk of wetland. Gareth didn't even fish the pond. He hated being cooped up in a johnboat. He liked to trout fish up at Bear Creek, wide open, thigh high in the rushing water.

So Halford's laying down their deddy here instead of a place like Cooper's Field where all the elder Burroughs were buried always struck Clayton as a little odd, but Clayton stopped trying to figure out why his oldest brother did most of the things he'd done a long time ago—and now it didn't matter. Halford was dead, and he was dead by Clayton's hand. He was dead because that was the way life had played out, leaving neither of them little choice in the matter. At least that's what Clayton tried to convince himself of at night before he medicated himself to sleep.

Clayton poured a little whiskey from the second bottle over the coarse granite of his brother's headstone and watched the liquid absorb into the stone as it ran down across the engraved letters. He almost spoke out loud to the captive company of ghosts, but the knock of a rebuilt V8 engine coming up the road stole his attention—and anything he might've had to say. He took another pull of whiskey, and tucked the bottle into the pocket of his Carhartt jacket. Scabby Mike circled the clearing and brought the obnoxious-sounding old beater to a stop by the pond. He'd been driving that same truck since he'd been able to shave, and there was more rust covering the old step-side than paint. "Scabby" Mike Cummings came by that horrible descriptive after an unchecked case of chicken pox scarred him real bad as a child. Clayton used to feel sorry for him when they were kids. People who didn't know him found him tough to look at. He was pitied and often avoided. Clayton considered it their loss, because the people who did know him barely noticed the scars.

Good people were just good people, and despite Mike's position as Halford's left hand during the past several years, that's exactly what he was—good people.

Today the leathery pockmarks that covered 60 percent of Mike's face were a bright, puffy pink that resembled a case of the hives. From a distance his face looked like a thin layer of chewed bubblegum could've covered it. His scars were always pronounced like that during the summer's high heat or when he was stressed, and that troubled Clayton because it wasn't that hot out now. Mike stepped out of the truck and took off his hat. He always did that. He smiled a crooked smile from the unscarred side of his mouth. It wasn't the warm smile he wore for occasions that involved cracking open beers to discuss how shitty The Braves were doing this year, but a smile Clayton recognized as a precursor to some sort of unpleasant news. He wondered if anyone on this mountain smiled out of just genuine happiness anymore. He couldn't remember the last time he had.

Another man got out on the passenger side of the truck and tipped a well-worn Cattleman at Clayton. He wasn't sure who it was, but he looked familiar. The man was tall and fit with chiseled features. He was clean-shaven and handsome. The absence of a beard, or at least a few days scruff, on a grown man around here was uncommon, and made him look odd. Clayton tended not to trust a clean-shaven face. He thought he looked like a goon. He nodded back and watched the two men as they approached.

"Clayton, this here is Mark—Mark Tuley. He's one

of mine." That meant he was to be trusted with what they were about to say. He extended his hand to Clayton and his entire arm was covered in exotic black-and-gray tattoo work. Monochrome tentacles of some half-hidden sea creature slithered out from under his clean, fitted white T-shirt. That meant he wasn't from around here either.

"Do I know you?" Clayton took his hand and shook it. He noticed the man's knuckles were scraped up and raw.

"It's been a long time, and I wouldn't say we were friends, but yeah, we've met."

Clayton studied the man's face, and Mark held his stare.

"Damn, Clayton," Mike said, "I just said he was with me, what's with all the eye-fuckin'?"

Clayton let go of Mark's hand. "Who else is in the truck?"

"What?" Both Mike and Mark looked behind them. A younger man was fidgeting around in the cab of the truck. When whoever it was saw everyone looking at him, he waved. Clayton took him for a kid. Mike shook his head, and scratched at the back of his neck. "That's T-Ride, my sister's boy. I told him to stay put. He ain't quite ready for all this."

"Right," Clayton said. "*All this.* Why don't you tell me what *all this* is about, Mike?"

Mike pushed his greasy brown hair out of his face, and seated the just-as-greasy baseball cap back tight and low on his head. He gave Clayton—and then Mark— a look as if he were unsure of how to proceed. He took a deep breath, looked at his truck, and then walked over to it. He stopped at the far corner of the tailgate and untied the bowline knot holding down the edge of a canvas tarp that covered the entire bed. He moved to the other corner and did the same. After another deep breath, he tossed it back, and moved back around to the side of the truck. "C'mon and take a look at this." He motioned for Clayton and Mark to join him by the tailgate.

"Grade school, right?" Clayton said as they walked.

"That's right," Mark said. "Sixth Grade. Mrs. Summers' class."

Clayton stopped walking. "Wait a second. You were Kate's boyfriend."

Mark laughed. "I was twelve years old, man. That girl scared me to death."

"Well, I can certainly understand that," Clayton said, and they continued toward the truck.

Mark said something else, but by that time Clayton could see what Mike had uncovered in the bed of the truck, and all the small talk he had in him dried up quick. Surrounded by a littering of faded empty beer cans, and lying in a thin bed of matted pine straw, was a boy about eighteen to twenty years old. He had a thick tuft of dark-brown hair, a chubby face, and a dark burst of fresh purple bruises under both eyes and across the bridge of his broken nose. He was bound, but he was moving, so immediately Clayton was relieved that he wasn't looking at a boy's dead body. The captive adjusted himself from lying on his belly to look up and his eyes were wide and jumpy, filled with fear and confusion. His frantic demeanor calmed a little as he finally settled his attention on Clayton. His mouth was wrapped in duct tape, as were both of his hands and feet. His feet were also bare and filthy. Clayton figured Mike had taken the kid's shoes in case he got loose. Bare feet made it tougher to run. He hated that he knew things like that. The white part of the boy's left eye was completely red from a busted blood vessel where he'd obviously been dealt a good one, and the swelling was still puffing up, so it must not have been too long ago. He thought about his new friend Mark's knuckles from a few moments ago. A trickle of dried blood from some unseen head wound had caked up the boy's hair, and the left side of his face was lined with indentations from where it had been lying against the pine straw and ribbed metal of the truck bed. Clayton swung his head from the kid to Mike and Mark, and then back to the kid. On instinct he took a quick survey of the pond and the surrounding area to make sure no one else was seeing this, although he knew no one was. No one came this close to a Burroughs graveyard and Mike knew that. That's why he picked this place to meet. Clayton moved back from the truck, and Mike and Mark moved with him. He took in a deep, settling breath and blew it out slowly before speaking. When he did, he spoke as precisely and controlled as his buzz would allow.

"Who the hell is that? And why was it so important to bring him here—to me?"

"He's a fuckin' Viner!" T-Ride yelled from the sliding back window of the truck.

"You shut up," Mike said, "and shut that goddamn window too, before I take a boot to your ass."

T-Ride slid the window shut and watched as Clayton waited impatiently for someone to start talking.

Mike tipped his chin up at Mark. "Go ahead, Mark. Tell him."

Mark watched the beaten boy in the truck flop around violently and grunt from under the silver tape. "His name's Joseph Viner. They call him JoJo. He's Twyla Viner's grandson."

"Are those names supposed to mean something to me?" Clayton said flatly.

"Not likely. They're a small outfit outta' East Georgia. Would never have made McFalls County radar. The old woman isn't really a concern anyway; she's more of a figurehead these days since her husband died a few years back, but her son—this little shit's deddy—Coot, they call him—he's about as mean as they come. The whole crew hails from a place called Boneville."

"Where the hell is Boneville?"

"Exactly."

Clayton was getting tired of the cryptic answers. "Mike, you and your buddy here need to start tellin' me what the hell is going on here."

"Boneville is a piss-ant little town down around the eastern border of Carolina."

Clayton's blank expression never changed. "For the last time, why do I give a shit?"

"Well," Mark continued, "this peckerwood kid was

part of a crew that botched a robbery out by Prouty Hollar. You know the place? A club called The Chute—" He stopped and looked at Mike, unsure of what he was allowed to say.

"It's fine, Mark. Go ahead."

"Right, The Chute. A big fella named Freddie Tuten runs it. It's an old outpost building that your deddy was using as a dry-house until—"

Clayton took the small bottle of whiskey from his coat. "I know where it is, Mark. I've lived here my whole life." He sipped the bottle and put it back in his coat. "I still don't even see why you even give a shit, Mike. Why would anybody want to rob old Tuten's place anyway? He's never got more than a few hundred bucks in the safe. What were they expecting to find?"

Mark tried to answer, but Mike cut him off. "That ain't the point, Clayton. I don't think you're seeing the big picture here."

"Well, then why don't you enlighten me, Mike? I keep asking for the point, and I keep getting more bullshit."

Mike stepped up close into Clayton's face, frustrated that he needed to even explain. "The point is, that club they tried to hit? It's been an unofficial cash cow for the Burroughs family for years. You know that. Everyone knows that. And because of that fact, the place carried a certain amount of untouchability. It's one of the only places still earning anything at all for the people up here after the Feds came through and shut almost everything else down."

"And you said Tuten handled it, so why should you or I care about some group of two-bit tweekers robbing a bar?"

Mark stepped in between the two men. "Because, Mr. Burroughs, if we are now living in a place that isn't feared by the 'two-bit tweekers' of the world, then you, your wife—and most importantly—your son, are all in danger. In fact everyone living on this mountain is."

Clayton was quiet for a minute as he stared at this man with the clean-shaven face. He didn't look like a goon anymore. He looked genuinely concerned. He looked at Mike, who nodded in agreement. Mike was the one in charge of things up here now that Halford was dead. It was odd to see him take a backseat to this Mark fella.

"Do you believe my family is in danger, Mike?"

"I believe if something isn't done about what happened last night, then it will be."

Clayton lit a smoke. "Where are the rest of them?" he said, and walked past them to the tailgate of Mike's truck.

"The rest of who?"

"The rest of this kid's crew. You said he was part of a group."

"Nails McKenna happened to them."

Clayton coughed up a lungful of smoke. "No shit." He hadn't heard that name in a while. Everyone standing knew no further explanation was necessary, so he looked down at JoJo. "Cut him loose, and send him home."

"Clayton, I think that's a bad idea."

"He's a kid, Mike. He's just a dumb kid who did something stupid that got all his friends killed. It's a lesson learned." He was still staring at JoJo. "Right, son?"

The kid grunted under the duct tape.

"This *kid* threatened your life, man. Once Tuten got him talking, he wouldn't shut up. All he talked about was how the Burroughs' time in North Georgia was over. He talked about how it was only a matter of time before him and his deddy come to claim it. He also said... Wait a minute, you know what? Why don't I let him tell you?" Mike raised his hands in mock defeat.

"Go ahead, Mark," he said. "Do it."

"You've got to be kidding me."

"The man said cut him loose, so cut him loose. And start with the gag."

Mark didn't argue. He pulled a fixed-blade knife from a sheath attached to his belt and bent over the tailgate. The kid pulled back at the sight of the huge blade and grunted again beneath the gag, but Mark grabbed a handful of the kid's hair, yanked his head across the truck-bed, and pinned it down.

"I'm going to do my best to only cut that tape off you, but if you keep wigglin' like a sissy, I might end up cutting off some other shit, like a nose or an ear. You listening to me, JoJo?"

A muffled consent came from under the gag, and the boy held still while Mark cut across the back of the sticky gray tape and not-so-gently yanked it free, along with some skin and clumps of dirty hair. The boy tried to talk, but despite being freed of the duct tape, his voice was still muffled.

"Now open," Mark said. "And I swear, boy, if you try to bite my fingers, I don't give a damn what this man says, I'll gut you like a pig right here." He gave the kid another good look at his knife and JoJo lay as still and quiet as a copperhead. He opened his mouth as wide as he could, and Mark used two fingers to slowly pull out about four feet of slobber-covered pink cloth. Mark felt a little strange doing it, like he was performing a magic trick, and then finally tossed the belt to Freddie Tuten's bathrobe into the gravel. JoJo hacked and licked at his dried-out teeth as everyone watched. When he could talk, he did.

"My deddy is gonna fuckin' kill y'all."

"Your deddy is a crack-head who couldn't kill time."

"Fuck you, faggot."

Clayton put his hand on Mark's shoulder and moved him aside. The kid stared at him with a teenage cockiness, pumped up more on adrenaline and curiosity than fear.

"You ain't been talkin' five seconds, and already I don't like you, but you're in a hole, son, and I'm gonna try to help you out."

"You want to help me, ginger? Then make that ugly motherfucker and his boyfriend cut me all the way loose, and then go lock your doors, before Coot gets here with the cavalry."

"There ain't no cavalry comin' for you, son. I'm the only shot you got."

The boy squeezed his eyes into slits and stared hard at Clayton's face. The red hair, the calico beard. The tan shirt and hat. Clayton saw the recognition wash over the boy's face.

"Well, fuck me, you're him. The sheriff that shot down his own brother."

"Careful, boy."

"Man, that's some cold shit, right there. I heard all that business left you a drunk with a gimp leg."

Clayton stood back and let the tailgate down.

"You got a limp dick, too? That'd be a shame 'cause I hear you got yourself a real pretty wife."

Clayton tilted his head a little, and Mike put a hand on his shoulder. Clayton shuffled it off, and put his cigarette out on the rusty flap of metal. "This is your last chance, JoJo. Shut up and listen before you lose the only friend you got here."

"Friends? We ain't friends. But that pretty wife of yours? Now, we could be friends—real good friends. I'll tell you what. I ain't makin' no promises for you three homos, but you let me go, and I'll see what I can do about lettin' her off with just a little kiss on my pecker."

Mike swung so fast that Mark didn't even see him throw the punch until it connected to JoJo's jaw, but Clayton pushed him back. "No," he barked and moved back to take his coat off. "Get this piece of shit out of there and bring him over here." Clayton walked into the soft earth near the edge of the pond. Mike and Mark each grabbed JoJo under his armpits and dragged him out of the truck. He hit the ground with a thud, taking the force of the fall to his shoulder, but the boy just started laughing. "Go ahead," he said. "Rough me up all you want. I can take it, but y'all know as well as I do why you didn't kill me last night, and it's the same reason you ain't gonna kill me now."

"Bring him right here."

Mark and Mike dragged JoJo to the water's edge and laid him on his back. His head touched just enough of the pond to send ripples out across the green sheet of glassy water. Clayton ignored the pain in his leg and squatted down next to him. "And why's that, boy? Why do you think you're still breathing?"

JoJo smiled wide like a shark, a bit of blood smeared across his yellow teeth. "Because you know I'm tellin' the truth. You know my deddy will rain fire down on this place like you ain't never seen. You know you ain't got the juice no more to stop us, and we're gonna start with that sweet piece of tail back at your place."

Clayton smiled at the boy, right before he grabbed him by his shoulder and his belt and flipped him over face down in the pond. Clayton stood and watched JoJo try to raise his face out of the three to four inches of water, but with his hands bound behind his back and his feet taped together, all he did was cause himself to sink deeper into the muck. A gurgling sound came from the water and Clayton cupped his ear. "What's that, JoJo? I can't hear you. How's that shit-talkin' working out for you now?" Clayton wiped his muddy hands down the legs of his pants while JoJo flopped around like a fresh-caught fish. Mike and Mark moved closer to the water, but Clayton held out a hand and the two men stayed back. Clayton picked up his coat from the ground where he'd tossed it and fished out the whiskey. He cleaned it off and tossed the empty bottle into the water behind him. By the time he'd put his jacket back on a fine layer of bubbles had formed around JoJo's head and his body began to twitch in the sand.

Clayton lit another smoke from the pack in his coat and pulled on it deep. He stood there with his back to Mike and Mark.

"Now cut him loose and take him home. I'm not going to say it again." He started back toward the Bronco. He walked with a limp now, overexerted and unable to hide it. "I want him dropped on his granny's front porch. I want Coot and the Gang to know what's waiting for them if they decide to follow in this idiot's footsteps. Now I'm done talking about it. I'm gonna need to change clothes, and I'm late for work."

"Yes, sir," Mike said, removing his ball cap again. He glanced at Mark who had already lifted JoJo's face from the pond water, and neither of them said another word while Clayton pulled a fresh uniform shirt from a duffle bag in the Bronco. They watched him remove the silver McFalls County Sheriff's badge from his chest and pin it to the clean shirt and then put it on.

"Clayton," Mike said. "The sit-down with Florida. We talked about it. Remember?"

Clayton rubbed the bridge of his nose, and then looked

out toward the three headstones in the clearing. Mike and Mark looked, too. He felt the headache coming, and he scratched at his beard.

"Clayton?"

"Just set it up, Mike. I'll be there."

"All right, then."

Clayton never turned back around to face them, but he stood there staring out at those slabs of granite for another minute or so until his hands stopped shaking. Then he climbed behind the wheel of the Bronco and disappeared down the mountain.

"Who did that remind you of?"

Mark took off his hat and knocked a little dirt from it. "I must admit, Mike. I didn't think he had it in him."

"Well, Halford did. If you ask me, I think it's why he hated Clayton so much."

"Because he had just as much Gareth Burroughs in him as Hal did?'

"No. Because he had more."

Mark rolled JoJo onto his back. "Well, I'll be damned. I think I had Clayton all wrong. Come here and look at this."

Mike leaned down and looked into the boy's lifeless eyes. He reached down and moved JoJo's head from side to side, and then sank his own chin into his chest. "Well, shit." He stood and grabbed the tape between JoJo's ankles, and with Mark's help, they tossed the body into the back of the truck. T-Ride looked through the window with significantly less bravado. He'd never seen a dead body before. Mark gave the kid a nod. T-Ride nodded back and tried to toughen up his expression, but couldn't, and turned away. Mike was right. The kid *wasn't* ready for *all this*. Mark flipped the tailgate up and immediately forgot about the dead problem lying in the back of the truck. "I still can't believe little Kate Farris ended up house-wifin' to a Burroughs."

Mike chuckled. "Kate ain't nobody's housewife, Mark." He walked around to the back of the truck to tie down the corners of the tarp, and lowered his voice to keep out of earshot from T-Ride. "You heard about the Federal that came knocking last year, right? The one that gave Clayton that limp. The one that nearly punched his clock?"

"Yeah, Agent Jolly, or some shit like that. Last I heard he was MIA."

"His name was Holly. Simon Holly. He was an ATF agent."

"Was?"

Mike smiled.

"You killed a Fed?"

"No, sir. It wasn't me. Your girl did it. She insisted she be the one."

Mark pulled the tarp tight. "No shit?"

Mike cinched off the knot. "Welcome home, Mark."

4

CRIPPLE CREEK ROAD

Kate Burroughs stared out the window above the kitchen sink that looked out over a small, dried-up cornfield. The field gave way to a massive expanse of sugar maple and yellow pine, with the occasional Jiffy-Pop burst of dogwood blooms scattered wild. The pink and white flowering this time of year allowed the Georgia state tree to show its utter disregard for the autumnal equinox. Like most of the people that lived in the foothills of McFalls County, the Dogwood tree did whatever it damn well pleased, but Kate barely noticed the flowers or the dogwoods anymore. On most mornings she fixated on a jagged stump that used to be a thirty-foot magnolia tree that loomed over the far corner of the pasture. She'd loved that tree. She used to sit in the shade of its waxy green leaves for hours during the summers before Eben was born. She read almost every book she owned under that tree. She'd read in the afternoons, and then collect the pearly white blooms for centerpieces on the kitchen table.

They made the house smell clean and sweet, like honeysuckle after the rain. She could still picture the clothesline tied high to the trunk that led all the way up to the front porch. She'd even talk to that stupid tree sometimes, mostly about someday becoming a mother, while she hung clean linens to dry in the breeze. She wanted to be a mother so bad back then, but now that she was, that magnolia wasn't around anymore to see it. She cried the day she cut it down. A fungal rot had begun to cover the tree—a fuzzy gray cancer too far-spread to try and stop. At seven months pregnant, Kate spent an entire day cutting it down with a homemade pole-saw and an old rusted chainsaw she'd never even touched before that day. With every limb that fell to the ground, her heart broke a little more. That's how it was sometimes. No massive blow from an axe, just a series of little daggers and cuts that left her a sobbing mess in the heat where there used to be shade.

It had been a hard year. Right about the time Kate noticed the rot in her favorite tree, her husband, Clayton, was nearly shot to death while working a case involving his gangster family. By the time he'd recovered enough for Kate to bring him back home from the Trauma Center in Atlanta, Clayton was just as much a hollow husk as her sweet magnolia. When the thumb of God gets pressed into the earth, it takes everything. Not even the trees are spared.

The saying goes, if something doesn't kill you, it makes you stronger, but the past year had taught Kate better than that. Just because something doesn't kill you, doesn't necessarily mean it makes you anything at all. Sometimes this world can summon up just enough meanness to beat you to the brink of death, but you don't die. You move on, and you recover. That recovery isn't the result of some newly imagined inner strength, it's just the stubborn refusal to feel any more pain. What doesn't kill you, makes you numb, was more true to the point.

The tree was dead. She salted the stump. She moved on.

Kate opened the window and pulled in a deep breath of mountain air through her nose. She turned on the faucet and waited for the well water to run hot. The air outside was cool but not cold, and the breeze helped expand the room—pushing back the walls that seemed to be moving in closer as each day passed. She glanced around the property until her eyes settled on the empty patch of gravel next to her Jeep. Clayton was gone again before sunrise. It was getting more and more frequent, as he was better able to get around. She'd been a sheriff's wife for nearly twelve years, but it felt like she saw less of him now than she did then—before he was injured—before he became a father.

Sort of became a father, she almost said aloud.

She could feel the daily twinge of resentment kicking in early, so she decided to make some coffee to combat it. Coffee could beat back anything if you drank enough of it. Using the scalding hot water from the sink, she poured it over some fresh-ground beans and let the hot liquid steep in the pot. The smell of her favorite vice mixed with the breeze and helped push back the walls even further. She drank her coffee with a heavy dollop of fresh cream from Harper's farm down the road, and looked at the Kit-Cat clock on the wall. She had about ten minutes left before the day stopped being about her. She looked at the note Clayton had left hanging on the refrigerator door explaining that he was headed out to Pollard's Corner for a few things they didn't need. His latest reason for disappearing while his family slept. She sipped her coffee and covered the silver star logo of the McFalls County Sheriff's Department with both hands. That mug had sat on Clayton's desk in the den every day since he'd taken the oath. It used to mean something to him. Now it was just another cup in the kitchen.

Clayton had defined himself as a good sheriff—a good man and husband. The only good son born of a crooked tree. Kate had defined herself as the wife of that good man. She was content with that. *They* were content with that, but now she wasn't sure he was any of that—not anymore. And that blue ceramic mug in her hand did nothing but fill her with resentment.

She took another mug from the cabinet, a plain white one, and dumped her coffee from one cup into the other. She sipped it again. It tasted better. For Kate, things were mostly that simple. If your coffee cup is the problem, pour it into another cup and move on, problem solved. There was no point in ever thinking on it again. Clayton was the exact opposite, he held onto everything. He hoarded guilt and pain the way some people did magazines and newspapers until it just became part of the everyday landscape. For over a decade she'd watched all the violence and depravity that rolled down the mountain pile up square on his back. Only now, after what had happened, he barely had the legs to stand and support the weight. She shook her head and felt guilty for being so resentful and dismissive about Clayton's condition. She didn't want to feel like this today. He lost a lot and she understood that, but life was moving in fast forward and the wound wasn't healing. She was getting tired of waking up to an empty bed and a cold house, instead of a morning kiss and a sleepy smile from the man that used to adore her.

She crossed the kitchen to the front door and picked up the walking stick she had made for Clayton after he got injured. It was a seasoned length of hickory that she hoped would make a suitable replacement for the badge, but it had stayed in the crook by the front door since the first day she'd brought it home. She had been the only one to ever touch it. It was almost part of her daily routine to pick it up from where the morning breeze caused it to slide down the wall to the hardwood floor. He said he didn't need to walk with a cane. It made him look weak. She wanted to tell him that being a drunk made him look weak, not an old stick. She leaned it back against the wall beside the door.

She'd thought about leaving him. She thought about that a lot lately. Especially after a good old-fashioned shouting match like the one they had last night. She'd forgotten what it was even about. It didn't matter. It was the same fight over and over now, and it always ended the same way. She would go to bed early, but leave the door unlocked. She'd hide beneath the quilts and blankets and wait for the knob to turn, followed by an unspoken apology, and his warm breath on her neck, but more often than not, she waited in vain. While she lay alone in the dark, waiting for some elusive revelation that would miraculously transform her husband back into the man he used to be, Clayton would be purposely banging cupboards, and pacing the kitchen like a caged animal waiting for the same transformation to happen to her. Neither of them ready to admit the real damage being done to them wasn't in the war, but in the waiting. Those hours of silence that follow the shouting is when the real madness sets in, and the devil got to get his licks in.

Kate sipped at her improved coffee again and looked out at the empty gravel space in front of the house. "Okay, Kate. Stop," she said. "That's enough." This wasn't going to be the kind of day she saw it becoming. It wouldn't be fair to anyone. She closed her eyes, and shook her head defiantly, as if she could physically shake the melancholy off her like a heavy blanket, and then she spent the next few minutes heating up Eben's bottle under the still-running hot water. Fifteen years together wasn't about to unravel because of the last one. They'd get through this. They had to. She had to believe it because it wasn't just about the two of them anymore. And as if on cue, Kate heard the first sounds of rustling from Eben's room.

Seconds later she heard her son's first cry of the day. She smiled, and all the resentment she'd spent the morning building up vanished—just like that.

Kate and Clayton had been trying to become parents for nearly half their marriage and had almost given up. Hell, they had given up. Babies don't come easy to forty-year-old couples, and they both knew it. Eben, being conceived and born on this mountain, was living proof that miracles can still happen even in a place that doesn't deserve them. That rosy-cheeked baby boy, now lying on his back in the den like a turtle trying his best to figure out the mystery of his feet, kept Kate from dwelling on any single regret or bad decision in her life. If the past year had been a tragic disaster movie, then Eben Burroughs was the happy Hollywood ending. She wished Clayton would figure that out. The key to a happy ending was knowing when to roll the credits before the next tragedy struck, but how many miracles was she allowed? Two would have to be enough.

She finished warming the bottle of milk under the hot water from the faucet and sprayed a warm stream on her wrist to test the temperature.

"You ready to eat, little boy?"

Eben grunted, and Kate melted. That's about all it took.

She scooped the infant up off the floor and wrapped him in a red wool blanket she'd crocheted while she was pregnant. She carried the baby outside to the porch swing and stood for a moment in the warming sunlight before settling down on the pine slats of the swing to feed her son. From the porch, the mountain was beautiful—all greens and blues, with an ever-present halo of clouds that made the summit both ominous and majestic. She used to love this place, but these days it felt more and more like just a cold rock. Eben was indifferent. He made for the bottle. He was cranky and ready to eat. He reminded her of his father right then, and she was surprised by the disgust she felt.

"*Men*," she whispered. *So needy. So obtuse.* She was projecting. Clayton might have been lost, but Eben was right here. He still had her. She eased back and forth on the swing and stared absently into the cornfield. A song-bird was nesting in the head of a scarecrow. Eben greedily sucked at his bottle, spilling warm milk down his chin and soaking the red wool. The mama bird was feeding her babies as well. Kate had seen that bird a few times before. She watched the fledglings and listened to them squawking. It was as loud as thunder, spoiling the serenity of the moment. She wrapped her own blanket a little tighter around her shoulders, and wondered what else could rob her of the morning. She leaned her head back and closed her eyes—right before the phone rang.

Of course.

She gently pulled the bottle from the boy's tiny suck-ing lips and hushed away his distress. "Sorry, buddy. We got to go find out what new reason your father has for not coming home." She knew it would be Clayton, calling to explain why he wasn't coming back any time soon. She was sure it would be something foolish and irrelevant.

It always was, but it didn't matter to Kate if the world was on fire. Nothing was more important than the boy in her lap waiting to touch his father's face, or tug on his beard. With Eben balanced on her hip, she made her way back to the kitchen and picked up the phone.

"Husband."

"Hey, baby. Listen…"

"I know," she said. "You got to work and decided they could do without you and you're headed straight home." She regretted voicing that fantasy as it rolled out of her mouth because of the coming letdown.

"Well, no."

You asked for it, Kate.

"I had a little business out by Burnt Hickory this morning, but I'm headed in now."

"A little business," she repeated flatly.

"Yeah, nothing to it. Just wanted you to know I was out there." He paused.

"Kate."

"You don't need my permission to keep beating yourself up."

"Kate, I'm not trying—"

"No, Clayton, you're not. You're not trying."

"C'mon, Kate."

"C'mon, Kate, what? How many times do I have to do this? I'm not having this conversation again. You want to go get drunk, and wallow in your own self-pity? Go. Just don't bother me with it. I just don't have it in me today to care."

"I'm not drinking."

"I don't care."

"What the fuck, Kate?"

He was drinking. He never cussed her without whiskey in his blood. He said something else, but Kate was already tuning out. She looked at the Kit-Cat clock hanging on the wall by the dining room table. She counted ten clicks of its pendulum tail, and shook her head in disgust. She closed her eyes, and leaned her head back against the wall. She wanted to scream, but this tired argument had scabbed over months ago, and at this point they were just picking at the scar, and then it just came out. "I love you, Clayton, but maybe you and I should take some time." She lifted her head up off the wall, surprised at herself for saying something like that so easily—something so finite—so casually cold and honest.

"What the hell does that mean, Kate?"

"You're the detective, Clayton. Figure it out."

"Let me get this straight."

Here we go, Kate thought, and shifted Eben to her other hip.

"I call you to tell you my whereabouts, like you insist that I do, and you tell me you need time? I can't catch a break. I don't call and I'm an asshole. I do call and I'm an asshole. I can't win with you."

"There's isn't supposed to be a winner when it comes to your family, Clayton. Why is that so hard for you to understand?"

Silence flooded the line as both husband and wife

waited for the other one to say the right combination of words to undo the damage being done, but the cream was in the coffee. There weren't any right words. Nothing but the clicking sound of that Kit-Cat clock's tail filling the tiny kitchen.

Tick-tock, tick-tock.

That black plastic tail might as well have been a timer counting down to the next series of hateful words and wrong turns that would widen the great divide. When Clayton finally broke the silence she didn't even hear what he said. His tone was belligerent, and that was enough. She hung up—hard—and then lifted Eben off her hip. The phone rang again and again. She let it. She walked back outside, letting the door slam behind her. She heard the walking stick slide down the wall and hit the floor. She let it lie. The phone stopped ringing by the time she had settled back out on the porch and so she finished feeding her son. She kept her eyes on his face, and off the magnolia stump and the scarecrow. She stared at the boy, while her brain cycled from calm to angry, to profoundly sad, and then eventually back to angry. She burped the baby and was just about to stand up, to walk off her mood, when the phone rang again. She knew nothing she had to say at this point would be productive. He was going to want to prove his point, to argue his case. That's what he did when he drank. Voices would rise, they'd talk over each other, and soon they'd be acting like two people she didn't even recognize.

She went in the house anyway.

When she put her hand on the receiver, she paused and tried to will it to stop ringing. She could just go back out on the porch, or get in her Jeep and drive—anywhere. Anywhere but here, but she didn't. Despite what she'd said, she wasn't really ready to give up. She refused to believe they were completely broken—yet. So she snatched the phone off the cradle.

"What, Clayton? What do you want? I'm not going to do this—"

She knew before she finished her sentence that it wasn't Clayton on the line.

"Hi, Kate? It's Mark. How you been?"

5

"Yeah, baby. I'll be home late tonight."

Bob Kane pressed the phone to his ear with his shoulder as he paid the convenience store clerk for the bag of ice. "Yeah, I know. I swear, that goddamn new kid, Pooler, keeps jacking up the system down here and there's no one else can fix it." He laid a ten on the counter and stuffed his wallet back in his pants. "You're damn right, I deserve a raise. These ports would all go to shit if they didn't have me around to keep them runnin'. How was your treatment today?"

The kid with his hair pulled back in a man-bun, rang up the ice and handed Bob his change. Bob hoisted the sweating plastic bag onto his shoulder and fumbled to grab the money and keep the phone to his ear. "I'm sorry, baby, but the doctors are right about this. You gotta hang in there." Bob dropped a quarter back on the counter and it bounced to the floor. The kid with the bun smirked. Bob stuffed the rest of the cash into his pocket and then held the phone to his chest, ignoring what his wife was saying.

"What the fuck kinda hair-do is that?"

The kid just kept smirking. Bob shook his head, and put the phone back to his ear.

"What?" he said. "No, no, I didn't say anything about your hair. It doesn't bother me at all. I like the wig. You know that."

He didn't see the kid give him the bird as he left the store. That was probably a good thing.

After spending a few more minutes on the phone with his wife under the fluorescent lights of the storefront, he tapped the phone and ended the call.

"It never ends," he mumbled to a man walking into the store, and re-situated the ice on his shoulder. He walked across the lot, waited for a break in the traffic, and then hustled across the four-lane highway back to the motel.

Once he'd made it across the blacktop, he cut across a Denny's parking lot and tried to remember a time when he wasn't serving at the whim of some woman. His mother passed away last year, and although he'd never admit to it out loud, he was relieved. He'd spent every day since his father died in 2002 being that woman's on-call do-boy. It was no wonder his dad checked out early at fifty-three. His mother had whittled the man down to a nub. Now his wife was sick, and ever since the day they found the lump, she'd expected him to be at her beck and call, morning, noon, and night. He and Kelly hadn't even got it on in almost a year, mostly due to the chemo. She was tired all the time. But to be honest, even before she got sick the sex was as cold and emotionless as a tax audit. No one would blame him for stepping out.

For stepping out on my sick wife, he thought, and almost laughed out loud. *Who am I kidding?*

Of course they would blame him. Everyone would hate him.

Everyone except Penny.

She understood how tough he had it, and she had the means to push Kelly and all her medicine bottles and doctor visits right out of his mind, at least for tonight. After he picked up the damn ice, anyway. Of all the rat-trap motels located off the ports, Bob had to pick the only one with—not one—not two—but three—busted ice machines. That skank at the front desk with a mustache thicker than his could've told him that when he checked in, but whatever.

Chicks with mustaches and guys with hair-buns. The world is going straight down the shitter.

Bob wiped at the sweat on his balding head, and rounded the corner of the motel.

Room 104. Penny. Finally.

He reached into the pocket of his khakis for the key card and then stopped cold. He didn't need the key. The door was already slightly open. He'd told Penny to dead-bolt it behind him when he left. This wasn't the worst part of the city, but why invite trouble?

Women expect you to wait on their every whim, but can't follow an order as simple as locking a damn door.

He grabbed the doorknob as a rush of panic hit him. Maybe Kelly found out about Penny and followed him there. Maybe she was sitting inside with that ridiculous wig on. The mind of a cheater was always on the defensive.

No way, he decided, and pushed the door open wide.

"Penny?" Bob looked around the empty square box of a room. "Penny?" he said again, sounding a little more concerned. "Baby, I'm back." The purple crushed-velvet comforter was still made up tight across the bed like it was when they'd arrived. He half expected to see Penny already laid out across it, wearing that black lacy number he'd bought her, but he could still bounce a quarter off that queen-size mattress. It hadn't been touched. He set the bag of ice on a small table and the condensation immediately began to pool and drip onto the carpet.

The TV was off.

He knew for a fact he'd turned it on before Penny started bitching about the ice. She knew Bob liked ESPN muted in the background when they got down to business. She thought it was because he liked a light on so he could see her, and that was part of it, but it was mainly to give him something other than her taut little body to focus on. Without something to distract him, he would barely last through the foreplay.

"Penny?" he said a third time. His voice was loud and impatient.

When the toilet flushed, Bob relaxed. *Game on*, he thought and grinned.

"Damn, girl. You scared me. You left the door wide

open. I thought somebody done come in here and stole you away." Bob turned and pulled a fifth of Bacardi Silver and a plastic bottle of club soda from a paper bag. The faucet in the bathroom cut on. "No need to get too clean in there," he said, and dumped two fat limes onto the counter from another bag. "Because you're fixing to get real dirty." He tore open the bag of ice, ignoring the wet mess it left on the table, and dropped a couple cubes into the motel-provided plastic cups. He poured the rum strong and added the soda water. "I got you all set up, girl. Whenever you're ready." Bob fumbled through the bag for the knife he'd brought to cut the limes. The sound of rushing water from the bathroom sink stopped and the door opened.

"Well, thank you, Bob, but I'm more of a bourbon girl, so I think I'll pass."

Bob spun around when he heard the voice that wasn't Penny's. He held the small paring knife in one hand and a ripe green lime in the other.

"Damn, Bob. I drive all the way down here to see you, and you pull a knife on me?"

The tall, pale-skinned woman smiled, unbothered by the small knife despite what she said, and finished drying her hands with one of the motel's small hand towels. Confusion danced across Bob's face like a chorus line. The tall woman's smile flashed and showed off a set of snow-white teeth, polished to a high gleam. She furrowed her brow and crossed her arms, and then spoke with the tone of a kindergarten teacher. "Would you mind putting that away, Bob? It's making me a little uncomfortable."

She tossed the damp towel onto the bed. Bob Kane looked down at the two-inch paring knife in his hand as if he were unaware of what it was, and then shook his head rapidly like he were trying to prompt himself awake after nodding off.

"Vanessa?" He spoke the woman's name like a question.

Vanessa put her slender clean hands on her hips. "Bob, seriously, the knife."

Bob slapped the knife down on the counter next to him, as if it had suddenly become scalding hot, but still held onto the lime, squeezing it like a baseball.

"What the hell are you doing here, Vanessa? Where's Penny?"

Vanessa was wearing a white pantsuit and had thick black hair she wore in a long, messy tangle down the length of her back. She pulled the tuft of hair over one shoulder of her suit, and then sat on the edge of the bed. She smoothed out the velvet cover with both hands, and then leaned back to rest on them. Without looking up, she answered. "Penny? You mean the young girl you were shacking up with tonight? She had to go. I'm sorry, Bob. I'm sure that's a real stinger."

Bob watched as the woman continued to rub at the purple velvet and then cross her legs. He watched her lean back further on her hands and get comfortable. Comfortable on the bed he'd paid for. Bob squeezed the lime tighter and pointed it at his uninvited guest.

"Just what the hell is going on here, Vanessa? Why are you here, and what the hell did you do to Penny?"

Vanessa looked offended. "Do? We didn't *do* anything to the girl. She left. What can I tell you?"

"We?" Bob said, and suddenly felt unbalanced. He abandoned all thoughts of the pretty young waitress.

"Of course *we*, Bob. You don't think I'd come to a strange man's motel room in the middle of the night without someone to look after my best interests?"

Bob, still clutching the lime, looked nervously around the empty room, before letting his eyes linger on the bathroom.

Vanessa turned to look at the door behind her as well, and then back to Bob. "There's no one in the room but us, Bob. I assured my associates that you were a man of reason and that we could work this out. I asked them to stay outside."

Bob relaxed a bit, and finally set the lime down next to the knife. "Look, Vanessa. I don't know exactly what it is you want from me, but you can't just bust in here and start acting like we're old friends. I barely even know you."

Vanessa stood up, brushed at the back of her legs, and took a seat at a small table by the wall. Bob noticed for the first time a stack of papers on the table next to the Knight's Inn channel guide. Vanessa slid them over toward the other chair. "I was under the impression, from the last time we spoke, that you did know exactly what I wanted from you, and you were willing to take the appropriate steps to get to know me a lot better."

"Well, lady, your impression was wrong. You asked me to falsify documents in the shipping computers. I told you I'd see what I could do. I took a look at it, and the risk wasn't worth the reward. I'm sorry, sweetie, but I can't help you."

"No, sweetie," Vanessa repeated the sentiment with disgust, "we had an arrangement."

"You're wrong about that, too. We have never had an arrangement. I had a small operation going that only a few people knew about, and it wasn't something I was real happy about to begin with. I'd still like to know how you found out in the first place. I need to plug that leak."

"It doesn't matter," Vanessa said casually, and studied the tips of her French-manicured fingernails.

"The hell it don't, but the point here is, moving a few can numbers around is one thing, but what you're asking is an entirely different ballgame. Too much oversight. I can't cover that kind of heat, so like I said before, I can't help you."

"Yes, Bob, you did say that already. I just don't think you understand the unique position you're in. I still believe you can be a big help to me."

"Goddamn, lady, are you deaf? I don't know you, and I don't owe you shit." Bob motioned toward the papers on the table. "So I suggest you listen closely to what I'm saying, and take whatever that is and hit the road." Bob crossed his arms and leaned back on the Formica counter, and then gave Vanessa a good once-over. Up until now, they had mostly just communicated by phone. She was a beautiful woman. Her eyes were huge and icy blue. They set sad at the edges, and burned with a quiet intensity. Her skin was so pale it shimmered like brushed pearl under her expensive tailored suit. She was a major step up from Penny, and light-years above the wife, but something in her eyes was just—off. There was a coldness in them that made Bob restless and uneasy. She must've been very aware of the effect they had, because she burned those eyes straight into him with all the heat of a blowtorch. She uncrossed her legs and spread them apart just a few inches. She arched her back off the uncomfortable wooden chair, knowing what effect that would have, too. It was a practiced move that put a strain on the lower buttons of her blouse, pushing her cleavage up front and center. Bob's eyes fell right where she wanted them. She smiled. To command a grown man using only her posture was empowering.

Bob spoke as if he were reading from a script Vanessa had written herself. "Listen, why don't we forget about all this nonsense with the docks, and you and me make us a different kind of arrangement. I mean, the room is paid for and all."

Vanessa faked a coy expression and spoke with mock embarrassment. "Now, Bob, do I look to you like the kind of girl that goes home with her panties in her purse?"

"I'd be willing to bet you're the kind of girl that doesn't wear any in the first place."

"You're a confident man, Bob."

"You have to be in my position."

Vanessa stood up and slipped from vixen mode right back into business. Her tone was cold and precise.

"Then be confident about your ability as the Ports of Tampa Shipping Foreman, and entertain the proposal I'm here to make. Do that, and you can also be confident that this little tryst with a woman half your age doesn't make it back to poor, sick Mrs. Kane."

Bob's flirtatious manner evaporated as well. His voice rose at the threat. "So you're here to blackmail me? Wow, you really are a dumb bitch."

Vanessa's eyes narrowed slightly, but not enough for Bob to notice. His face was flushed red, and he was shouting. "You think you can force me into doing something that could land me in federal prison by threatening to tell my wife I'm banging a little cooze on the side?" He laughed. "Go right ahead, honey. Tell her anything you want. You'd be doing me a favor. Maybe when you're done, I'll be through having to deal with any of you bitches."

Vanessa didn't flinch at the second insult. "Listen, Bob, I'm not here to blackmail you, or to try and convince you to break any laws. I can see that ship has sailed— forgive the pun. I just thought I'd put myself out there one more time since we were being so—friendly and all." She tossed her hair back over her shoulder. "I won't pressure you anymore about it."

"Great, so get out."

"Of course, but before I leave, I'm going to need for you to sign off on these." She rested a pale hand on the paperwork sitting on the table. "I had the appropriate pages tagged for you—to make it easy-peasy. Two shakes and I'll be out of your hair."

"And what exactly is it you think I'm going to sign?"

"Your resignation." The cold intensity returned to

Vanessa's eyes. "And your recommendation for your replacement."

Bob stared at her blankly, and then erupted with laughter. "My resignation?" He leaned over the table, and flipped though the sheets of paper, scattering them across the table. He laughed again, and his belly shook. Vanessa started to laugh with him. "You think I'm going to just walk away—and leave that dip-shit kid, Pooler, in charge—just because you said so?"

"Yes, Bob. Yes, I do."

Bob's laughter died as he read. Vanessa's did, too. She moved away from the table, but her smile stayed in place.

"You're outta your fucking mind if you think I'm going to sign this shit. There ain't no way I'm ever gonna do that."

Vanessa backed further away but kept her smile. "Just keep reading, Bob. Look there on the last page. I promise you'll at least find it pretty interesting."

Bob looked back down and flipped to the last page. It was a goodbye letter to his wife. Perfectly forged. So finely done, he was baffled as to when he might have written it. It went on to say how he was leaving Florida, leaving her, for another woman. It was so painfully honest, as it went on to talk about the cancer and how it sickened him. It went on to say a lot of things. Things he'd always wanted to say. Things he did say—to Penny. Bob's eyes went dark, and he slung the stack of paperwork across the room.

"No one is going to believe that shit."

"Yes, they will, Bob. As soon as they talk to Penny and she corroborates the story."

"You crazy bitch. Do you know who I am? I know people. Powerful people. You think you got power over me because you caught me with some redheaded slut in a motel room? Or because I got me a snitch on the docks who ran his mouth about my business? Well, guess what? All that adds up to jack shit. You don't know me. I survived the strikes in 2012. I took on the fuckin' president and I'm the one still standing—me—Bob Kane. I've got the union. I've got real power, and you don't have the slightest clue who you're fucking with."

Vanessa remained unfazed by the foreman's outburst and kept smiling.

"I know exactly who I'm dealing with, Bob." Her smile faded. "Just another soft, weak pig with a big mouth—most likely to compensate for his smaller assets."

"You bitch." He lunged at Vanessa. She sidestepped, putting the bed between them, as the bathroom door opened. Bob barely had time to react to the noise, before a thin figure in a black hoodie stepped out and lifted a pistol with a long silver tube screwed onto the barrel. The man fired a single muffled shot, and the bullet entered Bob's head right above his left ear. There was no exit wound, no momentum from the blast, and no blood, as the bullet bounced around inside Bob's skull. The former shipping foreman just stood there, staring into Vanessa's stormy blue eyes. He looked startled and confused, but completely unaware that he'd just died. Vanessa watched with wide-eyed fascination that quickly turned into disappointment when Bob's body collapsed in a heap at the foot of the bed. The thin man with the compact .22 caliber pistol unscrewed the silencer and tucked both pieces of hardware into the pockets of his hoodie.

"I'm not sure why you like to play these head games, Vanessa. You knew he wasn't going to sign this." The small man bent over and began to gather up the paperwork scattered across the carpet.

"I like to give people the benefit of the doubt."

"People will let you down every time."

"You haven't yet, Chon."

"The key word there, Vanessa, is *yet*."

"You're such a pessimist, Chon."

"No, I'm a realist, and the reality is we just wasted a lot of time on this. I'll finish up here, and toss the rest of the room to make it look like a bigger struggle. You should leave. Go home and let me handle the rest the way I wanted to in the first place."

"Goddammit!" Vanessa said loud enough to startle the little man. Chon fumbled for the gun in his pocket. He looked around the room and saw nothing. When he looked back at Vanessa, he sighed. She was focused on a small drop of blood no bigger than a ladybug that had landed on her thigh. "This is never going to come out. Shit. I said no guns and no blood for a reason."

"And that reason was your wardrobe?"

Vanessa glared at him, and Chon just shook his head. She looked around the room and fixed her eyes on the open bottle of soda water on the counter. "Can you believe the luck?" She snatched up a bottle of club soda from the counter, and then limped toward the bathroom, as if she'd been the one to get shot, careful not to let that pebble of red break and soak in.

"Vanessa, we need to focus here."

"Give me a minute."

"Vanessa, all due respect, I—"

She turned in the doorway to face him.

"That's enough, Chon. I'm not going to tolerate some-one else acting like he's my boss. You work for me, so call those biker friends of yours, and make sure they are handling their end of things, and don't worry about how I handle mine."

"The Jackals are on point, Vanessa. I can promise you that."

"They better be."

"I've yet to see Bracken and his people drop the ball on anything this big."

"The key word there, Chon, is *yet*."

Chon chewed his lip, but had no response.

"Right," Vanessa said. "Now make the call, and finish up this room however you see fit. I'm going to go in this nasty motel bathroom and handle this stain before I have a meltdown. Are we on the same page now?"

Chon wasn't pleased, but there would be no debate. He nodded. "Sure, Vanessa. Is that it?"

"No," she said, just to be combative.

"What else, then?"

Vanessa had nothing else. "I fucking love these pants." She slammed the bathroom door behind her, and Chon stared at it with tempered amazement. A few seconds later, he pulled out a set of latex gloves and went to work.

Vanessa sat down on the commode. She poured soda water on another hand towel and blotted it down on the bloodstain. "These pants cost six hundred dollars. Fuck. I don't care how much you have, six hundred dollars is a lot of money to just toss in the trash. Would you agree with that?"

The petite, redheaded girl who sat half naked and puffy-eyed in the bathtub didn't say a word.

"Well, it is," Vanessa answered for her. She dabbed at the drop of blood with the towel. "The secret is to blot it, not wipe it, but blood is the absolute worst. I might as well have just set six hundred dollars on fire." She did her best with the stain, and then pitched the towel into the sink with a huff. "Asshole," she said, and shot a loaded middle finger at the bathroom door. The girl in the tub still said nothing. She tried to be still by squeezing her knees tight to her chest, but all she had on was a cheap baby-doll teddy and panties and she was freezing. The fear in her blood and the cold porcelain on her skin made it impossible to control the shivering. Her stomach cramped from trying. Vanessa rested her elbows on her knees and let her dark hair fall over her face. The sound of the girl's teeth chattering filled the tiny room, and it brought Vanessa back to the moment. She pushed her hair back over her ear and then turned to the girl.

"Penny, right? That's short for Penelope?"

The girl nodded.

"Use your words, Penny."

"Yes." Her voice was timid and soft. "It's my grandmother's name."

"Well, it's a much better name than Penny—if you're gonna be a whore, anyway." Vanessa looked pensive. "In fact, Penny is probably the worst name ever for a girl who fucks for money."

Penny found a little more of her voice. "I'm not a whore, ma'am, I—"

Vanessa put a finger to her blackberry lips and shook her head. "Listen, honey, I get it. Boys your age ain't buying, and married men never ask how much. Every girl around your age, with a decent set of tits and half a brain, figures that out, and every one of us at some point considers taking the low road, believe me." Vanessa sat up and pushed her breasts together with the insides of her arms. She looked down at her cleavage as if it was more of a burden than a blessing, and then hunched back over, resting her elbows back down on her knees. "But not all of us take that road. The smart move is to make them play by your rules. Show the boys you can do it without them. Open your own doors. Buy your own drinks. Pay your own way. It confuses them. It breaks their spirit and puts the power back where it belongs. You do that," Vanessa said, and slipped a finger under the thin black strap of Penny's teddy, "and you end wearing six-hundred-dollar slacks instead of shit lingerie from Target." She let the elastic go, and it snapped down hard against the girl's bare skin.

Penny pulled her legs in even tighter and thought she might throw up.

"Are you taking any of this in, Penny?" Vanessa leaned in to read the girl's face, and sighed with disappointment. "No—I can see you're not. Most whores don't, but I'm going to give you the benefit of the doubt, here. I'm not completely jaded like my associate out there." She softened her voice. "Look, do you want to be shivering in bathtubs your whole life while pigs like Bob Kane demean you? Is that really who you want to be?"

The girl said nothing.

"Answer me, Penny."

"No, ma'am."

"Then consider this your opportunity to turn it around. My gift to you."

The girl looked at Vanessa, but only briefly, before staring back down at the tub.

"Here's what's going to happen next. You're going to sit in there for a while, while my friend in the other room sets the stage—for you. In about an hour or so, you're going to use the motel phone and call the police. We'll be listening, so I'll know when and who you call. The gist of the story you're going to tell the cops is that asshole you called your boyfriend—who, by the way, referred to you as a *cooze* and a *slut* within the space of eight minutes—was going to leave his wife, quit his job, and run away with you into the happily ever after. But right after you checked in, three or four unremarkable men harassed you two lovebirds in the parking lot. Eventually Bob ran his mouth to the point that a fight broke out. That's when you ran in here and locked yourself in the bathroom, afraid for your life. Before you even knew what was happening, one of these indistinguishable thugs followed you and Bob in the room and shot him. After that, they all got spooked and ran away. I'll leave all the other details up to you. You're a bright girl. You'll be able to sell it to the idiot cops in this town, I promise."

"What if they don't believe me?" Spurred by hope, Penny's voice was more her own now.

"Penny, I told my friend with the gun out there you could pull it off. So, can you? Can you pull it off, or do I go tell him I was wrong?"

"Yes, ma'am." Penny was crying now, but her shivering had settled.

"Good girl, because I hate being wrong. Now, after they let you go, you're going to have to deal with the fallout that follows, and you're going to get through it. Once everything settles down, the rest is easy-peasy. What you do after that is up to you." Vanessa leaned in again. "But I suggest you finish your English degree at that Appalachian University you left back in North Carolina, and make your grandmother proud. She's sweet, by the way. I love that little dog she has. Old women and their little dogs, right?"

All the blood fell from Penny's face, and it hurt to breathe.

"Are we understanding each other?"

Penny nodded—sharply—her eyes closed tight.

"Open your eyes and use your words."

"Yes, ma'am, I understand."

"Good, because if you fuck this up—" Vanessa snatched Penny by the chin and twisted it hard, until their eyes met. "I don't believe in third chances, or mercy for the undeserving. I know where you live, Pen. I know where your parents, Ron and Sabrina, live, too. I know where your little brother's special school is, and how easy it is to visit. I'd hate to see any of them suffer for your inability to take solid advice."

"I understand, ma'am. I swear. I can do this."

"That's good." Vanessa let go of Penny's face, stood, and tossed the neatly folded pile of clothes from the counter into the girl's lap. "Now get dressed, and start practicing what you're gonna tell the police. And remember—"

Vanessa's phone rang. "Excuse me a minute."

Penny gripped her clothes tightly to her chest, as Vanessa pulled a cell phone from her hip pocket and read the display. Vanessa looked ill. "You've got to be kidding me." She tapped the phone and held it to her ear. "What in God's name do you want, Coot?"

"Hey, Bessie May. Long time."

"I don't answer to that name, Coot. I haven't in over six years and you know it. So I'll repeat myself. What do you want?"

"You need to come home."

"I am home."

"Naw, Sis. You need to come on back to your real home."

"And why the hell would I ever wanna do that?"

"Because JoJo is dead is why. He was drowned to death. Held underwater like a stray cat."

Vanessa was silent. She held the phone loosely in her hand and waited for the rest.

"Bessie May. You still there?"

"I told you that ain't my name no more." Vanessa's North Georgia drawl slipped out so easily, she almost didn't recognize her own voice.

"Well, whatever the hell you're callin' yourself down there, it don't matter. You need to come on home and I ain't askin'. You see, somehow that boy and his dumb-shit friends got some hare-brain idea to rob some big dogs in North Georgia."

It was Vanessa's turn to lose her breath and she gripped her phone hard enough to crush it.

"The same folks in North Georgia you come around here talkin' at Mama about a few months ago. Now isn't that some interesting shit? You know that boy didn't have the sense God gave a goat, much less the balls to knock over some heavy hitters, so I'm guessing he must've thought he was onto a sure thing. You still listenin', Bessie May?"

"I hear you, Coot."

"I wonder where he would'a got an idea like that from?"

"What exactly are you trying to say, Coot?"

"I done said it. Get your ass home. Pronto."

"How did it happen?"

"We'll talk over the details when you get here."

"Fine. Give me a few days."

"The funeral is—"

Vanessa ended the call. She stood silent and put the phone down on the counter. She looked up at the ceiling and watched the green light on the smoke detector blink at least twenty times, before she blew out a long, frustrated breath, and turned to look at Penny.

"I don't suppose you have any cigarettes?"

6

THE COMPOUND

Forty-eight hours of excruciating quiet and tedious office work filled the McFalls County Sheriff's office before the secondary cell phone Clayton kept for off-the-books activity finally rang. Mike dropped the news that his contacts in Florida had crossed the state line and were headed north. Clayton spent the remainder of the day staring out the window, and spit-polishing his sidearm. When the time came, he dumped the majority of his workload and paperwork on his sole deputy, Darby Ellis. He paused and looked at the office phone on his desk. He should call Kate. He reached toward the phone but picked up his Colt instead. He slipped it into his holster, grabbed his hat and jacket from the rack by the door, and left the office without a word to anyone.

Cricket, the office receptionist and the county's only dispatcher, watched from behind her desk as the door eased closed behind him. She turned to Deputy Ellis and whispered as if it wasn't just the two of them in the room.

"Do you ever think we'll get him back? You know, like he used to be?"

"I don't know," Darby said. "I honestly don't know." The muscular young deputy slid into an office chair next to Cricket. "He just seems to be getting worse. Did you catch a whiff of him when he came in? He's drinking in the mornings again."

Cricket pushed her glasses up on her nose. "Yesterday his pants and boots were covered in mud—pond mud. I spent most of the morning cleaning up what he tracked in, and he didn't even seem to notice. I wish I knew what to do—what to say."

Darby put his hand over Cricket's. "I know. I do, too, but the only person that can save him from what he's going through is him. All we can do is be here."

"I talked to Kate the other day. I went out to see the baby. She said he's never there, and I didn't have the heart to tell her he's never here either. Where is he spending all his time?"

"Burnt Hickory, I suppose."

Cricket pulled her hand away and sat up straight in her chair. "Maybe you should follow him, Darby. I mean, maybe you can get through to him."

Darby tipped his hat back a little on his forehead. "Cricket, there was a time, I'd follow that man to hell and back. You know that's true. I've done it. But wherever he's going now, ain't nowhere you want me to be. I can promise you that."

Cricket didn't bother to hide her disdain for that answer,

and went back to typing away at the report she'd been working on earlier. Darby sat and watched her for a moment and then stood up with a huff. He walked over to the door and grabbed his own coat from the rack. "I'm going to get some decent coffee. You want some?"

"No." Cricket didn't bother to look up from the computer screen.

"Well, then I'll see you later?"

Cricket didn't even bother to answer that time. Darby shook his head and put his jacket on. "All right, then."

Clayton climbed into the Bronco, pulled out onto Main Street, and drove north to the summit of Bull Mountain. He chain-smoked the entire forty-five-minute drive and tossed each fresh butt out the window onto the pavement and then onto the dirt where the pavement stopped— the road that led to his father's house, or the compound, as it was called now. His last trip up here ended pretty badly when Halford instilled in him with his fists how unwelcome he was. Now he was here by invitation.

The king was dead. Long live the king.

Clayton had just put another cigarette between his lips when static burped on the radio followed by the timid sound of Cricket's voice. "Sheriff? Come in."

Clayton lit his smoke and waited for Cricket to call for him again before he grabbed the handset.

"What is it, Cricket?"

Static.

"We got a call about a rancid odor coming from a trailer on White Bluff Road. House number 1128."

"A rancid odor?"

"Yes, sir. The caller said it smelled like ammonia and—cat piss—her words."

"Who called it in?"

"Reba Brown, sir. She said the smell was so bad from the road it made her eyes water."

Static.

Goddammit. Clayton rubbed the handset against his forehead to push back the headache. After Cricket called for him again, he tossed his smoke and keyed the mic. "Give it to Darby."

Static.

"Sir, 1128 White Bluff is the Cole house."

"I know that, Cricket. What's your point?" He knew her point.

"Sheriff, I don't mean to sound combative, but if Sonny Cole is up there, do you think Darby is ready to deal with something like that?"

"He's a McFalls County Deputy, ain't he?"

"Yes, sir. But—"

Clayton could see the compound up ahead. "Cricket, I ain't paying the kid to work out every day and sit around the office and flirt with you. The boy needs to earn his keep. Now give him the call."

Static.

"Yes, sir."

Clayton listened to Cricket call for Darby over the

radio before reaching out and turning the unit off. The wood around the dirt path had broken into a clearing, and a bone-thin kid in a red flannel shirt, and a long, stringy goatee, the kind that forms before you can grow a real beard, stood from his post at the main gate and spoke into his two-way radio. The kid let his automatic rifle hang loose over his shoulder by the leather strap as the eight-foot-high automated aluminum gate began to crank open. Clayton nodded at the kid as he waited to pull his county-owned vehicle through the huge chain-link fence that surrounded the epicenter of criminal activity in all of North Georgia—his childhood home. The fence had been put up recently. It wasn't there the last time Clayton was this high up the mountain. The thin young man waved him in, and tipped his ball cap to him as Clayton crept his Bronco past him, and parked it in the dirt lot. The man at the gate, who was really no more than a boy, hollered out as Clayton cut the engine. "You can go right on in, Mr. Burroughs. Everybody is waitin' for you."

It struck Clayton as odd that just one man—a boy, no less—was left by himself to man the gates of Burroughs Summit, so he hollered back, as he tried to place where he'd seen him before. "Why are you out here, all alone?"

"I promise you, Mr. Burroughs, I ain't alone." He pointed to the security cameras that topped each fence post. They surveyed the entire property. That was new, too. Clayton remembered the number of men guarding this place when Halford was alive was in the dozens—an army of shadows all ready to light up anyone who came calling if the big man gave the word. Now there was a skinny kid with a rifle and bunch of cameras. When Halford ran the mountain he kept things old guard like their father had done, but Mike had embraced the concept of the *High-Tech Redneck*, and taken advantage of the available modern technology. Either that, or the stories Clayton had been catching wind of recently about Halford's dwindling crew held more truth than he previously believed.

But why the hell wouldn't they scatter? What was left up here for them? The empire had fallen.

Clayton had seen to that himself when he pulled the trigger on his own kin, and executed their leader.

"They call me T-Ride!"

"Huh?" Clayton looked back at the kid by the gate. He was smiling and holding his hat with both hands, and the recognition set in. He was Mike's nephew. The kid in the truck from that mess at Burnt Hickory the other day.

"I know who you are, son. How's your mom and them?" Clayton didn't really care. It was a reflexive response, and so was the boy's answer.

"Can't complain, I reckon, and it wouldn't do no good if we did."

"I heard that." Clayton looked up at the blinking red lights on the cameras as the gate closed on its own between them. "Listen, kid, I don't care how many cameras Mike's got on you out here, you watch your six."

"Yessir." T-Ride tapped the rifle hanging at his side. "I got this watchin' my back."

Clayton nodded, and unpinned his badge. He tossed it onto the seat of the SUV. Everyone up here knew who he was, but he didn't see the point in rubbing salt in the wound. He walked over to the passenger side, reached through the window and slid his Colt from the glove box. He winced a little as he slid it into the holster strapped to his bad leg. He moved with a slight limp, but not enough for the kid by the gate to notice. "Just be careful out here, son."

"Yessir, Mr. Burroughs." The kid waited for the gate to click closed before he sat back down on his perch near the tree line. He laid the rifle across his lap, and winced a little himself as he thought about the man he watched drown to death in three inches of pond water at Clayton Burroughs' feet. Clayton didn't notice the kid's hands shaking either. In fact, he forgot about the kid the instant he turned and headed toward the house.

The sun had already begun to set in the lowlands, but from this high up, the sky was still a soft tangerine behind the endless rolling backdrop of the Blue Ridge Mountains. The orange burn of the evening was slowing lulling the giants to sleep, stealing their details. The ridges and ravines had disappeared, leaving only the Goliath silhouettes towering in the distance. It was beautiful—and telling. That sky would only last a few minutes. It was the perfect example of how fleeting beauty could be up there before everything was swallowed by pitch black.

The dirt-and-pea gravel surrounding the compound that used to be a grassy front yard, was filled with trucks and Jeeps and ATVs, matte black and primer gray, some new, some old—mostly old—some only held together by spite and free time. It wasn't a yard anymore. It was a hillbilly motor pool. Halford had turned the house into an armored fortress. The whole place took on the look of a miniature state prison. Motion lights, cameras, and razor wire replaced wooden slat shutters and hand-carved rockers. Sleeping bloodhounds on the porch were gone now, replaced by highly trained pit bulls tied to the chain-link fence.

This used to a *home*, now it was a *home base*.

Clayton and his brothers grew up here, but nothing about the compound resembled the place he remembered. The house still remained at the center, a simple, pitched-roof structure made mostly of yellow pine and cedar. There were two windows on each side of the front door. Only now, they were covered by hinged sheets of galvanized steel—pocked and marred by gunfire. Concrete-block additions were built onto the sides of the house for added protection and muscle. He looked at the roofline as he crossed between cars. Massive floodlights had been added, the kind you'd see at a high-school football stadium, and once he saw the high-end security camera's blinking red lights at the fence, he began to see them everywhere. They were nestled into everything. He looked for the bench by the fire pit where he first tried to hold Kate's hand. It was gone. The fire pit was, too.

The huge birdhouse that once sat atop a wooden pole on the side of the house was also gone. The pole was still there, but only tatters of duct tape and paracord hung from it now. He could only imagine what it had been used for over the years.

Clayton remembered there always being a faint smell of blood and fresh venison, cornmeal, or homemade bread in the air at this time of day when he was a kid. Despite who his father was, he always spent the time to gather all the boys together for family dinners, but that was gone, too. Now the air smelled of gun oil and diesel fuel. The compound had consumed the home the way a copperhead would a field mouse.

He walked up the steps to the door, and watched a camera mounted above it swivel and follow his movement. He stared at the red light, knowing full well the color red meant stop, another sign he was going to ignore, like the call from Cricket he'd just passed on to his inexperienced deputy. The guilt of that was beginning to set in when he heard the loud click of the lock. Without realizing he was doing it, he let the fingers of his left hand rub at the wooden grip of his Colt, as he pushed open the door.

Clayton wiped his feet on a tattered chunk of yellow carpet just inside the door. It was filthy. The hardwood floors were stained and buckled in places, but still felt as solid as the floors in his own home. Gareth Burroughs built things to last. He searched the cedar-paneled front room for a familiar face. The lamplight from the house's original fixtures filled the interior with an electric amber glow that caused the pine rafters to cast distorted shadows all over his brother's clubhouse. Clayton zeroed in on Scabby Mike, who stood up and removed his hat as he walked in. At least a dozen more men wearing clothes the color of sun-bleached straw and dried mud stopped talking when the Law invaded their domain. The place stank of spilled whiskey, cigarette smoke, and men gone days without soap or a shower. He wondered if Halford would have stood for the people he commanded letting their father's home be defiled like this, or had he let it get this way himself? He could feel the burn of every set of eyes in the room on his skin like a rash, and he was suddenly aware of the sweat beading under the coarse red hair on his upper lip. He didn't belong in this place anymore. He wanted a drink. More eyes peered at him from the kitchen. The yellow-and-cornflower-blue wallpaper in the kitchen triggered a memory about a fistfight he and his brother Buckley got into in there the first time he brought Kate home to meet his family. Clayton nearly beat his brother to death that night for saying something about her that he couldn't even remember. He did remember how his father did nothing to stop it, how he smiled and just moved Kate gently out of the way. He also remembered the look of disgust in Kate's eyes that night. It was the last time she ever came to dinner.

Mark Tuley was in the kitchen, standing with a man at least three times his age. Mark lifted his beer bottle off a makeshift table made out of plywood and stacked ammunition cases and tipped it to Clayton as he crossed the room. Clayton nodded in hopes of getting his hands on one of those beers. He tipped an imaginary bottle to his lips and Mark smiled before moving to the fridge. As Clayton moved further into the snake pit, he started to recognize more and more of the men in his company. Frank Wells, a local fireman with more children at home than Clayton could count, sat with the Rosier brothers—twins—both of them named Robert, although one of them went by Bobby. He didn't know which one. He didn't think anyone did. That was a common occurrence around the foothills. Clayton's train of thought screeched to a dead halt when he saw another face he'd not seen in years. It was the large, misshapen face of a man named Nails McKenna, who sat by himself on a dingy sofa in the darkest corner of the room. Clayton hadn't seen him in person since before he and Kate were married. They used to be friends. The three of them. Nails sat by himself, not just because his appearance frightened people, but due to his reputation as a stone-cold killer. Nails had the ability to scare the un-scareable, but Clayton was glad to see him. He'd known Nails back when people didn't fear him, and they still called him Nelson. Back before decades of ridicule about his mild retardation or his incestuous family turned him into the brooding loner that he was. Back before the people sitting around this very room stole his childhood and turned him into a hardened killer. Everyone called him Nails because of the deformity in his left hand that made his fingernails resemble animal claws. Clayton felt the nickname suited him, but not because of his hand. Nails McKenna might just have been the saddest story on Bull Mountain, but he survived it. He was still here. Clayton believed that to get through a life like that, someone would need to be made of steel—or hard as nails. He held his right hand out to Nails, and the big man half stood to shake it.

"Good to see you again, Nelson." Clayton offered a half-smile, but Nails offered nothing in return. He'd lost the capacity to smile a long, long time ago.

"How is Katelyn?"

"She's good, Nails. Better than I deserve."

"And the little one?"

Clayton shrugged. He really didn't know.

Nails let go of Clayton's hand, let out a small grunt, and settled back into the sofa. He stared into his beer and Clayton let the conversation die there.

The old man standing with Mark was Ernest Pruitt, and after seeing the two men standing there side by side, it was easy to see the relation. Ernest had been inner-circle when Gareth Burroughs was alive. That made Mark kin. Now Clayton understood why Mike seemed almost subordinate to him the other day at the house. Ernest lifted his gray-whiskered chin to him and tipped his hat. Clayton nodded but thought it was a little strange that this old-timer showed him any respect at all. He never had before. None of them had, but things had changed, and the room buzzed with it. In fact, most of the men in the room had either removed their hats, or stood up when he came in.

"Clayton," Mike said, squeezing the brim of his hat as he greeted him. Mark handed him a beer, and Clayton took it without a thank you.

"Let's just get this over with."

"Okay, come with me." Mike led Clayton through what used to be the living room where a huge, ornate television had been the centerpiece of the room. It was empty now except for the ammo cans that lined the walls and a massive stocked long-gun rack. They walked through a thick oak door that led to a room Clayton had never been privy to when he lived here. It was his father's private office—the war room, his brothers called it. Once they passed through the door, three men stood up from their seats along the left side of a smooth and ancient oak farm table. The men dressed in leather and denim looked to be as out of place as Clayton did, yet a lot more at ease. They stood and waited for the introductions. Clayton shook hands with a man named Moe. He was short and wide, and wore his hair in a ponytail. His handshake was a dead fish. The second man, a younger one with a crew cut and bright eyes, cupped Clayton's hand with both of his and introduced himself as Jay Martin. He looked more like an insurance salesman in a biker costume than he did an actual biker. They both wore cuts of leather with patches indicating their rank in the Jacksonville Jackals Motorcycle Club. Clayton had been a distant observer to these people his entire life. Now he was shaking their hands. He didn't know how that made him feel. He wanted a cigarette. The air felt thinner in the small meeting room as if it had somehow elevated another ten thousand feet while they stood there. His chest felt tight, and it tightened even more as he caught the stare of the third and final man he had come there to meet. This one was in charge. He stood at least a foot taller than anyone else in the room, and his skin appeared to be carved out of granite. Not just his skin, but his eyes, his lips, his fingernails, even the denim he was covered in was completely void of color. A few days' growth of gray stubble around the edges of his head had blended into his salt-and-peppered beard, and his age was impossible to guess. He was fifty if he was five hundred. His face carried age-lines, but they didn't soften him or make him appear fragile or old. They were carved into him—the way water eroded rock over time, cutting grooves in sandstone. Clayton stared at the gray man's hand for too long before shaking it. It made him look weak, and all at once he knew he'd made a mistake. He was sure of it. This stone man had been staring right through him since he walked in the room, and knew Clayton had to build up the nerve to stare back. He would see Clayton for the frightened rabbit his father saw him as and it would get them all killed. He felt the sweat on his lip spread and moisten his forehead and neck. Stars burst at the edges of his vision and he thought sure he might faint.

Goddamn, Clayton. Get your shit together. This is

*your deddy's house. Don't you let 'em do this to you.
Don't you dare, you stupid old bastard.*

"Clayton," Mike said, putting his hand under Clayton's
elbow, to keep him steady.

The stone man spoke. "Mr. Burroughs, my name is
Bracken Leek, President of the Jacksonville Chapter of the
Jackals Motorcycle Club. I'm also a friend to your family."

It was comical in the most tragic sense to see how small
his own hand looked inside of this giant's. Bracken could
squeeze his fingers around his and crush every bone in
Clayton's hand if he wanted to, but it didn't go that way.
Bracken shook his hand firmly and held it long enough
for Clayton to feel the warmth of blood behind the stone,
and then let go.

"I know who you are, Leek."

"I have no doubt you do, Sheriff."

"So what is it you want?"

"Why don't we have a seat," Mike said, cutting in
and motioning for Clayton and the bikers to sit. Clayton
began to sit in one of the chairs along the opposite side
of Bracken and his men, but Mike discreetly nudged him
toward the larger chair at the head of the table. Clayton
sat down, and the comfort of easing his weight off his
left leg was evident on his face. What wasn't apparent to
anyone in the room but Mike was the strange blend of
emotion that had to be churning through Clayton's blood.
He was sitting in the same chair that had belonged to his
brother Halford, and to his father Gareth before him.
The same chair his grandfather Cooper had steered the

Burroughs empire from before them all. It filled his chest with something hot, something he wasn't used to, or could recognize right away. No one really believes that anything in life is more important than money, or love even, until it's their turn to sit at the head of the table—until they truly know power. That was what Clayton felt as he sat in that chair—power. Mike couldn't help but smile as Clayton took off his hat and laid it on the table like it belonged there. He leaned forward and repeated himself.

"So—what is it you people want?"

7

SERVICE ROAD NINETEEN

"Copy that."

Deputy Darby Ellis hung the handset to his radio back in the cradle and turned the 2002 Crown Vic around, careful to avoid the ditches that lined both sides of the road. *Thank God*, he thought. He'd only been a few miles behind his boss when Cricket called him off. He'd much rather be on his way to a call than anywhere Clayton was headed to.

"A possible cookhouse on White Bluff Road," Cricket told him.

"Possible, my ass." Darby knew full well what went on at that address, but at least now he knew what he was getting himself into.

Sonny Cole was a run-down lowlife who had spent most of his adult life in and out of prison. It was a cycle that kept his wife and son in a constant state of disrepair. The trailer they lived in mirrored that fact. It may have been white or beige at some point in history but a decade of mildew had built up over every square inch of the thing, painting the entire rectangular box a dull green. There weren't any cars parked out front, but that didn't mean anything; Darby had never known Sonny to own one. He had other things to buy with the family's money like liquor, beer, and crank. Darby pulled the Crown Vic up to the front door and cut the engine. He stepped out and put on his hat. The new hadn't worn off the stiff Stetson yet and he still liked the feel of authority it gave him. Darby had wanted to be a cop his entire life, and it was still a little hard to get his head around the fact that he actually was one. He tucked at the back of his shirttail to make sure he looked presentable, and ran his hand across the cuffs on his gun-belt, letting it rest slightly on his county-issued Glock 9. He knocked once on the Plexiglas trailer door, and after no response he knocked again a little harder. The acrid smell of ammonia was thick in the air, and his eyes teared up from the sting of it. He looked down at the sticker-covered BMX bicycle lying in the dirt by the steps and the fresh tracks tailing the back tire and rubbed at his eyes.

What kind of asshole does this kind of thing with his own kid around?

Darby already knew the answer to that question. He was standing in front of a trailer that belonged to precisely that kind of asshole. Darby hoped this wouldn't be a family affair. The bike belonged to Sonny's boy, Reggie, but the kid could be anywhere. Darby keyed the radio on his shoulder. "Cricket, I'm not getting a response at the door, but there is definitely something rotten in the crock pot. I'm going to go scope it out some. Five-minute check-ins."

Static.

"Copy that, Darby. Five minutes. Be careful."

"Aw, you worried about me, girl? I like it. Don't worry, I'll be done here in no time and you can show me over a pizza and Netflix how concerned you are about me."

"Just focus, Darby. Five minutes."

"Yes, ma'am."

Deputy Ellis backed down off the brick stoop, took out his weapon and walked around to the side of the trailer. He stepped over a rusted-out wheelbase and avoided some fresh dog shit. He held his free hand over his nose and mouth to fend off the pungent odor of both chemicals and feces. The air was thick and hazy, but he could see a shed twenty or so yards around back, a makeshift building made out of galvanized steel sheeting, nails, and particleboard. A shop-light hung free in the wide entrance connected to a long, bright-orange extension cord that snaked through the grass and disappeared behind the trailer. Darby shook his head, and wiped at his eyes. The shed was an open-air cookhouse and apparently Sonny Cole didn't care who knew about it, because it was up and running at full steam. Darby could see two men in their skivvies wearing nothing else but gas masks standing just inside the shed, pouring something from a huge plastic jug into an even bigger plastic tank. Darby wiped at his eyes again and watched as the two men set the jug on the ground, but after a clearer look, he realized it wasn't two men at all. It was two boys—two very young boys. It wasn't Sonny Cole. It was his son, Reggie, and another kid about the same age.

"Son of a bitch," he whispered and slipped the Glock back into his holster. "It's a bunch of damn kids." He grabbed the radio on his shoulder, but before he could key it up, the sound of a shotgun being racked froze him in place.

"Git yer hands off that radio, boy, and put 'em straight up in the air before I blow the back of that pretty blond head off."

Darby did, but not before pressing a small orange button on the side of the lapel mic. The distress call went right to dispatch—and right to the sheriff. "Sonny, now listen here—"

"Uh-uh. Not another word. I ain't playin' neither. Now back yer ass up until I tell you to stop."

Darby took a hesitant step backwards.

"That's it. Keep movin'. C'mon now."

Darby took another step, and then another, and then one more, until he was back around the corner and the shed was out of eyesight. His heart dropped when he felt metal press into his spine.

"Feel that, boy? I reckon that's far enough. Now turn around real slow and keep those paws where I can see them."

Darby turned and lowered his hands a few inches. Sonny raised the shotgun to his shoulder.

"Put them fuckin' hands back up high, the way they were."

"Sonny, I'm a sheriff's deputy now. You don't want to do this."

Sonny took a step forward, shoving the shotgun in close to Darby's face. "Didn't I just tell you to shut the fuck up?"

Darby winced and closed his eyes as Sonny looked him up and down, and saw the deputy's badge. He laughed, and lowered the gun a few inches. "Well, look at that shit. Clayton done made a snot-nose punk his deputy? He really must be as fucked-up as I heard."

Darby slowly opened his eyes. Sonny Cole was as thin as a fence post, and he stood there holding that heavy long gun, staring at Darby through a cheap dollar store pair of swimmer's goggles. He was shirtless, wearing nothing but a pair of filthy Levi's and combat boots. And although Sonny Cole was a black man, he was shiny bald, and the patchwork of gray and bluish prison tattoos that covered his light skin made him look more like a Nazi skinhead—a Nazi skinhead about to go for a swim.

"Sonny, I ain't out here looking for trouble, but I can't allow what them kids are doing back there to go on."

"I'd say the minute you decided to come here, pretending like you got some kinda say-so about what happens on my property, you came lookin' for trouble." Sonny kept the barrel of the rifle about a foot from Darby's chest and the deputy kept his hands in plain sight.

"Your boy is back there cooking dope, Sonny, and I'm

a sworn deputy of this county. That means I do have some say-so about what you're allowing to happen back there, and you holding that gun on me like that is enough to get you locked up again—maybe this time for good."

Sonny just stood there twitching and chewing on his lip.

"So why don't you lower the gun, and let's put a stop to all this while we still can. I ain't looking to come down on your family, man. I'm just trying to keep the peace here."

Sonny's dark eyes glazed over under the plastic goggles, and he just continued to twitch and chew until he started to smile. His smile turned to a chuckle, and then to a full-on belly laugh.

"Keep the peace? Are you shittin' me, son? You been watchin' too much *Gunsmoke* or something. There ain't no peace to keep up here. That badge don't mean shit no more. Hell, your boss—the sheriff? He's the one callin' the shots up here now. He ain't no fuckin' lawman no more, and neither is your dumb ass, so go ahead and climb your white-boy ass back into that shit-trap over there and git the fuck off'a my land before I seriously have to—"

The screaming coming from behind the trailer caused both men to turn and look. One of the boys was yelling. Darby and Sonny both moved to the edge of the trailer to see Reggie running straight at them, holding his gas mask in his hand. The other boy was nowhere in sight, but a flash of flame blew out from the entrance of the shed and another scream came from inside. When the second boy appeared, he was engulfed in fire. He only made it out of the shed a few feet before dropping to his knees. Darby only made it a few feet toward Reggie before the explosion knocked him backwards and everything went white—then black.

8

"Did they really just dump JoJo's body right there in the front yard?"

"I heard it was right on the front porch. In broad daylight even."

"That's balls."

"That's not balls, man. That's straight-up crazy."

"Hell, they treated Coot's boy like a flamin' bag of dog shit. They might as well have rang the bell and ran."

"Whatcha' mean? Like nigger-knockin'?"

"Watch your mouth, Donnie, or I'll nigger-knock your fronts out."

"Shit, Tate, that's not how I meant it."

"Ain't no other way to mean it, you prick."

"Will you two keep your voices down, and show me and my mother some respect?" Coot Viner glared at his cousins, Donnie and Tate, and both men went back to ignoring each other and trying not to look indifferent about JoJo's passing. Neither of them liked the little shit that much anyway. His own father could hardly stand him. He was always running his mouth about something. He had always been the type that if he heard you'd been to the moon and back, he'd been there twice already. Everyone knew he'd end up like this sooner or later. It was just a shame he had to take Clyde Farr and the rest of the boys with him. It wasn't like the whole family hadn't told him to stay clear of North Georgia, but he was Coot's only son so they all had to play the part. More importantly, he was Twyla's only grandson, so they kept their opinions about the boy to themselves for her sake.

"Sorry, Coot. I didn't mean no disrespect."

"I don't care if you meant it or not, Donnie." Coot took a swig from a silver flask and rubbed at his nose. "And the next time you wanna throw words like *nigger* around in front of Tate, church or no church, I'm gonna let him stomp a mud hole in your repugnant ass. Now apologize to him, too—quietly—and then shut your trap."

Donnie looked down at his dingy work boots and rubbed them together. Coot leaned over him and waited.

"Sorry, man."

"I said to him, dumbass, not me."

Donnie turned to Tate. "Sorry, man."

Tate sat up a little straighter in the pew, crossed his arms and puffed his chest out. He liked having Coot take his side for once, even though Coot said the word *nigger* more than anyone else he knew. "Damn right, you're sorry."

Coot sat back and yawned. No one else in the cramped chapel hall said anything, as the preacher delivering the eulogy droned on and on about how JoJo's suffering had finally come to an end. A few heads nodded in agreement right on cue like puppets, but Coot just stroked his white-blond goatee, and yawned again. He knew all that mess about a great reward waiting in the afterlife was a load of shit. Dead only meant dead—no more, no less—just dead. Anyone pretending to know any better than that was just a damn fool trying to make sense of their pointless existence.

The obese preacher had dark, wet stains on the armpits of his powder-blue shirt and kept wiping at the sweat running down his forehead. He looked more afraid of saying the wrong thing in front of the deceased's clan than he did worried about his eternal soul. He was just following the same old script he used on everyone who cut him a check for his services. He was a cereal-box preacher—all sugar and tooth decay, dressed up like a can of soup to look wholesome and good for you. He made Coot ill. He hadn't been inside a church, or a chapel like this one since grade school, and regardless of the reason for being there now, he couldn't wait to get the hell out. There were enough gaudy plastic flower arrangements around the simple wooden casket holding his son's body to crowd a landfill, and Coot hoped that was exactly where they ended up when this circus was over. He didn't want any of that garbage coming back to his house, although he knew his mother would want it to.

He slumped down on the uncomfortable wooden bench to get some shoulder room and stretched his legs. His suit was secondhand. It used to belong to his father, but it wasn't cut right and itched like crazy. He pulled at his collar to loosen the clip-on tie biting at his Adam's apple and began to feel even more claustrophobic. He was wedged into the front-row seat reserved "for family" between his two cousins and his mother. It was a good thing these places sat the mother of the deceased on the aisle seat, because it allowed room for Twyla's portable rolling oxygen tank to be close to her without all the plastic tubing getting tangled all over everything. Every few minutes or so, the old woman would lift her veil and hold the breathing mask to her nose and mouth to ward off the emphysema. Twyla Viner was old as dirt and not in the best shape, but Coot was convinced the tough old bird would outlast them all.

She also had yet to shed a single tear.

That irritated Coot. He figured had it been his sister, Vanessa's, son lying in that pine box, his mother would be a blubbery mess, but there she sat shrouded in that look of *I told you so* that made Coot want to fill a few pine boxes of his own. He reached into the inside pocket of his jacket for his whiskey, but Twyla reached over and put a cold, frail hand on his knee. The skin on her knuckles was as thin as paper. She peered through the flimsy black curtain of lace obscuring her face and silently warned him to keep the flask put away. That irritated him, too, but he did. She leaned her head slightly onto his shoulder and wheezed a little in his ear. He knew what she was going to say before she opened her mouth.

"Where is your sister, Daniel?" she whispered.

Coot looked back over his shoulder, across the faces of his friends and the sea of people there only to kiss his and his mother's ass, to see if his little sister had slipped in and taken a seat in the back. She had not.

"I don't know, Mama, but she said she'd be here, so she'll be here. You know Bessie May. She don't operate on the same schedule as the rest of the world."

"Her nephew is dead, Daniel. Your son."

"I know, Mama."

"My grandbaby is dead."

"I know, Mama." Coot put his hand over hers.

"She should be sitting here with us."

"I know, Mama."

Twyla lifted her head off his shoulder and took a deep hit off her oxygen mask. She pulled her hand away from Coot's leg, but not before giving it the motherly "good boy" pat he'd grown to hate, and they both went back to listening to the Jesus-crispy salesman. This part—the church bit and all the preacher's hoopla—this was all for Twyla. She needed it, and Coot allowed it. His part would come later. After the food got eaten back at the house, and the liquor got drunk out by the pond, that's when his time would come. That's when he'd get to plan the real party, and the thought of that was the only thing keeping the rage building just under his skin contained. He sat and waited until the sweaty fat man at the podium said his final "Amen."

9

The Compound

One of Scabby Mike's men, a younger man with a scar that circled his left ear and a massive pink goiter on his neck, came into the war room and set a pitcher of iced tea, a bowl of farm-fresh apples, and a sleeve of red Solo cups on the table.

"Thanks, Tank."

"No problem, Mike."

How hospitable, Clayton thought. *Southern gangsters still retain their raisin'*.

"How about something with a little more teeth?" Clayton said, waving his empty beer bottle at Tank.

"You got it, Mr. Burroughs."

Tank left the room and Clayton retuned his attention to the men at the table.

"Now then, Leek, how about we get right to it? Why are you here?"

"I don't mean to sound presumptuous, Mr. Burroughs, but I think you already know why we're here."

"Then let's not presume anything. Talk to me like I'm a five-year-old. Straight answers to straight questions."

Bracken let a slight smile invade his stony face.

"Is something funny?" Clayton could feel his heart racing, but kept his exterior hard.

"No, Mr. Burroughs, no disrespect. It's just a bit jarring, how much you remind me of—"

"Of who? My brother? Listen, let's clear that up now. I'm not my brother. Halford was a selfish prick that didn't care about anything or anyone but himself—and he was a drug dealer, who turned this mountain into a haven for other drug dealers. It's important you know the distinct difference between us before you go to reminiscing."

Mike shifted uncomfortably in his seat, and Tank retuned with a jar of pecan hooch and a rocks glass already filled with a half-inch of the clear white lightning. He set them both on the table and Clayton wasted no time draining the glass. No one said anything until he set the empty glass back down. "I'm nothing like my brother."

Moe motioned for Jay to slide him the jar of shine.

"No," Bracken said. "You aren't like your brother. I was going to say you remind me of your father."

Clayton wasn't sure he cared for that comparison either, but he said nothing. His face flushed red from the whiskey, and rode out the after-burn. He'd forgotten how powerful the shine up there could be; still he motioned for the return of the bottle. Once Moe poured himself a nip, Jay slid the bottle back to the man at the head of the table.

"Listen, Leek. The Feds raided all the cookhouses you and Halford had up here. They're shut down—permanently. The marijuana crops are dried and fried, and now this whole place is on the government's radar. It's over up here, so even if I had any interest in allowing that kind of commerce to begin again, and I don't, I couldn't if I wanted to. The jig is up. Bull Mountain is a bust."

"I'm aware of all that, Sheriff. We aren't looking to reestablish production of anything in your mountains."

Clayton looked at Mike and poured another drink. That wasn't what he was expecting to hear at all. He studied Leek's face, but could read nothing. He'd also forgotten how fast the shine could dull his senses. "Then what are you doing here?"

"Straight answers to straight questions." Bracken repeated Clayton's own words. "Bottom line?" he said. "My club still needs access to the routes we spent years building through here into Tennessee and the Carolinas. Alabama we can handle on our own, but Halford and his father had cultivated a relationship with your state police, Georgia Highway Patrol, and all the other state-level law-enforcement agencies that operate in this region. Those relationships are quickly drying up. You're in a unique position to help us maintain those relationships, even more so than your predecessor."

"My predecessor?"

"I'm sorry, Mr. Burroughs. Again, I mean no offense, I'm simply trying to be delicate here. I mean your brother."

Clayton waved it off. "And my unique position is that I happen to be the county sheriff."

"Yes. We've spent a lot of time and money building a vast blind spot stretching from Valdosta to Gatlinburg, and this area is crucial to our business, seeing as it's the gateway to so many other regions that we do business in. We need that blind spot to stay blind, and we need the guarantee of safety we've received in the past to continue our operations."

"What operations?"

"That's our concern."

"No, you're making it the concern of everyone who lives here by wanting to travel through our mountains. It's a fair question that everyone in this room needs to have answered to know whether it's something to even continue talking about. I've already told you I won't help reboot the meth trade up here, even if that just means my office turning a blind eye, while you hustle it through. If that's what we're talking about here, then it's no different than what you had going on before, and my answer is no."

"No amphetamines, Mr. Burroughs. We are moving the club into something else. Something legitimate. We have contacts in place within a group of medical professionals based in Tennessee and North Carolina that wish to expand their business, and they need our help to do that. They are also prepared to pay everyone who helps facilitate that a handsome and ongoing sum."

"Medical professionals?"

"Yes."

"What kind of business are they looking to expand?"

"They operate a number of medical clinics already, and wish to open more."

"Clinics?"

"Yes."

"Specializing in pain management, I suppose."

Jay and Moe glanced at each other and then at Clayton. They were impressed.

"You'd suppose correctly," Bracken said.

"You're talking about OxyContin," Clayton said, and Bracken didn't even blink. Clayton was beginning to think he didn't know how. He figured out the rest without any coaxing. "And you need safe passage to move stolen drugs from Florida to these clinics north of us."

"Yes, that's right, except that the medication isn't being stolen. It's being purchased."

"Okay, if you say so, and Halford's relationships with the police will keep them off your back, while Mike here keeps the unruly locals from jumping you in transit, right?"

"Yes."

"And you're calling that legitimate?"

"I'm calling it progress."

"And you're telling the local sheriff your intentions because I just happened to be named Burroughs? Ballsy move."

"No, Sheriff. It's not balls, or because of your name alone. It's respect. Respect for your father—for your brother."

"I told you, I'm not Halford. And I may be a sheriff, but I don't know anyone—not like that."

"Mike here can facilitate that."

"Then why not just deal with Mike?"

"Because Mike knows his place at the table."

Clayton waited for that indignity to play out across Scabby Mike's face, but it didn't happen. He simply nodded in agreement again.

"My family. Right. And you're telling me I get to make the call as to whether or not this happens? Just like that?"

"Yes, Sheriff. You have the ability to turn us away, without debate—just like that."

Clayton didn't even hesitate. "Well, then—no." He let that hard syllable hang over all their heads, while he hammered his second shot of hooch. He sat the glass down, and rubbed at a knot in the wooden table as if to signal that the meeting was at a close. "Well, that's that. Drugs in the hands of children and the poor are the same to me, whether they're made in a bathtub in these mountains or a lab in India, and I won't be a part of it. So if you're shootin' me straight, and all this is truly up to me, then my answer is no—hell, no."

The room stayed silent. Clayton thought about saying it again, but he didn't have to.

"Sir, if I may," Jay said smoothly, breaking the silence. "Children are not the recipients of legally prescribed narcotics. And Sheriff, I hate to break it to you, but the impoverished are able to get the same thing from any Walmart or local drugstore in the region, so I fail to see the difference in what we're proposing, outside of you letting fat-cat corporations make a boatload of cash that could rightfully benefit your own constituents."

"Fancy talk there, son." It was clear that Clayton's shine buzz had begun to melt his inhibitions. "Legally prescribed narcotics?" he said and leaned forward onto the oak table. "Jayden, is it? That's a fancy name, too. Let me ask you something, Jayden. Do you think I'm fuckin' stupid?"

"Hold on, Clayton," Mike said, cutting in to stop the escalation. "Maybe you could let Bracken and his people explain why allowing this partnership could benefit not only the people in this room, but everyone on this mountain—including Kate, and Eben."

Clayton narrowed his eyes at his scarred friend. "Use as many familiar names as you want, Mike. It's not going to happen."

"Well, hell, I'd like to hear it."

Everyone turned. Mark Tuley poked his head in from the open doorway he'd been leaning on. "I mean, c'mon, Clayton, these men have come a long way. The least we can do is hear everything they have to say before we send them packin'. Right?" Mark sat down next to Mike like he belonged there and poured some iced tea. He was the first to touch the sweaty pitcher. Clayton sat back, and scratched at his beard. He liked this guy, Tuley. He didn't want to, but he did. Bracken waited for Clayton's permission to continue.

"Okay, Leek. Tell me what I'm missing? Humor Mr. Tuley, there."

Mark sipped his tea, and nodded at Clayton. "Thanks, Sheriff." He turned to Bracken. "Now sell it, big boy. The table's yours."

Clayton almost laughed out loud.

"Okay, Mr. Tuley. As you know, your people have a huge problem up here. We can help you solve it."

"Enlighten us."

"Halford's unfortunate death and the federal raids that stripped this place of everything he and his father built, have created a vacuum up here—a void if you will—that an extremely troublesome element is going to want to fill. That black hole is at this very moment attracting a lot of wolves directly to your front door mainly because of your name. These people know the Burroughs organization is crippled and will be looking to reestablish that flow of dope and money, and the last living Burroughs is now, and always will be, a threat to them."

"I handle myself just fine, Leek."

"I wasn't referring to you, Sheriff. I meant your son."

Clayton said nothing.

"You can't pretend to not know this is happening, Mr. Burroughs. You even had an incident with some of the people I'm talking about a few days back."

Clayton shot Scabby Mike a hard look. Mike just shrugged, and nodded in agreement.

"This kind of thing isn't going to stop," Bracken said. "I know. I've seen it happen a hundred times over in this business. And yes, that's what it is, a business, and if you want to define your role in all this as the man who keeps the peace, and keeps crank off of Bull Mountain? Then work with me. I can help that happen. What is it they say? If you don't maintain the land, you'll get overrun with weeds and vermin."

"Do much farming back in the day, Bracken?" Mark grabbed an apple from the bowl.

"Sixty acres of orange orchards was how my father fed us, Mr. Tuley, but that's irrelevant. The point is, and someone of your intelligence and history knows as well as I do, that if this vacuum goes unregulated much longer, you're going to have much worse than some kids from Boneville to deal with. People will die—your people. You don't want that. I don't want that."

Mark let Clayton pick up the volley. "And what are you offering here, Bracken? Guns?" Clayton made a show of looking around the room at all the firepower already present. "How many guns do we need?"

Bracken leaned down on his elbows. "Sheriff, the people conspiring against you have the same truckload of scatter guns and hunting rifles you do. The difference is more and more people are going to side against you if the other side offers to pay them. Mike here is having a harder and harder time convincing them to stay. Just ask him."

Again, Mike nodded in agreement.

"So, guns? Yes, I can provide firepower to replace everything the government confiscated after Halford's death. I can also bring in another chapter of the Jackals to help out with manpower, but, most importantly, I can cut your family into my deal with these doctors up north. It's incredibly lucrative and the cash in hand will calm the natives. I can help your mountain survive this."

Again the room went silent. Mark sipped at his tea. He'd also taken out his knife and was carving off pieces of his apple. He smacked his lips while he ate them. Clayton was beginning to get irritated with how relaxed he was.

"Why are you asking, Leek?"

"I don't understand, Sheriff." Bracken leaned back in his chair.

"Neither do I. I mean, why ask us? Why not come in here guns blazing and just take it? Take the routes, claim it all without a second thought to what I think?"

"Because family is important."

"We aren't family, Leek."

"Not by blood, but neither am I blood related to these two men sitting next to me, and I'd give my life for each of them, as they would for me. Family goes beyond blood in my world, Sheriff, and my club has broken bread with your kin for a very long time. That means something to my club. It means everything to me. I am not your enemy."

"You keep talking about my family as if I have ever been a part of it. Let me tell you something about family, Leek." Clayton's belligerence was beginning to rear itself, and a slight slur had attached to his words. "Do you remember the floods that came through here in 1985?"

"Clayton, maybe now isn't the time." Mike put his hand on Clayton's arm, but the sheriff snatched it away.

"No, Mike. This fella here has all the respect for my family. So I want to tell him a little bit about them." He looked at Bracken.

"I do remember the flooding. It stalled our business with your father for months. What about it?"

Mark sat upright. Wondering what the hell this had to do with anything.

"That crazy rain we had back then washed out the whole valley. We were kids." Clayton looked at Mark. "Were you still here? You remember that?"

"Yeah. I'm tracking."

"The rain. It didn't stop for days. It was like the end of days or something. I remember that shit like it just happened."

"Clayton—" Mike said, trying to reel Clayton back into the moment.

"Just hold on, Mike. Listen. This is important." Clayton cut his eyes at Bracken. "Family is important, right?" he said, feeding the big man's words back to him. Bracken didn't seem to mind listening, and that was a good thing, because Mike knew once a Burroughs got started on a tangent, folks were going to hear the story whether they wanted to or not, so he scooted back in his chair and stretched his legs under the table.

"I was eleven," Clayton said. "I didn't even know Kate yet—but he might've." Clayton tipped his glass at Mark, who showed no reaction. "I remember that summer and that rain so well because it was the first time Halford tried to kill me."

"Clayton—"

The sheriff didn't even acknowledge Mike's interruption that time. He just kept talking.

"The rain caused Bear Creek to overflow and it ran as wild as the Mississippi all the way down the mountain. It hit Clark's Hill pretty hard as it passed through, snatchin' up trailers and mobile homes along the way before it finally washed out Main Street in Waymore. The Hill never recovered." Clayton looked pensive for a moment and then continued. "All kinds of stuff from those homes, like books, furniture, baby dolls, toilet-bowl scrubbers, you name it, were rushing down the waterway, getting thrown all over the place. It was a mess. Anyway, Buckley had this crazy idea that we should snatch up something to use as floats and ride the current from up here all the way down into Waymore. He said we could go loot Main Street since most of the townsfolk had evacuated. Hell, back then I didn't even know what looting meant. I only agreed so I could hang out with my brother, since most of the time he treated me like shit. Buck found himself an old corduroy sofa cushion, and I found a big, round, plastic garbage-can lid. At first it was crazy fun. The creek was flowing so fast, every time we got in, it would slam us into the sandy bank by the bend at Johnson's gap. We'd hit the sand and roll into the grass and trees. We got filthy as hell, and it was one of the few times I ever saw Buckley laugh without it being at my expense." Clayton poured a little more shine and slid the jar over to Moe, who was the only other person at the table drinking it.

He was getting comfortable in his father's chair. "After a little trial and error, we finally got a pretty good handle on how to maneuver our trash-floats and thought we were ready to take the bend. We hoofed it way up to Red Rock before we dropped back in, so we'd have some real speed pushin' us, and then gave it one more go." Clayton sipped at his whiskey. "Most fun I ever had in my life," he said, and leaned back in his chair lost in the memory. He scratched at his neck and beard.

"Well, then what?" Moe blurted out like a third-grader during Story Time. Mark nearly laughed out loud at the rotund biker's eagerness to hear the end of his new drinking buddy's story.

"We cleared that fuckin' bend, is what," Clayton said, still in a fog, and then focused back on the point. "We pulled it off and made it, but that trash-can lid was round and it spun me the whole time like a pinwheel. I got it under control in the straightaway, but not before I hit a huge branch—or a log, maybe—I don't even know, but whatever it was, it had snapped down from the rain and there it was, out of nowhere, lying across that side of the creek. I straightened out just in time to face-plant right into that son of a bitch. I cracked my head real good and it stopped me cold. That trash-can lid flipped out from under me and blew down the creek and I got more and more entangled in that overhang. I was jacked up on that branch something fierce, and the current was steadily trying to pull me under. It had my legs pulled straight out in front of me, and I didn't have the strength to force them down. The water ripped my boots off and my feet felt like they were being sucked off my ankles, too. Buck made it through the bend but cleared the branch that had me. The last thing I saw was him looking back and hollerin', but he was haulin' too much ass to stop. A few seconds later he was gone."

Bracken didn't appear uninterested but poured himself a glass of iced tea.

"Anyway, here I am getting pulled deeper and deeper under that mess until I finally got my foot stuck on something under me to brace myself, but not before my face done slipped about a half-inch or so under the surface. I couldn't get any air. I stretched my neck until I thought it might snap but I just couldn't get clear. Every breath came with a good swallow of that nasty-ass river water."

"Drowning is a horrible way to die," Bracken said. That made Clayton think about the young man he left gagging on the edge of Burnt Hickory Pond, and wondered if that was Bracken's intention.

"Second only to fire," Mark said over his tea glass, and Bracken actually stiffened. Mike shifted again in his seat. Clayton wasn't sure what that was about but had enough shine in him not to care. He kept talking.

"I could see the sky and treetops above me distorting through the water, and up to that point in my life it was the most scared I'd ever been. I couldn't breathe. I thought I was going to die. I knew I was going to die. I couldn't stand up. I couldn't get free. I couldn't do anything. I was sure I was about to check out, and the sad part was I remember thinking how relieved my father was going to be to find out the son he *didn't* want had drowned to death in about four feet of water."

"That's a horrible thing for a boy to think."

"Bracken, my father never cared if we lived or died out here. He only would've been concerned with how, and if we deserved it or not."

"That isn't the Gareth I knew."

"And that's the point here. They weren't your family."

"But you didn't die."

"No, I didn't."

"So what happened?"

"I was able to get free. I don't know. The branch shifted or something, and I was able to claw my way to the shore."

"So in what way do you interpret what happened to you that day as an attempt on your life? You said it was the first time Halford—"

"He was there." Clayton sat up sharp and angry. "Right there, sitting on a broken tree stump just a few feet away, watching the whole time."

Mike sat forward as if to say something.

"No, Mike," Clayton barked and shut him down with his tone. "That son of a bitch sat there and watched—waiting for me to drown. Don't say he was about to help or he didn't understand what was happening. Don't defend him. He saw me going under, and he sat down to take in the show. Once I got done hackin' and could breathe right again, I watched my big brother stand up, brush the mud off his pants, and walk away—disappointed. And that's my brother, Mr. Leek. That's the family you're here to honor. And that's why my answer is no. The burden my family has been to the people who live on this mountain has finally been lifted, and I'll be damned if I let it begin again—much less be an active participant." Clayton slid his chair back and stood up. The pain in his leg became secondary to his anger. "We're done here."

Bracken studied him and then nodded. "Okay, then. I need to make a phone call."

"Of course," Mike said, and stood. Clayton was almost to the door when he finally noticed the orange blinking light coming from his portable radio. He'd silenced it before the meeting, but that indicator light meant someone had initiated their emergency-response system, and there was only one other person in the county who could've done it. He eased up the volume knob, and keyed the mic.

"Cricket, what's going on?"

Static.

"Sheriff, where have you been?" Her voice was frantic. "There have been several calls about an explosion on White Bluff Road."

"That's where we sent Darby?"

"It's where you sent Darby, yes. He went dark over ten minutes ago. Clayton, he's in trouble."

"Dispatch county fire."

"I already did, sir. No word yet."

"Fuck. I'm on my way." He slipped the radio into his belt. "Mike, get that gate open."

"Yessir."

Goddamn you, Clayton. That boy is your responsibility and you just sent him into a shit-storm so you could play outlaw. What is the matter with you? If something happens to Darby Ellis, it's on you, you old fool.

Clayton hustled to his Bronco as fast as his gimp leg would allow.

"Clayton!" Mike yelled from the porch, and the sheriff turned to look.

"What?"

"That day at the creek. It wasn't what you think. I mean, it was, but not the way you think."

"I don't care, Mike." Clayton slammed the truck door and headed out toward White Bluff Road, where he should have been in the first place.

10

When the Jackals reached the cabin a few miles off the summit of Bull Mountain, Bracken waved Moe and Jay on into the house and stood silently by himself on the porch. The night air was thin and the slight breeze on his neck brought little comfort. He despised the humidity of this state. Florida wasn't that much different by way of the heat, but back home, the smell of salt in the air was a constant reminder of how close he was to the sea and the freedom that came with it. Long ribbons of blacktop and wide-open spaces made up for the furnace-fan weather. Here, there was no compromise. The wet heat just pounded you into submission, even in the shade. It was a filthy feeling that even after decades of dealing with, he'd never gotten used to.

He wanted to ride, no helmet, no weight, no worries, with the wind in his face, and the beach to his back—but that day was still a long way off. He would be here trapped in this myth of mountain culture until this latest business was done. Of course, there would always be more business to tend to—always one more problem to deal with. And now, yet another man named Burroughs—just as stubborn as his predecessors—was standing in the way of his next long ride. Bracken unbuttoned his jacket, hoping to feel a little more of the breeze on his chest but no such luck. It only allowed sticky fingers of sweat to run down his body that only a shower could relieve. He stood on the far edge of the porch, stared out into the woods, and punched an encrypted number into his sat-phone.

"Yes, Bracken." A woman's voice answered.

"As of right now, the Burroughs option is a no-go."

"That's unfortunate."

"Yes, it is. It seems the youngest brother has no interest in keeping the family business alive."

"He does realize that this meeting was just a formality? We don't really need his permission. And that by saying no, he isn't showing much interest in keeping himself alive either?"

"I don't think we are at the point where threats are necessary, Vanessa."

"I assumed when you asked for this sit-down, you knew the outcome already. You told me it was a lock."

"I thought it was. It's the smart move for him—for everyone up here."

"So much for your code of honor, Bracken. Now there's a wild-card lawman out there who knows what we are trying to do."

"It's not like that. He isn't interested in stopping us. He just doesn't want to throw in. He didn't show any disrespect."

"But he didn't play ball."

"It was the first time he was up to bat. He's in a dark place with what happened to his brother. I believe he's just confused."

"I don't have time for confusion."

"I still believe it's the right move."

Vanessa was silent for a moment before she brought on more bad news. "I suppose you heard about the robbery up there. I'm guessing that didn't help the negotiations."

Bracken switched the phone from one ear to the other. "How do you know about that?"

"I believe I might've been responsible for that."

"What are you talking about?"

"I'm talking about my idiot nephew and his buddies. The last time I was in Georgia—when I first heard about what the Burroughs had up there—that moron must've overheard something he shouldn't have, and thought he'd act on his own to go looking for it."

"Your nephew? You mean one of the men that robbed the bar was your kin?"

"Not just one of the men, Bracken, but the one your sheriff friend killed."

The big biker closed his eyes and scratched at the silver stubble on his neck. "Jesus Christ, Vanessa. How could you let that happen?"

"Thanks for the sympathy, Bracken."

"I don't have time for sympathy. The ramifications of this could lose us everything. How could you be that sloppy?"

"Don't go getting all worked up, old man. I can contain it."

"Is that right?"

"Bracken, out of my respect for you and everything we've done together, I'll forgive your tone, but don't forget who's taking the biggest risk here. This is my deal. I brought you in on this, because of your connections to those rednecks, and so far, that has amounted to jack shit. So cut me some slack. I can handle my own family."

"You said your nephew. Would that be your brother's boy?"

"Yes."

"I've never known anyone to be able to handle Coot Viner on the warpath."

"Does my brother frighten you, Bracken?"

"Now is not the time for games, Vanessa."

"You're right. I'm sorry. Listen, just deliver what you said you could deliver, and I'll handle the rest. Coot won't be a problem."

"You're asking me to put a lot of trust in you, Vanessa. More than I originally envisioned."

"I know that."

"You understand the consequences of breaching that trust?"

The line was silent. Bracken watched Moe and Jay through the broken slats of one of the cabin's windows.

They were laughing about something. Bracken felt the weight of them on his broad shoulders. He turned back to facing the woods and lowered his tone. "I believe the sheriff needs more time. He isn't ready to admit to himself how bad it's going to get up here, or how important a role he can play in stopping it. He will come around. He doesn't have a choice. He's just being stubborn, and it's a trait I'm used to dealing with up here."

"Okay," Vanessa said, keeping her answer curt. "And the other thing?"

"We've got our ears to the ground. We've been treading lightly since we've been here, since our priority is to reopen the routes, but one of the men at the head of the table up here is someone I didn't recognize, so Jay did some digging and it turns out he's a tracker from Atlanta. He's got skill and a reputation for getting the job done."

"What's his name?"

"Mark Tuley. He's one of Jack Parson's crew. Do you know that name?"

"Of course I do. Everyone in the Southeast knows that name."

"Good. Then you know that confirms we are no longer working on a possibility anymore. Tuley's a native to this place, but he was just brought in a few months ago. I can only assume that's why."

"So we are working against a tighter clock."

"We shouldn't be working against anything. If anything, the presence of this Tuley fella only reinforces that we should all be working together."

"Well, that's why you're there, right?"

"That's right."

"Okay, then, keep at it, and I'll see you soon." Vanessa hung up, and Bracken stuck the phone in his pocket. He looked over at his bike and sighed. He just wanted to ride.

11

WHITE BLUFF ROAD

The plot of land where Sonny Cole's trailer stood looked like a war zone. The building was still standing, but all of the Plexiglas windows had been blown out and there was flaming debris scattered all over the lawn. Clayton stopped the Bronco and got out, leaving it running. He zigzagged through the small patches of fire but tripped over a wheelbase and planted his good knee in the pile of dog shit his deputy purposely avoided. He would have been disgusted by it, but there wasn't any time for it to register. That's when he saw the bodies on the ground. Sonny Cole and Darby Ellis both lay sprawled out in the grass. A scorched deputy's hat lay on the ground just a few feet from where Clayton had fallen. He half-scrambled, half-crawled to the only one of the two bodies he was concerned about. He took a quick inventory of his deputy's body, patting his legs, chest, and arms, before grabbing and shaking Darby hard by the shoulders.

"Darby! Wake up, boy. Don't do this to me. Darby!"

Darby was completely limp at first but after being pounded a few times into the dirt, he grunted, and immediately Clayton could feel a swell of relief. The deputy hacked and coughed and brown drool spattered across Clayton's shirt. He was trying to talk, but couldn't. The air was acidic and Clayton could feel his own eyes and throat burning.

"Don't talk, buddy. Cricket's got EMS on the way. You're gonna be okay. Just hang on."

Darby pulled himself up from the dirt a few inches and Clayton tried to stop him. "Just take it easy, son. Help is on the way."

Darby pulled back from Clayton some more and moved his arm to point toward the bulk of the fire behind the trailer. He managed to choke out one word.

"Kids."

Clayton looked over and saw two more bodies on the ground—smaller bodies. "Oh, my God." He let go of his deputy and took off toward the two boys. He didn't get very far before the chemical haze that hung in the air stopped him in his tracks. He felt his throat constrict and he struggled to pull in a solid breath. He pulled his collar up and held it over his nose and mouth, but made no attempt to move any closer. He dropped back to his knees and his eyes began to sting to the point of tears. He wiped at them and through the blur of his vision he saw the two boys, only they weren't boys anymore. They were just charred curls of flesh that lay in the patchy grass barely distinguishable from the warped and smoking debris scattered all over the yard. He prayed it wasn't Reggie, but he knew it was. He threw up in the grass and pictured Reggie the way he looked a few days ago at Pollard's Corner. He threw up again, but nothing came from the dry heave except bile. He could hear sirens coming up the pass—getting closer—but it was too late for these kids. This mountain was a circle of tragedy that never stopped rolling. It held no bias against who it took—not even the children.

He finally willed himself back up to his feet, keeping his face wrapped in his collar. He fell back beside Darby and pulled his head and shoulders into his lap. He could see the flashing lights from the ambulance and called out. He glared at the body of Sonny Cole and yelled out to the emergency medics again. He didn't know if Sonny was alive or not, but he'd be damned if he let any medical help be wasted on that piece of shit before it got to Darby. He looked down at the bruises starting to form on the deputy's cheekbones.

"Boss, Cricket is gonna be so mad at me."

"She'll get over it, son. I promise." Clayton whistled, and two young medics in McFalls County uniforms slid Darby from his lap. "Besides," he said more to himself than anyone else, "this ain't your fault. It's mine."

12

Kate got her third call from Mark on an evening that Clayton and she were actually getting along. Something had happened a few days prior out on White Bluff Road that got a few local kids killed and put his deputy in the hospital. It was something he didn't want to talk about, but like everything bad that happened in this county, he'd blamed himself and he'd been staying home a lot more since. Only he wasn't drinking as much since it happened, so she decided that if he wanted to keep the details to himself, she wasn't going to pry. She was just thankful for the cease-fire. They were three-quarters of the way through an old spaghetti-western movie starring Yul Brynner when the phone rang. Mark had been asking to see her ever since his surprise call a few days ago and now he was calling when he knew full well Clayton was home. It was like he was testing her to see if she'd lie or finally tell him to fuck off.

While he talked on the other end of the line, she debated

whether or not to tell Clayton about her ex being back in town, and letting him handle it, but by the end of the phone call she'd agreed to meet him and thought up a lie. If Mark had been testing her, she just failed—miserably. But she and Clayton had made it this far, and she wasn't going to let some old boyfriend spin Clayton back into his downward spiral, so she decided to meet with him and tell him herself to go back to wherever he'd been the past twenty-five years and leave her alone. At least that was what she tried to make herself believe, anyway.

Once Mark had hung up, Kate held the phone to her shoulder and watched Eben rub at the scars on his deddy's chest. Clayton had let his copper-red hair grow long over the past year; when the baby pulled at it, he winced and started to laugh. She hadn't heard that sound in years. She almost laughed, too, at how stupid she was to do what she was about to do on a night like this, but maybe after tonight, after she shut this nonsense with Mark down for good, the laughter coming from the den could go back to being a permanent fixture in their house. That happy family on the couch in the other room was what she'd been praying for, and here she was coming up with an excuse to leave it. The irony wasn't lost on her. She felt like she'd just stepped into an episode of the *Twilight Zone*, where she and Clayton had reversed roles. She began to feel ill, but the dial tone buzzed from the phone in her hand, sharpening the moment, and she quickly hung it up. Part of her still felt spiteful, like she deserved a secret of her own.

"Charmaine is in serious need of some girl time," she said, and grabbed her jacket from the hallway closet anyway.

"Now? It's getting kinda late, ain't it?"

"Clayton, I love you, but if I have to watch this stupid movie one more time, I think I might run away and never come back."

Clayton looked offended. "This is a classic, baby."

"That's one word for it."

"We can change it. Find something else." Clayton fumbled around on the couch for the remote and when he found it, he held it out. "Here—"

"No, baby, you two men get in a little male bonding. I won't be long." She ran a hand over Eben's head. "Maybe you can convince *him* that this snore-fest is a classic."

"You're breaking my heart, woman."

She ran her own hand over the scars that crisscrossed his chest and ribs. "I think you'll survive." She leaned over the couch and gave them each a kiss on the forehead. "I won't be long."

"It won't matter. We won't be awake."

Kate pointed at the TV. "Of that, I have no doubt."

Clayton rolled his eyes.

"Listen out for the monitor after you put him down."

"I always do, Kate."

She smiled. She doubted he even knew how to turn it on.

13

Kate sat on the passenger side of Mark's Nissan Tundra, the newest and possibly the most expensive vehicle in McFalls County, and tried her best not to stare at him. She'd just left her Jeep in the hands of two men Mark introduced to her as Nipper and Lo-Fat, and it had become perfectly clear to her right about the time she handed over her keys, that she had lost her goddamn mind. This evening's rendezvous with a man who was nothing more than a stranger to her now had to top the list of the dumbest things she'd ever done. She'd never cheated on her husband. She'd never even considered it—and knew she never would—but she'd never lied to him either.

Not until tonight.

She felt dirty and wanted to rewind the past hour of her life and go back home, but still, she couldn't stop looking at this man sitting beside her. She remembered Mark being beautiful in high school, and nothing about that had changed. He didn't appear to have aged a day.

If anything, now that he'd been stripped of the smoothness of adolescence, he'd only become even more magnetic than she remembered.

"You remember this road?" Mark said, and Kate looked out her window. She didn't.

"No. Should I?"

"I suppose not. It's pretty strange for me to be back here. Everything is so different but so familiar at the same time. It's like being in a constant state of déjà vu."

Kate wanted to agree but didn't. It was bad enough she felt like a schoolgirl; she didn't want to sound like one, too. Mark's tattooed arm dangled over the steering wheel and he let his wrist guide the truck down the single-lane dirt road. As they made their way up the mountain, wrapped in awkward small talk, Mark paused to turn up the stereo. Taylor Swift's voice erupted through the static of an FM radio station. They navigated the mountainside listening to a sticky-sweet pop song about never ever getting back together, when Kate was suddenly overwhelmed at the ridiculousness of it all. She reached out and turned the radio down.

"Okay, Mark. What is this all about?"

"How do you mean?"

"I mean we haven't seen each other in over twenty years so get to the reason you're back here—and why you are all of a sudden so anxious to see me. You don't even know me anymore. I don't know you. So please just tell me what this is all about."

"I don't think it's fair to say I don't know you, Kate."

Kate's face went hot, and her back stiffened. "Don't do that. I'm happily married, and if that's what this is all about, then please just turn the truck around."

"Whoa, hang on, Kate. That's not what I meant. I just meant I don't think it's fair to dismiss what we had. It meant something to me."

"We were kids."

"We were nineteen, Kate."

"And that made us kids, Mark."

"Well, if it meant nothing to you, then how come your husband doesn't know anything about us?"

Kate was surprised. "Clayton knows all about you. I don't have any secrets from him."

"He knows we held hands in middle school, but he doesn't know about that summer after graduation, or—"

"Wait a minute." Kate held up a hand. "How do you know what my husband knows or doesn't know?"

"Because I talked to him. I saw him the other day."

"All right. Stop the truck. Tell me what the hell is going on here."

"Calm down, Kate. There's no conspiracy happening. When I first got back, I was out with Mike Cummings and we ran into Clayton. He recognized me, but nothing about what he said led me to believe you'd told him anything about us other than when we met."

"I can't believe I'm having this conversation. What was I thinking?"

"Look, Kate, I'll tell you anything you want to know. Ask me anything."

Kate stared at him a moment and then turned to look back out the window. "You can start by telling me where you've been all this time. You just vanished. You never said goodbye. Nothing. What happened to you?"

"I'm sorry for that."

"It's not important, but if you want to start somewhere, then start with that."

"It's not really as mysterious as you make it sound." Mark shuffled a cigarette out of a pack in the console. "You mind?"

"I do."

He looked at her again to see if she was kidding. She wasn't, so he slid it back into the pack.

"You were saying?"

"Right, well, you know me and my old man never really got along."

"Yes, I knew that."

"I was old enough to handle the old prick when he got to drinking and knocking me around, but my mother, and my little brother—"

"Raffe?"

"Yeah. I couldn't always be there to protect them. Raffe got the worst. He was just a kid. Deddy would've killed him one day if I didn't do something, so as soon as I squirreled away enough cash, I got them out of here. We ended up in Atlanta. I know, not very far away, but far enough from that bastard. We started using my mother's maiden name and scraped together a new life."

"Why didn't you tell me?"

"I didn't want to take the chance of anyone knowing where we went. My granddeddy was high rank with the Burroughs clan, and if Deddy really wanted to put the screws to someone and find out where we were, I didn't want that someone to be you."

Kate's face went hot again. The heat rushed through her. "Is your mother still there, in Atlanta?"

"She passed a few years after we got there."

"Oh, I'm sorry."

"No. It's okay. She got sick. Things happen. My brother and I were there with her when she died. She went peacefully, so she was okay with it all at the end. We were, too, but my brother needed looking after when she died, and that fell on me. Lucky for us, we met up with some good people that eventually offered us work. Lucrative work. The job took us all over the country—all over the world, really."

"Like where?"

"We spent a lot of time in Japan, Afghanistan, the Philippines. All over." He paused and looked distant.

"What kind of work takes you to Japan?"

Mark took a minute to answer. "Repossession."

"You're a repo man?"

"Yeah, you could say that. I recover things." He hesitated again. "Sometimes I make things disappear, too. It's complicated." It was obvious he was keeping his backstory intentionally vague, and Kate didn't press it.

"Clayton's mother had to leave this place, too. For the same reason you had to get your mother out."

Mark cut his eyes at her. "I know."

"But she didn't try and save anyone but herself. She left him behind."

"Lucky for him."

Kate was surprised by that response. *Lucky* was the last word she'd use to describe a child abandoned by his mother. "Lucky? In what way?"

"Well, if she had taken Clayton with her, he never would have met you."

Kate had no response to that. They rode for a moment in silence before another tune on the radio caught Mark's attention and he turned up the volume just slightly to fill the gap in conversation. They rode on for a few minutes as pop-country filled the cab of the truck. Kate hated that shit. This time she turned it off. "So what brought you back here?"

"You did," Mark said almost too quickly, as if he had been waiting for that question.

Kate felt the heat again. She really needed to send schoolgirl Kate packing. "What does that mean, exactly?"

"Well, not you, *per se* but your family. Your husband's family."

"How so?"

"Mike and I go way back. You know that. And this probably isn't going to help me out any with your trust issues, but I was a connection for Mike and Halford in Atlanta for years."

"Is that right?"

"Yeah, and despite what you might think, Scabby Mike's a good man."

"I know that, and I think it's horrible that you people that claim to be his friends still call him that."

Mark smiled at her. She could still surprise him. "Anyway, I was working a job on the Texas border a few months ago and Mike contacted me to let me know my old man died."

"I heard about that. I'm sorry."

"Don't be. It couldn't have happened to a nicer guy. The point is, Mike also caught me up on everything that's happened here over the last year. He told me about Halford getting killed and who shot him. He said he could feel the natives getting restless and said he could use some help keeping this place from becoming the Wild West."

"When wasn't this place the Wild West?"

"Believe me, Kate. It's a brand-new animal up here now."

"So why do you care? I mean, it seems like you've done pretty well for yourself in the lowlands." She rubbed the dashboard of the Tundra. "Why risk what you've got to come back and help out all us helpless country folk?"

Mark looked offended. "This is my home, Kate. You of all people can understand that. Imagine how surprised I was to first find out you married into the Burroughs clan. Besides, it got me worrying about Granddeddy. I knew he was sewn up tight with your husband's family and I didn't know how he'd be affected without Halford looking out for him."

Kate was already tired of hearing that man's name.

"You do realize Halford Burroughs was a lunatic, right? He didn't look out for anyone but himself. I'd say your grandfather is safer now that the psycho is dead."

Mark left that argument alone for the moment. "Well, regardless, Papa's getting up there in age, and I don't know how long he'll be with us, so I figured it was time to come home."

"Did your brother come with you?"

"Raffe? Nah. No way in hell he'd come back here. There's still way too much bad mojo up here. He's watching the shop back in ATL while I'm gone."

"I see."

"But I'm in no rush to get back."

"Why's that?"

"The scenery has changed."

Kate felt the flush of heat on her skin again.

Dammit, he was doing it on purpose.

Kate wiped her sweaty palms on her jeans.

"That's kinda why I wanted to see you. Put your seatbelt on. This road up here gets a little bumpy." Mark turned off the paved two-lane onto a grown-over dirt path on their right.

"Where are we going?"

"I want to show you something."

"Mark, I don't think this is a good idea."

"I promise it's not like that, Kate. It'll only take a minute, and then I'll bring you back to your Jeep."

★

Kate clicked her seatbelt and Mark maneuvered the truck down the rocky path. As the path widened into a clearing, the full dark around them broke open and Mark pulled the truck onto the soft ground at the widest point of Bear Creek. This section of the creek could be mistaken for a river and moonlight reflecting off the water looked like an endless colony of fireflies hovering over the surface. She did know this road. She knew this place—from when she was a kid—but hadn't been out here since then. She remembered a run-down trailer on blocks that used to sit far back on the other side of the water, but it wasn't there anymore. In fact, she couldn't believe what she saw there now. She thought about what Mark had just said a few minutes ago.

The scenery had changed.

He wasn't talking about her. He was talking about this. A small brick cottage, quaint and well lit, with a screened-in porch covering the entrance, had replaced the old trailer. There was a wood-framed swing set attached to a child's playhouse in the middle of the yard as well.

Mark cut the engine and Kate got out. She walked as close to the edge of the water as she could before her shoes began to sink into the marsh. Mark got out and followed. A man sat in the screened-in portion of the deck with a toddler on his lap. He'd been reading to the child under the porch light, but now he was staring back across the creek at Kate with a curious expression. Another child, a boy about eight years old, was on the steps with a sketchbook and some pencils not paying them any mind at all. Kate realized the man on the porch was Ernest Pruitt, Mark's grandfather. She turned to ask him who the children were, but Mark answered before she could.

"They're my half-sister's kids. She's had some problems over the years and Papa's been lookin' after them while she gets her shit together."

Kate nodded. "Are those roads paved?" she asked pointing to the drive leading away from the house.

"Yup. Underground power, too."

"You're kidding me."

"Nope."

"That's not the way I remember this place the last time you brought me out this way."

"So, you do remember?"

Kate didn't answer.

"No, I imagine it doesn't look the same. It used to be a shit-hole. Our rusted-up singlewide sat right past where that house is, a tin can on wheels with two bedrooms, a living room, a kitchenette, and a toilet that never worked. My dear old dad made one room a bedroom for me and my brother, made Mom sleep on the sofa in the living room, and used the other room to drink and shoot crank."

"I didn't realize you grew up there."

"I didn't. Not there, anyway." Mark pointed to his grandfather and waved. Ernest didn't wave back. He hoisted the small child from his lap, and then called the other one into the house. "I grew up in the place it was before that *lunatic* Halford Burroughs hauled that old trailer out of here and built what you're looking at now."

"And why would he do that?"

"For the same reason he did a lot of other things you don't know anything about, living life down there in that bubble called Waymore Valley."

"Give me a break. You sound like all the rest of the fools up here that thought Halford was some kind of hero."

"Hero? No. But, seriously, listen. When I was a boy, that singlewide you remember and a few others like it were all that was out here. You grew up around here. I'm not telling you anything you don't already know. There was nothing out this way but run-down firetraps owned by run-down ex-bootleggers all chasing the same nickel. This whole stretch of mountain was filled with bathtub cook-shacks being worked by some real bastards. My deddy included. They hustled that shit to make just enough cash to keep gas in the generators, whiskey in the cabinet, and beer on ice. Never mind things like food, or beds, or clothes for their kids. There wasn't even running water out here except for this creek. I remember having to fetch water from right over there for my mama to boil potatoes and cabbage while Deddy knocked back beer after beer, geeked out of his mind. It wasn't like most of the kids couldn't go to school if they made the hike every day to Waymore like I did, but who could blame them for not wanting to sit next to all the clean, normal kids with lunch boxes and bright-white running shoes?"

Kate thought about her old lunch box and her own

bright-white running shoes. She was one of those normal kids Mark was talking about, and he knew it.

"It was easier to just fall in line behind folks like Deddy and hustle dope or take a small step up and work for Clayton's father in the crops. I hated this place. All I remember back then was people hurting other people, and people hurting themselves. Hardly anyone here owned a truck or a car. Guns were plentiful enough, but anything that might make a home feel normal, like a fridge, or a TV, or a radio even, well—there was none of that. This was as trash as trash gets. I was as trash as trash gets. Now look, Papa lives in a real home. Those kids have a real yard to play in. They have a shot, you know?"

"And I suppose that's all because of Saint Halford."

Mark sighed, and pulled out the cigarette Kate wouldn't let him have earlier. He took a long drag and blew the smoke away from where Kate stood. "Did you know two kids were killed—blown up—in a meth-lab explosion over on White Bluff the other day?"

The wind off the creek was pushing hard, and Kate blamed it for the cold chill she felt. "No, I didn't."

"One of your husband's deputies was sent to intensive care just for being there."

Kate said nothing, but Mark knew she was piecing something together behind her green eyes. He pulled in another deep drag of smoke and blew it out slow. "There was a time when things like that just wouldn't have happened. As flawed as Clayton's brother might've been, he did make a difference in that sense."

"Flawed?" Kate said with disgust. "Halford and his father sold drugs and guns to anyone who paid them. The only Burroughs who ever really tried to make a difference up here is the one I married. The one who could barely walk on his own for a year because of your humanitarians."

"That's not entirely correct, Kate."

"What isn't?"

"Halford didn't sell it here. If anything, he kept it away from here. He rooted it out and kept it out. Do you know how many kids were blown to hell on this mountain while Hal was alive? I'll tell you. None."

"Take me home, Mark."

"I will, but answer me something. Do you regret it?"

"Regret what?"

"Killing that Fed?"

She was angry now. "I said take me home."

Mark held his cigarette between his thumb and pointer finger. He blew into the cherry and made the embers glow.

"Of course you don't. I do know you. You never do anything you don't believe in. So does that make you a lunatic? Or does it make you someone who did what needed to be done to keep her family safe? Now ask yourself how many men like the one that tried to kill your husband do you think Clayton's father, or Halford, encountered in their lifetime?" Mark crushed the fire off the cigarette with his fingers, before tucking the crushed cotton butt in his pocket.

Kate pulled her jacket in tight around her and pushed her hair back over her ear. She didn't want to talk anymore. She wanted to go home.

"Mark, I can appreciate your *outsider's* opinion of who and what these people are up here, and I'm glad your grandfather and those kids down there are being provided for, but why did you bring me out here and show me this? What does it matter to you or anyone else what I think?"

The lights went out inside the cottage across the creek and the two of them stood in the beams of the truck's headlights. Mark squatted down to pick up a smooth rock from the bank. He skimmed it across the water and they both watched it skip to the middle and sink.

"When the Feds raided this mountain last year, they took everything they found, pocketed what cash they could, and left the place in tatters."

"I know. So what?"

"So, they didn't get it all. In fact, we think they barely scratched the surface of what's out there."

"Ah." Kate suddenly became aware of her own weight. She felt anchored in place.

Money. This was all about money. Everything that happens on this mountain is calculated.

She pushed her hair back and picked up a rock of her own. "So calling me out of the blue, talking to me about our past, getting me to come out here with you, showing me all this, it's all just part of some pitch." She cleaned off the stone and slung it out over the surface of the creek.

They both watched it glide and jump clear across to the other side.

"Not entirely."

"Save it, Repo-man. What do you and Mike want me to convince my husband the sheriff to do? I'm sure it's something he's already said no to."

"You really don't trust anyone, do you?"

"Trust nearly killed the man I love, Mark, so just say what you brought me here to say, and be out with it."

"Maybe now isn't the time."

"Then take me back to my Jeep."

"If that's what you want." Mark moved behind her and reached out his hand. He placed it gently on Kate's hip. At first she didn't move at all, as if it felt completely natural being there. Then she turned to face him. She took a step back, and unzipped her jacket. The blouse she wore underneath was just low enough to show the smooth curves of her cleavage. She knew a man like Mark would be forced to look and he did. Then Kate tilted his head up gently by his chin until his eyes met hers. "I want you to take a good look, Mark. Stare as long as you need to in order to get it out of your system, because it is not going to happen. I am Clayton Burroughs' wife. I love him. You already know the lengths I would go for him. You just made a big point of that very thing a minute ago. Everything you think you know about what's happening here with you and me is wrong. You're no different than the rest of the men born of this place, but my husband is. And if you really need me to help you convince him of anything, then you need to drop the old-flame act and show him and me both the respect we deserve."

"Okay, Kate. I get it."

"Do you?"

"Yes."

"Then tell me what it is you're looking for."

"Millions, Kate. We're looking for millions. The problem is we aren't the only ones looking and if they get to it first, everything I just showed you, everything decent or good left on Bull Mountain is going to burn, and that's the truth."

"And you think Clayton can help you find it."

"I think he's the only one who can."

14

CRIPPLE CREEK ROAD

By the time Kate arrived home, the house outside was dark. The porch light was off. She quietly unlocked the door and stepped into the foyer. She kicked off her boots and slid out of her jeans, leaving them on the floor where they lay. She unzipped her jacket and hung it on the back of the recliner, and carefully sat down next to her husband who was snoring on the sofa. He stirred a little when she lifted a sleeping Eben from his chest, and held the baby tightly in her arms, covering his tiny forehead with a hundred mommy kisses. Clayton reached out to touch her bare leg as she stood. She let him, and then continued on to Eben's room and laid him in his crib.

Clayton was upright when she returned to the living room, upright and sober. Without speaking, she took his hand and led him down the hall.

"Everything good with Charmaine?"

Kate ignored him, opened the door to the bedroom,

and closed it behind them. Clayton reached for the light switch, but she stopped him. "Leave it off."

She wanted to fuck him, but not necessarily look at him.

She pushed him down on the bed, and unbuttoned her blouse, letting it fall off her shoulders. She couldn't see Clayton's sleepy high-school smile, but she knew it was there. His inability to think of anything other than her when they were like this was always a powerful intoxicant, and Kate wanted to feel powerful right now after feeling so helpless all night. She reached around her back, unhooked her bra, and let it fall.

"This is not at all what I expected when you got home."

Kate ignored him again, and climbed on top of him. He hustled to unbuckle his pants and Kate helped until he was able to kick one leg free. She kissed him—hard—not a trace of whiskey on his breath. His beard scratched her face. She didn't care. She didn't want delicate.

Not tonight. Delicate could wait until the morning.

15

Coot stared out the window into the pitch black of a starless night. He looked exhausted from all the glad-handing and the drugs, but thankful for the moment's silence. Donnie and Tate had put on a comfortable buzz and sat on the sofa as if they were waiting for permission to move. Twyla, as always, sat in her high-backed chair by the fireplace and flipped quietly through a photo album filled with pictures of a younger, prettier version of herself and her husband, Joe. The two people in the photos looked like strangers to her now. Joe Viner had been a good man—a good husband to her and a good father to the children. He'd always tried to do his best with Daniel, but when Joe first got sick, it was clear that the product of his first marriage was never going to be the same kind of hardworking and honest man his father was. His transition from Daniel into Coot was more than just a name change, as he got older. It was more metaphysical. He had molted into a different animal, like a snake shedding its skin. It wasn't until after her husband's throat cancer finally killed him that Twyla watched the real changes begin. Coot sold his father's interstate trucking business—one he'd taken over twenty years to build—and used the money to invest their family in the meth trade. Coot never could say no to anything that could kill him, so before long, he was doing as much as he was selling. When the violence became too much, Twyla's own daughter with Joe—Bessie May—had to leave. Although it broke Twyla's heart, and left her alone in Coot's world, she never tried to stop her. She understood it. She hoped that Coot's son Joseph would be a reason to hold on—a reason to believe she still had a family, but now Joseph was as dead as his namesake, and she believed it might as well have been by Coot's own hand. All the men she loved in this world were dead now, and the only ones left with her blood still running through them were the ones who'd done the killing. She had nothing now but the ache of her missing pieces. They created a vacuum that pulled what was left of her in on itself—a black hole in her chest. She held the oxygen mask to her face and tried to fill her broken lungs.

"What do you know about the people that killed my grandson?"

Coot turned to his mama. "I'm still waiting to hear back about one, but I know for sure that the other one is a fella called Scabby Mike. That name ought'a tell you why he was recognized. He's an ugly son of a bitch. His face is all burned up, or some shit."

"And who are their people?" Twyla sipped a glass of red wine.

Coot felt the irritation with his mother rise up again. Not because of the callous way she spoke about his son. He didn't really care that JoJo was dead. The boy was born soft. But the way she didn't seem bothered by how it might affect him. It just drove home the fact that he never did feel wanted by this woman. Not like his sister, her real flesh and blood. He almost smiled at his mother when he gave her the answer to her question.

"They come from McFalls County. Up in North Georgia."

Tate slid off the sofa and helped himself to a beer from the fridge. Twyla's hand started to tremble as she sat her wine down on a side table, and then nervously tucked at the red-and-green plaid blanket she had wrapped over her legs.

"Bull Mountain, Mama."

Twyla's eyes glazed over.

"That Scabby fella is a lieutenant high up the chain under Halford Burroughs." That name hung in the air as it became apparent to the old woman that this problem was much bigger than she had anticipated.

"I heard the Burroughs boy was dead." Her voice was thin and breathless.

"He is. His baby brother, the sheriff, shot him down over a year ago."

Twyla's face turned from plush cotton to stone. Her

voice lowered and lost all authority. "I have always told you to stay away from North Georgia. They don't bother us. We don't bother them."

"I wasn't the one that went, Mama."

"So why was my grandson anywhere near Bull Mountain?"

"You mean *my son*, Mama? *My son* and that cowboy, Clyde Farr, decided to go and pull a half-assed heist. Does that surprise you? Did you even know the boy?"

Tate returned from the kitchen with three bottles of High Life and a jug of sweet red wine. "They were looking to make a cheap score, Twyla." He handed a beer to Coot and another to Donnie and then carefully refilled Twyla's glass. He went on to tell the old woman about the plan JoJo had sold to his friends about the robbery at Freddy Tuten's bar in a much less emotionally charged voice. Coot moved to the front window and stared out at nothing again. As Twyla listened, the tremble fell from her hands. "I can't believe you all allowed this to happen?"

Coot spun around and slammed his beer down on a side table. "Allowed? I didn't 'allow' anything. I told that moron to stay the hell off that mountain. I had nothing to gain by him pulling this shit."

Twyla looked disgusted. "You had nothing to gain? That's always what matters to you, Daniel. What you can gain."

Coot knew she was just lashing out at him, because she had no one else to lay it on, but he was sleep-deprived and worn out. He needed a bump and his temper was hot, so he fueled the argument. "What can I tell you, Mama? He's grown."

"He's not grown. He's dead."

"And what are you saying? That it's my fault?"

"No, Coot. That is not what she's saying." Everyone looked toward the front door. Vanessa rolled her suitcase in and leaned it next to the doorjamb. "She's asking you what you intend to do about it."

"Well, goddamn, y'all. Look what the cat dragged in. It's about time you got here, Bessie May. You missed the funeral."

"No, I didn't. I was there, and I thought you looked real handsome in Deddy's suit." Vanessa set her purse on her suitcase, and crossed the great room to her mother's chair.

"Well, I didn't see you."

"That's because I didn't want to be seen." She knelt down at her mother's chair, and took both her hands into her own. "My presence would have distracted everyone from why they were there. Which was to comfort you and Mama, and pay respect to your son. Something I don't see any of here."

Twyla's expression softened back into warm cotton, as Coot's became steely and cold.

Donnie sat up and came alive for the first time in hours. "Damn, Bessie May, you're lookin' right."

"Go take my bags back to JoJo's room, Donnie." She squeezed her mother's hands. "And then you and Tate can go on home. We'll let you know what, when, and where, when the time comes."

Tate killed his beer.

"The hell they will." Coot motioned for Donnie and Tate to stay put. "That's some bullshit, right there, little sister. You ain't been around for years, and now you think you can walk in here and boot out all the people that cared about him?"

"Really, Coot? If y'all cared so much, then why are you in here yellin' at Mama and not out there doing what needs to be done?"

"I'm waiting on more intel."

"Well, that's a start."

Donnie set down his unopened beer, got up, and stood next to Coot by the front door. "I'm ready for anything, Coot. You just say the word."

"Get her bags."

"Huh?"

"I said get her bags."

"What?"

"My bags," Vanessa said, without looking back. "He said pick up my bags and do as you're told."

Donnie looked at Coot for reassurance but didn't find any. He stepped to the door, mumbled under his breath, and then snatched up the purse and hard shell suitcase with a huff. He disappeared down the hall into the back of the house, and only Tate watched him go. Coot kept his eyes drilled into Vanessa, who stayed focused on her mother.

"I'm here now, Mama, and we're going to make this right, okay?"

168

Twyla looked at her daughter, and nodded. That's when the tears finally came. Coot flopped down on the sofa and pulled a plastic baggie the size of a golf ball from his shirt pocket. He cut out two lines of crank on the coffee table.

"I don't need you makin' anything right. I'm going to handle this my way."

"No," Twyla said. "That's not what I want."

Coot rolled up a dollar bill and snorted the dope. He leaned his head back over the sofa to let the burn drain down his throat. The gray-and-black lion tattoo on the center of his chest heaved and showed its teeth through his unbuttoned flannel shirt. His eyes teared up from the burn and he set the dollar bill down on the table for Tate to use. He waited for Tate to lean down to do his line, and then told him to go join Donnie in the back of the house, and that he'd be right out. Coot focused his bloodshot eyes on the women in his house and spoke clearly so he wouldn't have to repeat himself.

"I would never hurt either of you"—he looked at Twyla —"because my deddy loved you"—and then at Vanessa— "and you're my blood, but here's the news. I'm going up Bull Mountain to get me an eye for the one they gouged out, and you're either on board or in the way, and that's all that needs to be discussed."

Twyla's tears turned to a full-on sob and Vanessa held her as Coot stood up and grabbed his beer. He took a long swig before smashing the bottle against the wall on his way out of the room.

16

THE COMPOUND

Mark pulled the Tundra up to the gate and let the window down. T-Ride had already jumped to attention the moment he saw the truck coming and was standing outside the truck's door like a puppy waiting to be let outside to pee.

"Hey, Mr. Tuley. Man, that's a nice truck. About how much does something like that cost? I want me a truck like that one day. You think you'd ever want to sell it? Hell, I mean, not now or anything, but if you did, I could make payments to you or something. It's pretty badass."

"Slow down, kid. You got your eye on the wrong prize. A truck is just a truck. Believe me. If you keep working hard like you're doing, then all good things will come." Mark turned his stereo down. "Hey, why are you always on gate duty by yourself? Doesn't Mike have anyone else he can put out here with you?"

T-Ride puffed his chest out a little. "Uncle Mike says I gotta get in my share of grunt work. He doesn't want the rest of the crew thinkin' I get a free ride just because him and me are kin. I can take it."

"I know you can, T. I'm just concerned about you out here alone."

"Don't sweat it, Mr. Tuley. I'm under constant surveillance out here, and besides, there's only one way in and one way out. Nobody is gonna get the jump on me. I can promise you that." He tapped at the assault rifle hanging off his shoulder.

"All right, kid. I hear you, but be careful all the same. It's a dangerous time up here."

T-Ride leaned down on the window ledge. "It's always a dangerous time up here, Mr. Tuley."

"I reckon you're right, son. Go ahead an' buzz me in."

"Roger that, sir." T-Ride looked up at the probing security camera and spoke into his radio. The gate clicked and the chain-activated pulley system roared to life. The gate started to move, and T-Ride tipped his hat at Mark as he backed away from the truck.

"Just remember what I said, kid. Always watch your six."

"Yessir. I will."

Mark pushed a button and the window slid back up. He eased the truck through the open gate and parked in front of the compound. A few minutes later he was seated at the oak table in the war room with Scabby Mike, Ernest Pruitt, Lo-Fat, and Nipper.

Mike sipped a beer. "So you finally met with Kate?"

"Yeah," Mark said. "And she's about as stubborn as she ever was."

"I told you."

"I took her out to Papa's place so she could see a little bit of the good Halford did up here."

Ernest spat tobacco into a Styrofoam cup lined with a paper towel. "Yeah, boy. I saw you. I also saw you tryin' to put your hands on her."

Mike shot Mark an angry look. "You did what?"

Mark made light of it. "Oh, c'mon. I was just trying to soften her up some. That's what I was there to do, right—soften her up in order to get her to get Clayton to play ball. That's what you asked."

Mike was genuinely pissed and slapped his ball cap on the tabletop. "I asked you to talk to her, you peckerwood. Not try to fuck her. Goddammit, Mark. Some things never change."

"Calm down. I didn't do anything of the sort. I was just softening her up."

"I'd like to soften you up."

"All right, Mike. That's enough." Ernest spit another string into the coffee can. "Mark is still my grandson, and I won't sit here and let you threaten him. Let's move on."

The table was quiet for a moment, and Nipper and Lo-Fat felt uncomfortable and out of place. Mike finally broke the silence and spoke with a more level tone. "So did you tell her about the money?"

"Yes."

"And what did she say?"

"After telling me we were a bunch of lying, thieving

heathens, she said she'd take bringing it to Clayton under consideration."

"And what exactly does 'under consideration' mean?"

"It means she's not that hip on doing anything that might involve her husband in something else that could get him killed, and frankly, I don't blame her. We don't need Clayton. I can find where Halford stashed the cash. I just need more time."

"Time isn't on our side, Mark."

"I'm aware of that."

Ernest spit again, and Mark took one of the apples from a bowl on the table and carved off a piece. Another man—the man with the scar around his ear—entered the room and waited for permission to speak. Mike tipped his chin to him. "What's up, Tank?"

"We've got a problem at the gate."

"What kind of problem?"

"Visitors. The unwanted kind."

Mark chewed and swallowed the apple slice. "What was that you were saying about time, Mike?"

Scabby Mike stood and hustled into the other room. He joined a half dozen other men who were already looking at a massive set of monitors in the living room. He returned almost immediately. "It's Coot Viner, and he brought himself a posse."

Mark laid his knife and half-eaten apple on the table. "Stay here, Papa. We'll handle this."

Ernest stood slowly with both Nipper and Lo-Fat's help. "I've been warrin' on this mountain long before

you were born, boy. I ain't about to sit this one out."
He grabbed a .30/30 from a rack on the office wall and
walked out the door. Nipper and Lo-Fat followed. Mark
sighed and pulled his gun. He dropped the magazine,
inspected its inventory and slapped it back in place. He
returned the gun to its holster and took another bite of the
apple. When he finally stood, he stopped in the kitchen to
get some iced tea before following his grandfather and the
rest of them outside.

The sound of racking shotguns and slides being pulled
back was loud enough to rattle the floorboards on the
porch, as Mark slipped out the door to see who Mike was
already aiming at. The convoy outside the fence consisted
of two mid-size pick-up trucks toting at least four men
each, and a Geo Tracker carrying the man in charge of the
parade. Mike stood on the steps and trained his .440 on the
ugly Tracker as it rolled to a stop at the edge of the fence.
The rest of Mike's men did the same. More than a dozen
barrels lined the porch rails. The Tracker's door opened
and Coot Viner stepped out. His blond hair and pale skin
glowed in the dark. He was tall and thin, but looked like
he hadn't missed a workout in ten years—he was prison
fit. His collared shirt was unbuttoned and his sleeves were
rolled up, revealing small patches of jailhouse tattoos. The
lion on his chest was clearly something he liked to show
off, but from the porch the tattoo looked more like he'd
painted chest hair on himself. Mike took the man for a

fool immediately. Coot's eyes were so blue they looked unnatural and Mike took notice of them even at the fifty-yard distance. Mike also took notice that Coot wasn't armed. In fact, as far as he could tell, none of the men that came with him were either. Two men that Mike assumed were Coot's first and second in command walked around to the driver's door of the Tracker and joined him. One man was thick and dopey looking. His shirt untucked in the back and a belly that hid his belt buckle—a hoss, Mike thought, but not much else. The other man was a midnight-skinned black man about the same size in bulk but much more proportioned. His movements were the exact opposite of the fat-boy. They were smooth and deliberate. He moved like a shadow. His skin color and dark tactical clothing made him blend into the darkness, and Mike had to squint just to make sure he was there. One thing that seemed easy to tell—at least outwardly—was that dopey and the shadow also appeared to be unarmed like everyone else in the party. Mike spat over the porch, and kept his gun firm to shoulder. "Turn it around, Viner. You got no business here."

Coot displayed his empty hands—palms out—and then crossed his arms and leaned back on the Tracker. "I'd say I got plenty of business here, Scabby Mike. I mean, you are Scabby Mike, right? If you ain't, I swear you need to be. You're one ugly motherfucker."

Mike took the insult in stride. "You're way out of your depth here, Viner. I'll advise you again that you have no business here, and it would be in your best interest to tell your buddies to turn them trucks around and head South. That includes Salt and Pepper there."

Coot looked at Donnie and then Tate, and then started to laugh. "You know what? I never thought about it like that before. You're funny—for a motherfucker with leprosy. I think I might like you."

"I'm not going to tell you again."

"First of all—"

Mark waved a hand to cut him off. He had yet to brandish his weapon, and was holding a red plastic cup of iced tea. "First of all," he repeated, mocking Coot's words, "I know you want everyone here to take you seriously with all your badass tattoos an' all, but let's be honest. It's hard to talk to a man who just drove up a mountain in a Geo Tracker." He looked around at the men on the porch. "I mean, am I right, y'all?" Some of Mike's men chuckled. "What would you call the color of that thing anyway, fuchsia or raspberry?" More laughing filled the porch.

"You must be Tuley."

"At your service."

Dopey chimed in. "I ought'a kill you right now, Tuley," Donnie said, and turned his hat around backwards. It made him look even dumber.

"You sure about that, Donnie?"

Donnie looked surprised at the mention of his given name.

"Yeah, I know who *you* are, too, and since we've both apparently done our homework, I'd suggest you choose your next words carefully."

"I can take you, man."

"Take me where, to the prom? Burger King, maybe?" Mark drank some tea. "Clearly you aren't going to take good advice, so how about instead of you doing all this flirtin', I put a couple holes in you and call it a night? Then, while you're bleeding gravy all over the dirt there, your dip-shit cousins can drive your fat ass back down to Boneville in that pink bitch-mobile."

"You can—fuck you—Tuley," Donnie said, stumbling over his words.

"Huh? I can what?" Mark looked at Mike. "Is he retarded?"

"All right, that's enough." Mike raised a hand to the sky. He was running out of patience. "Mark, if they ain't climbin' back into that weird Jeep-thing of theirs within the next thirty seconds, I want you to take out the squirrelly black one. I got Blondie."

"I figured as much, you blind sum' bitch." Mark sat his iced tea on the porch rail, and pulled out his gun for the first time. He racked the slide on a solid black .380 and chambered a bullet he'd made himself. He was fairly confident that bullet was capable of seeking out and killing anything—even a shadow. He aimed the gun at Tate Viner, who didn't move or seem to care.

Coot raised his hands. "Okay, fellas. Okay. No problem. We'll pack it up and head on out. Hell, there ain't a one of us that wants to be here no how, but can I ask you for just one thing before we go?"

"Thirty seconds," Mike said.

"We came here unarmed." Coot's voice had lost its bravado.

"I can't speak on stupid, son. Twenty-five seconds."

"You killed my boy. My only son."

"Can't speak on that, either. Twenty seconds."

"Do you deny it?"

"Your boy killed himself. Just like you're about to do. Fifteen seconds."

"My son was tied up and drowned to death, and then left on my mother's doorstep for her to find. That's some cold shit, and when I come here, unarmed, to speak to the men responsible, this is how I'm treated?"

"Ten seconds."

Mark couldn't help himself. "Okay, Coot. I'll bite. What is it you want?"

"One for one."

"Not gonna happen."

"Just give me the man who had his foot on my boy's neck, and it can all end right now."

"Scooter, it's already over." Mark shifted his aim and fired. Donnie's backwards trucker hat flew off his head as if an invisible string had yanked it off him. The big man cussed and grabbed at his head with both hands.

"The next one goes right through Pepper's brain."

Donnie started to say something but Coot reached out and put his hand on his shoulder. He said something in his ear that no one on the compound's porch could hear. Donnie glared at Mark, but turned, picked up his hat and walked to the other side of the Tracker. Tate stayed silent, but eventually walked over to join him. Coot moved forward and put a hand on the fence. He curled his fingers through the chain links.

"I was gonna give you a pass, Mike, out of respect for the crown. You, too, Tuley, on account of who your granddeddy is."

Neither Mike nor Mark said anything.

"It's important that you all know I didn't come here to flex on you. That's not what I wanted. I only came here to collect on a debt, one for one, a free shot at your friend the sheriff and you refused. So that changes my terms."

"There ain't no terms here, Coot." Mike pulled back the bolt on his rifle.

Mark got an uneasy feeling in his gut. "Open the gate, Mike." He spoke in a whisper.

"Shut up, man. I got this."

Coot let go of the fence and opened the door to the Tracker. "It ain't gonna be one for one no more." He climbed into the driver's seat, and shut the door. "I'm taking three of you now."

"I'm serious," Mark said a little softer—but more urgent. He laid his gun on the railing.

The Tracker's little four-banger cranked up, and Coot rolled the window down. "Remember what I'm telling you, Mike. I just wanted the one—the lawman. Everything that happens next is on you and that twat, Tuley, there. And speakin' of twats—I gotta admit, the old fairy we went to see first was about as tough as they come."

Nails McKenna pushed his way to the front of the porch from where he'd been silently listening and stood between Mike and Mark.

"But in the end, he broke. They always do."

"Mike, where is T-Ride?"

"I said shut up, Mark."

Coot tossed something about the size of a basketball out the window and into the dirt—a pink-and-red basketball. "Yeah, he held out for almost six hours, but he—or she—or whatever—finally gave up who was there when my son was killed at that pond of yours." Everyone stared at the pink fuzzy ball on the ground with mass confusion. It was Nails who first realized what it was. "NO!" he screamed. His deep voice thundered across the yard adding to the onset of confusion. He pulled his .45 and unloaded on the Tracker as he bounded across the yard. The shots were wild and not a single one connected. Coot cranked up the Tracker pulled away. Both pick-ups followed. Mark hopped the railing, knocking his gun and iced tea into the bushes, and sprinted behind Nails toward the fence. "Open the gate," he yelled. "Open the goddamn gate." Panic broke out across the front porch of the compound as everyone tried to piece together what Mark had already suspected. Mike turned to the man with the scar circling his ear. "Do it, Tank."

Tank ran into the house to flip the switch that controlled the fence. Everyone else just watched as Nails screamed and he and Mark made for the gate. It wasn't until the last truck pulled off that anyone saw the rope tied to the live oak just left of where the truck had been purposely parked. The rope was also tied around an unconscious young man with a stringy goatee and a red flannel shirt.

"T-Ride!" Mark yelled in vain in order to wake the boy up.

Mike lowered his gun and squinted into the darkness. "Jesus."

A few more men started to follow Mark into the yard as they put it together. All of Coot's banter—his insults and swagger—it was all a cover. The pile of rope on the ground by T-Ride was being pulled away faster and faster down the dirt road.

Mark hit the fence at the same time Tank hit the switch inside. The gate began to move and Mark pressed himself into the opening until he could squeeze himself through. Nails pulled at the gate behind him in an attempt to move it faster. Mark pushed himself through the opening, slid down into the dirt, and reached for his knife.

The knife he'd left on the table inside the house.

He fumbled with shaking hands to undo the knot. T-Ride's eyes opened slowly. "Mr. Tuley? What's going on?"

Mark worked frantically at the knot. "Just hold on, boy."

T-Ride's eyes widened as he felt the pressure around his waist. He had just enough time to say Mark's name one more time before the rope pulled tight and lifted him off the ground. It flipped him sideways and spun him in mid-air. Mark was thrown back hard into the dirt as the rope bit deep into T-Ride's belly, holding him there suspended and unnatural. Mark turned his head before the boy's body gave way, and was ripped into pieces.

Mark sat there in the dirt—peppered with T-Ride's blood—as men grouped around the boy's remains. Some of them cussed and made empty threats. One man threw up next to the top half of the body, but all Mark could hear was a strange moaning sound behind him. He turned and looked at the source of the noise. It was Nails. He was crying. The hulk of a man was sitting in the dirt behind Mark just a few feet away. He was rocking back and forth with his huge, shiny bald head hung low over his lap. He was cradling the balled-up bathrobe Coot had used to wrap up the pieces of Freddy Tuten—the only real friend Nelson Nails McKenna had left in this world—until now.

17

How in holy fuck do people eat like this?

Vanessa used a wet-nap to slide the Edmund's Kuntry Kitchen menu, sticky with dried jelly, to the other side of her booth. When she traveled with Chon, they always kept a relative distance between them as a precaution. Most of the time a few miles of separation worked out in her favor. She would normally find a decent place to eat, or read, and have a glass of wine, unbothered. Of course, this was Georgia, and aside from Atlanta or Athens, every establishment in the peach state was just another variation of Waffle House or Denny's. Edmund's was no different. It was a rectangular box of bright-orange booths with bright fluorescent lighting and a waitress who was born wearing an apron. This trip was just a long stretch of boredom and disappointment. How people preferred the mountains to the beach was a head-scratcher of the highest order. The lone waitress working this particular twenty-four-hour roadside eyesore had a name tag that read Jeremie—spelled with an "ie" instead of a "y." Vanessa supposed that witty variation was intended to clear up any gender confusion. Jeremie was also the type of woman who might benefit from the distinction—not a curve on her.

Vanessa sat at one of only two booths being occupied at this hour of the night. The other one was filled to capacity with three rednecks. Two were the size of an adult walrus and the third one was a thin, studious-looking kid with gold-rimmed glasses he had to have picked up from a Family Dollar store. The group of obvious locals had a round of sweet tea, and a basket of cornbread on their table, but as of the last ten minutes, all Vanessa had been able to squeeze out of this Jeremie woman was a glass of ice water that tasted like it had been drawn from a pond out back. *Fuck it*, she thought. She would never eat any of this deep-fried garbage anyway so she took a paperback copy of *East of Eden* out of her clutch and hoped she'd just continue to be ignored. Of course, three pages into the book, Jeremie finally decided to mosey over and ask if Vanessa was ready to order. She gently folded the corner of the page, closed her novel, and asked the extremely unremarkable blonde waitress if there was anything on the menu that wasn't fried. Jeremie was stumped. She had to pick it up and look at it to find out.

"Listen, Jeremie, I'm just waiting on some people and I'm not very hungry, so if I could just get a cup of coffee and a slice of the freshest pie you have available, I suppose that will do."

Jeremie looked uncomfortable as she switched her gum from one side of her mouth to the other. "Ma'am, I'm real sorry, but the booths are normally reserved for two or more customers."

Vanessa looked around at the twelve other empty booths. "It's almost two in the morning."

"A little after, I think." Jeremie was oblivious to the point.

"Are you expecting a mad two-thirty rush?"

"It's just the rule, ma'am."

"Okay. I can understand that, or at least I could, if there was any other business in here, but considering the crowd, Jeremie, do you think we can let that particular rule slide?"

"Yes, ma'am, I kinda already did when you sat down, but you'll need to at least order a full meal, or Karl is gonna get all in my crack about it."

"Get all in your crack?" Vanessa lowered her glasses, and slid a lock of her shoulder-length blonde wig back behind her ear.

"You know," Jeremie said, all surprised. "Like in, *chew me out*, or *give me a hard time*. You never heard that?"

"Not until just now."

"Look, I just work nights. It sucks. I really don't wanna rile Karl up, and never see a daytime shift, you know? I got kids, and an overnight sitter costs an arm and a leg."

Vanessa looked at the photo of two homey blonde children Jeremie had taped to her order pad. She took her Ray-Bans off and laid them on the table. "All right, then, I'll tell you what. Bring me the three most expensive 'combo meals' you have on the menu, and put them in to-go boxes. Will that be enough to justify my seating selection?"

"You mean, if you get all that, can you keep sitting there?"

Vanessa sighed. "Yes, dear. That's what I mean."

"Well, I reckon it would."

"Great." Vanessa picked up her book and flipped to the dog-eared page.

"You wanna know what all comes in those combos?"

"Absolutely not."

"All right." Jeremie scribbled in her notepad.

Vanessa looked for her place on the page.

"And you said all of those combos are to-go?"

Vanessa was getting tired of talking. "Yes, that's right."

Jeremie smacked her gum, and scribbled some more.

"And did you still want the coffee and the pie?"

Vanessa set the book down, spine up, and took a deep breath. "Yes, if it's not too much trouble."

"Oh, no, ma'am, it's no trouble at all. Would you like me to bring the pie out first?"

"As opposed to the food I'll be taking with me?"

"Um, yes, ma'am—that."

"Yes, Jeremie, I'd like to have the pie first. Now, are we all good here? I've read the same sentence in this book three times now."

Vanessa must have pushed a button. "Ma'am, there's

no reason to get all snippy. I'm just trying to make sure you receive the best service possible."

Vanessa pursed her lips and nodded at the empty seat across from her. "Of course, Jeremie. I'm sorry. I didn't mean to get all *up in your crack*."

The waitress smiled. "Aw, that was a joke, right? You're funny, ma'am—and you sure are pretty, too."

"Thank you." Vanessa picked up her book for the fourth time and Jeremie disappeared through the orange-and-white double doors that led to where the Edmund's magic happened.

She saw the idiot coming, before his huge ass even left the seat. The local boy in his early twenties stood, hiked up his jeans, and crossed the restaurant to Vanessa's booth. She let the bangs of the blonde wig drop into her face as she dropped her chin. The walrus put his hands on the table and introduced himself. "I'm Teddy."

She looked up. Teddy's T-shirt was a mustard color, but might not have started off that way when he bought it. It was just tight enough to give a perfect outline of his impressive man-boobs. She could see right through the mesh sides of his trucker-style ball cap that had the letters F.B.I printed across the front. Vanessa nearly laughed directly in his face. "So can I help you, Teddy?"

"I sure hope so. Me and my boys over there got us a bet going and we was wonderin' if you could help us out with it."

Vanessa closed her book, and slid it across the table. She wouldn't be opening it again. "How can I help, Teddy?"

"Well, we were just sittin' over there checking you out and all, and we were trying to guess where you're from, since it can't be from anywhere around here."

"Well, you're right about that, Teddy."

"So do you mind us askin'?"

"And what does the winner of this little wager get for guessing correctly?"

Teddy leaned in a little and grinned. His teeth were surprisingly straight and white. "Well, little lady, the winner gets the privilege of picking up your tab."

"Is that right?"

"Yes, ma'am, it is."

She looked past Teddy and over at the table where the other two boys were sitting. One looked like he might be Teddy's twin—*Freddy*, she imagined. He actually winked at her. The other one with the glasses smiled, and offered a shy wave. She didn't wave back, but thought the kid had a nice smile and a kind face. Vanessa even thought that the kid might have a shot in life if he moved at least two hundred miles away from here in any direction. "So what was your guess, Teddy?"

"Me? I said New York City, of course."

Vanessa put on an exaggerated expression of disbelief. "Well, hot damn, Teddy. You're the grand-prize winner."

He gave a "thumbs-up" to his buddies and sucked his belly in a little. "Hell, yeah, I knew it. I did. I knew it. But you know what?" Teddy held his arms up in front of him, palms out and stepped back. "That's as far as I'm going to go with all this. I know you don't know me from Adam, and I don't want you thinking anything weird. I'm just buyin' your food because that's the kinda fella I am. I don't have any expectations."

"Well, thank you, Teddy."

"I just like doing nice things for nice people who happen to be passing through our little piece of paradise. I'm not looking for anything in return."

"That's very kind, Teddy."

"I ain't even gonna ask for a hug or nothing."

"Great. Thanks again, Teddy." She beamed a gorgeous fake smile at him and held it there until he realized that the jig was up. He tipped his hat and smiled, knowing he had lost the real bet he made with his friends that he could get a hug from the hot blonde. "Well, you enjoy the rest of your evening, ma'am."

"Thank you, Teddy, I will."

Teddy slumped back into his seat and took the ribbing. He looked over at her just in time to see Jeremie sit three Styrofoam clamshells of Edmund's finest on the table. Teddy's disappointment increased. Jeremie walked off.

Still no fucking pie.

Vanessa stared at the orange vinyl seat across from her and practiced her breathing until Jeremie returned with a cup of coffee. "I gave the check to Teddy over there. He insisted."

"Nice fella, that Teddy."

Jeremie leaned in. "I don't think he knew what he was

getting into with that bill, but whatever, right?" She held her fist out and Vanessa assumed she was supposed to bump it. She didn't. Her phone buzzed inside her clutch. Chon was giving her the five-minute heads-up. They were heading out.

Thank God.

"Listen, Jeremie, can I ask you something?"

"Sure, I guess."

"Have you ever thought about going to college?"

"Sure, I guess."

Vanessa waited, but that was the entirety of her answer.

"Okay, then let me ask you something else. If you had five hundred dollars in cash right now, what would you do with it?"

"That's easy. I'd get my damn car title back, before I lose my ride. Those people are the absolute worst."

Vanessa stood up. She took five hundred-dollar bills out of her wallet, folded them in half, and then pressed the money into Jeremie's hand.

"Here," she said. "Go pay off your title, and use the rest to apply at a tech school somewhere. Let today change everything for you."

Jeremie beamed. "Thank you, ma'am."

Vanessa held a finger to her lips, and tilted her head toward the other table of customers.

Jeremie gave her an animated wink and traced the shape of a heart in the air with a finger. Vanessa put her glasses on, and tucked her clutch under her arm. "Where is your trash can, Jeremie?"

"Over there," she pointed, "right by the front door."

"Thanks." Vanessa picked up the twenty-five-pound stack of deep-fried Southern take-out and walked to the door. She turned and looked directly at Teddy, who was, of course, watching her every move. She smiled and dumped all three boxes into the trash. The dumbfounded look on his fat face was worth every bit of the time she'd wasted in this place. She gave him a flirty little wave, and pushed open the door with her hip.

"Dyke!" someone inside yelled before the door closed. *That was the best he could come up with? Sad.*

Vanessa was several feet from her car when she heard the front door to Edmund's open again and a voice yell, "Hey!" Her heart instantly started racing. She didn't respond and kept walking. "Hey, hold up. For real!" Vanessa felt her palms get sweaty, and the skin on the back of her neck get cold.

She stopped between her car and a red Chevy Silverado. She set her clutch on the roof of the BMW and slid her jacket sleeves up to her elbows. The voice behind her was practically in her ear now. "Damn, lady, you can't hear good?" Based on the approximate location of his voice, Vanessa swung around and came seconds away from shoving the handful of keys she'd arranged between her fingers like little razor blades into the face of the good-looking kid with the gold glasses. She pulled her punch and the kid jumped back.

"Whoa, lady, take it easy. You forgot this. I was just tryin' to catch you before you left." The boy held up the tattered copy of *East of Eden* Vanessa had left on the table inside.

"Oh. I'm—sorry. I thought…"

"No, it's cool. It's dark. You're alone. I get it. I just thought this might be important to you."

"You have no idea." Vanessa went to extreme pains to keep her identity under the radar during these trips. The wig and glasses, the wet-wipes in her bag, they were all there for a reason, but she'd allowed herself to get so caught up with embarrassing fat-boy back there, she forgot all about the book she'd been trying to read that was covered in her fingerprints.

That was sloppy, she thought. *Sloppy and stupid. Bless this kid.*

"It's a great book. I read it a few years ago. Here—" He held it out and Vanessa took it, letting her keys fall back around the ring. "Steinbeck is one of my favorites," the kid said.

"Well, I'm truly thankful. And again, I'm sorry for the knee-jerk reaction a minute ago. I thought it might have been your friend back there. I wasn't very nice to him. I'm sorry for that, too."

"Teddy?" The kid looked back at the diner. "Nah, don't worry about it. He's harmless anyway. He'd never have the balls to follow a woman to her car. Especially one who embarrassed him like that."

"Yeah, well, that wasn't my finest moment for sure, and I'm glad you did."

"No problem, ma'am. Have a good night."

"You, too."

The kid turned to walk back inside and Vanessa grabbed her clutch from the roof of the car. She needed some sleep. She was getting careless. She'd never allowed herself to be exposed like that before. She didn't even think about the book. She still mustn't have been thinking straight, because she also didn't hear the kid turn back toward her, or the swing he took that caught Vanessa right in the spine, between her shoulder blades. The force of the punch knocked her down to all fours, and the pain of it shot through her entire body in all directions. Her glasses flew off her face and landed on the pavement.

"That's not my friend in there, bitch. He's my cousin. He's kin, and he's a good guy."

She tried to get up, but the kid kicked her in the ribs. She hit the side of the Silverado and fell flat on the ground by the back tire. She could feel herself blacking out. The unassuming kid with the kind eyes and the gold glasses squatted in front of her.

"How you like that shit, princess? You get off on treating people like shit? You think you're better than us country folk? Teddy wasn't tryin' to do any wrong by you. He was just looking to get a hug from a pretty girl. No big deal. You could'a just said no and left it at that, but no, you had to go and make an ass of him like that for no reason. Just because bitches like you think you can do whatever the hell you please just 'cause you got a set a fake titties and mall clothes. Well, guess what, princess? That shit ain't gonna fly out here. This is our town. We live here.

My cousin lives here, and you don't get to come through and cut the man's balls off like that just because you think your shit don't stink. It's about time somebody taught your skinny ass a lesson." The kid drew back to punch her again.

"Wait," she grunted, and held her hands up to protect her face.

The kid slapped her open palmed but mostly just connected with the backs of her hands. "Stop," she said.

"Stop, hell. Maybe if you got your ass kicked one good time, Your Highness, next time you'll think twice before you piss all over us peasants." He stood up and grabbed a handful of blonde hair. He yanked hard, but all that came up was the wig. "What the hell?" He looked at it, confused, and that was all the distraction Vanessa needed. She swung her left foot wide across the pavement and swept the kid off balance. He fell hard onto his hipbone and Vanessa's training took over. She wrapped her thighs around his neck and locked her ankles. She twisted onto her belly and tensed her whole body.

Sleep, motherfucker.

She let him go when she felt the pop. When she lifted her leg off him, his head wobbled all wrong before it fell off her other leg and slapped down hard on the asphalt.

What the fuck just happened? Was this kid that fragile? Vanessa was heaving and rolled over on her back.

Fuck. Fuck. Fuck. Her head was spinning. She meant to put him to sleep, not snap his neck. She didn't even think she could that.

But you did. Now deal with it.

Her back still hurt from the initial sucker punch he gave her, but she came off it quickly and looked around the side of the truck. No one else had come out of Edmund's—yet. She checked the spongy flesh of the kid's neck for a pulse she knew wouldn't be there, and then tried to lift him up by the shoulders. Vanessa gauged him to be around two hundred pounds. Defense training was one thing, but moving dead weight was another. Trying to get this idiot into the car was going to take too long. She needed to leave him. "Goddammit," she huffed, and dropped him flat. She checked his hands for any scratches and his fingernails for any sign that he might've scratched her. There was no sign of any fight, not even any bruising on his knuckles, just a kid in a parking lot with a snapped neck. She searched his pockets and found a folding knife, some loose change, a sealed condom, and finally his wallet—that contained thirty bucks in cash and a scratch-off ticket.

A robbery. The kid just got robbed. Control your breathing. Slow it down. Just slow it down. You can contain this. Just slow it down. Leave nothing behind. Just like Chon taught you. Remember your training. You've got this.

Vanessa stayed low and gathered up her things—her glasses, the book, the wig, her clutch, and her keys. She loaded the mesh liner of the blonde wig with the contents of the dead kid's pockets, and then picked up one of her shoes that had come off during the struggle. She did a final scan of the lot for anything else that could implicate her—nothing. She was shaking.

Stay calm, girl.

Vanessa hit the button on the keyless entry and slid inside. Once she was behind the wheel, she ran through it all again, replaying the events. She looked at herself in the rearview. Her black hair was slicked back in a tight bun, held in place with bobby pins, but there was no damage done to her face—no cuts and no blood. Her hands were shaking, but there were no cuts or scratches on them either. She was whole. There wasn't any trace of her on him or him on her. She was right. This could be contained. She exhaled slow and crept the BMW out of the lot through the back drive by a row of dumpsters and disappeared on to the highway. Within ten miles, she was laughing. Within fifteen, she was howling out the open window. She had invited it on, and she'd held her own. She might not have known what she was doing as she was doing it, but somewhere deep down inside the girl named Bessie May Viner, there was her new persona, there was Vanessa, and Vanessa had something to prove. And she just did. She was nobody's victim. Not anymore. Not Coot's, not anybody's. By the time she hit McFalls County, Vanessa's biggest concern was whether or not her clothes actually looked like they'd come from a fucking mall.

18

COOPER'S FIELD

Clayton had spent most of the day out by Cooper's Field. He hadn't been out that way in a while, and with no one to maintain the overgrowth, most of the grave markers that covered the left corner were impossible to read or even see from the road. Halford normally had someone out here handling things like that, but without a whip being cracked, no one felt the need to get out here and take care of the place. Clayton supposed he should be the one to do it and he would—eventually. Part of him was glad the field had remained untouched for so long, because it meant not only the weeds and hay grass were tall, but all the wildflowers that usually got mowed down were growing in bright-colored clumps scattered across the hillside. The orange-and-yellow blossoms Kate loved were everywhere. She called them firewheels, and he spent a great deal of time pulling them up by the handful. He couldn't remember the last time he brought her flowers. He also couldn't remember the last time she'd ever lied to him. Until the other night, he didn't think she ever had.

They'd showered together the night before, and while he washed her hair, she said she was out late with Charmaine Squire catching up on *girl shit*. She said she'd had a few glasses of wine and waited out her buzz before driving home, and there wasn't much else to it. That was what she said, but around ten o'clock that night, about two hours before she made it home, Darby had called him from the hospital to ask him about the reporting system software on the station computer. With him laid up and recovering from the lab explosion out on White Bluff Road, there was no one to cover the night shift but Clayton's new hire, Woodson Squire, and the boy just wasn't catching on to the computer system. He also told Clayton how nice it was having the new guy's mom comin' around all the time to bring them food. She was an amazing cook. In fact, he said Woodson was at the station that very night eating some monkey bread she'd dropped off just a few minutes before he called. He said he hated being at the hospital because Woody's mom's monkey bread was to die for. He said she baked it special since it was the first official night her son was manning the McFalls County Sheriff's office by himself. She was so proud. For one brief, panic-filled moment Clayton thought Kate might be having an affair, but Kate was nothing if not fiercely loyal. She'd leave him before she'd do anything like that to him—or herself, and then she made it perfectly clear by the way she practically attacked him when she got home that an affair wasn't the case. That's how they ended up in the shower, but still—she'd lied.

Something was off.

Clayton wandered around Cooper's Field pulling up handfuls of firewheels until he felt a buzzing on his leg and pulled out his phone. The name on the display was one he hadn't seen in quite some time. He smiled, tapped accept, and put the phone to his ear.

"If it ain't Charles Finnegan. How is Georgia's finest junior G-man?"

"Well, my doctor says I need to lose fifty pounds, my prostate is inflamed for some reason, and the AC is broke in my office so I'm battling the worst case of swamp-ass I've had in ages. How 'bout yourself?"

"Yeah, well, until you painted that lovely picture for me, I was doing just fine standing out in my grandfather's pasture picking flowers for the wife."

"You in the doghouse?"

"Man, I live in the doghouse."

"I can relate."

"So, did you just call me to talk about the various conditions of your ass, or did you actually need something?"

"Believe it or not, as important as it is, my ass does indeed come in secondary this afternoon. I'm calling for a favor."

"Well, that's a first."

"I know, right? It's normally your country ass that

needs my vast superior knowledge and experience, but for once, I've got a case that might benefit from talking to a bumpkin."

"Well, since you asked so nicely."

"Okay, like I said, I'm looking at a case up around your area and—"

"Hang on, Charles. I don't know if you've heard, but I'm semi-retired. I'm a little slow-moving these days. My Deputy Darby is handling most of the casework and will most likely be taking over for me come the next election."

"Yeah, I did hear. That's another reason why I'm calling. I'll get to that. But this case I'm looking at doesn't require much; it just needs a few more sets of eyes up there around McFalls County, and the GBI is a little short on manpower."

"All right, then. Whatcha' got?"

"Do you know the sheriff over in Fannin County? He's another hayseed like you. A fella named Dane Kirby."

"I know Dane. He's a good guy. I campaigned for him in 2010. What happened?"

"He caught himself a homicide."

"No shit."

"Nope. Some local kid got his neck broke—nearly snapped clean off—in the parking lot of a chicken joint called Edmund's Kuntry Kitchen."

"Witnesses?"

"Not anyone reliable, just a drunk across the street who remembered a fancy car in the parking lot before it happened. He said the only reason he even remembered that much was because there is never any fancy cars parked at a shit-hole like Edmund's."

"He get a plate?"

"Yes and no. He couldn't remember any numbers but said the last two letters were ED. That, and the plate had a peach on it."

"That's it?"

"Yup."

"That ain't much."

"I know, but I let the guy look at some photos of different cars and got it narrowed down to a late-model BMW—black in color. I know that's not much to work with but I don't reckon there are too many eighty-thousand-dollar BMWs driving around those foothills, and if someone was to be looking, it would stick out like a sore thumb."

"Yeah, I suppose it would."

"So you'll pass the word around?"

"Sure, Charles. We're a little understaffed ourselves lately. Darby got himself hurt the other day at a meth-lab explosion, but I'll see what I can do."

"Jesus, Clayton, is the boy okay?"

"Yeah. He's gonna be all right. He's as tough as an ox, but I'll tell him you were asking about him, and tell Dane I hope he gets his man. I know nothing much happens around Fannin and he could use the win."

"I'll pass that along. Now about that other thing I mentioned."

"What thing?"

"The thing about you not being hayseed law enforcement for much longer."

"What about it?"

"Is that a decision you're dead set on?"

"It's not really a decision, Charles. I feel like I need to step down. I can't get around like I used to. If that had been me out on White Bluff Road the other day instead of Darby, I don't think I'd be talking to you right now."

"I am talking to the man who took two high-powered rifle hits to the chest and lived to talk about it, right?"

"Yeah, you are, but how many times can someone do that before it catches up to him?"

"So you're saying you're turning into an old fart like me. Mortality is knocking and all that shit, right?"

"No, Charles, I'm saying the first time I need to chase some peckerwood down into the woods for shoplifting from Pollard's, I'm going to fall on my face and not be able to get up. That doesn't really instill confidence in the people of McFalls County. You know what I mean?"

"I suppose, but what if you didn't have to chase down peckerwoods for shoplifting anymore?"

"What do you mean?"

"I mean, what if you were working from an office instead?"

"What are you getting at, Charles?"

"I'm offering you a job, you dumb hillbilly."

"With the GBI?"

"No, Clayton, at Walmart as a greeter. Yes, the GBI. We are hemorrhaging good men. Everyone we train up that's worth his salt moves up the chain to a federal level. So a seasoned detective without the inclination to move anywhere could be seen as a real asset."

"You mean a detective who also happens to be a cripple."

"I mean a detective I could rely on who knows those mountains better than anyone else."

"I don't know, Charles. Kate and I are just starting to sort things out, and you're talking about relocation, and we have the baby, and—"

"Say no more, buddy. I didn't call to pressure you. I'm just putting it out there. You think on it. Maybe talk to Kate. Maybe down the road, if you want to hang up the sheriff's hat and you need something else to focus on, you take me up on it."

"Thanks, Charles, but right now the only thing I need to be focused on is getting these flowers home to the wife."

"That's a smart man. Only proves my point. So anyway, put a black BMW on your radar, tell your boy scouts to be looking out, and give me a shout if anything pops up."

"Will do, Charles."

"Okay. Take care of yourself, Clayton."

"You, too, Charles."

Clayton ended the call, and looked at the phone for a long while. Deddy would really be proud to know his baby boy was a G-man. He'd almost walked back to the Bronco with his hands tucked in his coat, almost forgetting to do what he'd come there to do. He scooped up the few bunches of firewheels he'd tossed back into the grass and slung them onto the seat of his truck. Tomorrow was another day, but today was a day for atonement. He held a hand over his eyes and looked up. The sun was at five o'clock. It was the perfect time to stop by Lucky's for a drink. He knew when he got home he'd need to talk to Kate about her whereabouts the other night, and he was dreading it. A fight with the wife wasn't what he wanted at all. He was hoping the flowers were a step in the right direction. He knew stopping down at Lucky's Diner for a drink would be a definite step in the wrong direction. There was no way he was going to do that, no matter how good it sounded.

19

Clayton stared at the red-and-white sign hanging above Lucky's across the street from his office. The sign said, "Come on in…" and Clayton reckoned he would.

He walked into the diner and crossed the dining room to the bar. Lucky's was as he thought it might be at that time of day. The place served as a diner and Main Street's largest eatery during the day, stationary bar stools, laminated menus, and plastic salt-and-pepper shakers on the tables, but it doubled as the town saloon after six p.m. every day of the week except Sunday. Nicole, the bartender, a beautiful little thing in her early twenties that most of the women in Waymore hated for being a beautiful little thing in her early twenties, was behind the bar making the transition. The lights were still bright and the shades were still up, but the tablecloths were already folded and put away. The menus were stuffed under the counter and cases of Bud Light and Yuengling were stacked on the bar about to be iced for the night. Two hunters sat at one of the tables eating an early dinner, a slim blonde woman drinking a glass of white wine sat at the bar, and another young man in a dirty orange T-shirt sat a few stools over chatting up Nicole as she cut up lemons and limes for cocktails she'd be making during the next few hours. She smiled and flirted with the boy with roofing tar under his nails as she tossed the wedges of fruit into small plastic containers she had lined up on the bar. Nicole sat the knife down on the cutting board when she saw Clayton plop down at the bar.

"Hey, Sheriff, we eating or drinking our lunch today?"

Clayton tried to smile, but his mood wouldn't allow it.

"Drinking it is." Nicole poured a double bourbon neat and set it down in front of him. He looked at his reflection in the amber and hated his own face. That boy shouldn't be dead. He could've stopped it. He could've stopped it a few days ago at Pollard's instead of roughing him up like he did. "I'll just take the one, Nicole." He reached into his pocket for his wallet, but Nicole waved her hand.

"Already started a tab, Sheriff. Your friend said she had it covered."

"What friend?"

Nicole looked confused. "Um, her?" She pointed at the slender blonde with the glass of wine. "She said she was waiting to meet with you."

Clayton looked at the woman with bright blue eyes sitting a few stools over. She offered a polite wave.

"I don't know her."

"But I know you, Sheriff Burroughs," the woman said. She picked up her glass and moved over to the stool next to Clayton.

"Well, I doubt that."

"It's true. I know all about you."

Clayton sipped his bourbon. "Then you know I'm married, right?"

"Yes."

"Then what do you want?"

Vanessa wiggled her glass in the air like a dinner bell, and Nicole brought her a fresh full one to replace it. "My name is Vanessa Viner."

"And?" Clayton hadn't looked up from his drink since the first time he looked at her.

"A few days ago, my nephew was killed up on Bull Mountain."

"And?" Clayton took another hard swallow. He did know the name Viner. Vanessa turned in her stool to face him.

"And I believe you were the one who killed him."

20

Having guns pointed at him was something Clayton had grown used to in his past line of work, but having guns pointed at him by two men on his own front porch was something entirely different. Clayton instinctively swerved the Bronco to the left, placing as much U.S. steel between himself and the guns on his porch as possible and snatched his own rifle off the mount in between the seats. He was out and crouched behind the front quarter panel and ready to return fire before his brain had even caught up with what he was doing. A third man appeared in the doorway, a scarred man with a bushy beard that only covered the one half of his face. Clayton dropped his forehead to the warm metal of the fender well and exhaled. He felt relief wash over him, but he kept the rifle in place anyway. Scabby Mike swatted one of the men aiming at Clayton across the back of his head, knocking off his ratty baseball cap. Both men lowered their guns and sulked back to their assigned positions at the sides of the front door like scolded children.

"Clayton," Mike hollered. "My bad. They should'a been told about your truck."

Clayton stayed crouched and trained. "What the fuck is going on here? Where's Kate?" Before Mike could answer, Kate appeared at the threshold. She held the hickory walking stick he kept by the front door, and used it to push past Mike and the men on the steps. Finally, with his wife in sight, and clearly safe, Clayton lowered his gun and stood. The furious pain in his hip shot down his leg like a length of rebar being shoved through his thigh all the way down to his kneecap. It brought a tear to his eye. He'd pushed his physical limits too far today. When Kate made it out to him, she mistook his watery eye as a tear of worry for her. It softened her, and he let it. She smelled the whiskey stink on him from Lucky's immediately, but she held back the lecture and hugged his neck regardless.

"What the hell, Kate?" The rush of adrenaline in his blood allowed him to stand on his own, but he took the stick from her anyway.

"Everything is okay, baby."

"Is it? Is that why Mike and two assholes with guns are on my front porch?"

Kate wiped at the wetness on Clayton's cheek, stroked his beard and kissed him, sweet and light, over and over. That softened *him*, but only a little.

"He'll explain everything," she said. "Just come inside."

"Where's Eben?"

"He's fine. He's in his playpen waiting to see his deddy. Now come on." Kate took Clayton's hand and he slung his rifle across his back by the strap.

"Hold on," he said, and pushed the still-open door of the Bronco shut with the end of the hickory cane. He forgot all about the bunch of wild flowers that were now scattered all over the floorboards. He let Kate lead him inside, passing the two men on the porch. They were too embarrassed to hold Clayton's eyes as he walked by. Scabby Mike followed the couple inside and stood in the foyer, his hat in hand. "Good to see you, Clayton."

"No offense, Mike, but maybe you want to start this conversation with something other than bullshit. Why didn't you tell me about the kid you brought to the pond the other day? That he—that I—"

"It's not important, right now."

"Not important? Are you kidding? Mike, I—"

"Did what you had to do to protect your family."

"I didn't mean to kill him."

"C'mon, Clayton. What did you think was gonna happen?"

"I'm not a murderer, Mike."

Mike didn't argue any further. He knew it wasn't him Clayton was trying to convince. Clayton turned to Kate to back him up, but he could see in her eyes that she wasn't going to. He felt sick and stared at the floor.

"Clayton, it's okay."

He lifted his head back up to look at his wife. He expected to see disgust or fear in her eyes over what he'd done, but he didn't. He just saw concern. Clayton could feel real tears swelling in his eyes now. "He was eighteen years old."

"How do you know that?" Mike said.

"It doesn't matter right now. What matters is another child is dead, and it's my fault."

"He wasn't no child, Clayton."

"Then what the hell was he?"

"A threat."

Clayton just stood there. He stared at this man with the scars on his face who he'd come to know as his brother and didn't recognize him at all. "Jesus Christ, Mike. Who are you? You knew that kid was dead, and you let me go through with that sit-down the other night anyway."

"He threatened your son."

"He was a kid."

"Stop saying that," Kate said.

"Why? He was. He was a kid, and I killed him. I took somebody's life, and to top it off, I took a meeting with known criminals like I'm not the sheriff of this county."

"You're a father first."

"Kate, he was just an innocent kid."

Kate came off the counter. "No, he wasn't. He was a killer from a family of killers. That boy in there"—Kate pointed down the hall toward Eben's room—"he's an innocent kid, and you need to sit down and listen to what Mike has to say before he grows up to die in his underwear and a gas mask."

Clayton was slack jawed. He looked at Mike as if every cat had been let of the bag, but by the look in Mike's eyes he knew there was more to come. He sucked up his guilt and tried to focus on why these men were at his house in the first place. Something must've happened. He slid his weight into one of the dining room chairs and relieved the pain in his leg. "Well, okay, then, what is going on?"

Mike took a seat at the table and Kate followed suit. Mike took off his hat and tried to figure out where to start. "Okay, the boy at the pond. The robbery over at The Chute."

Kate winced. "The name of that place is disgusting."

Mike ignored her and kept going. "We believe it wasn't just a random robbery. We think they were looking for something. Something a lot bigger than what they found."

"And what is that?" Clayton said, and scratched at his beard.

"We think they were looking to find your brother's money."

"What money?"

Mike leaned back. "All right, let me back up. For the last few years, before the raids, long before you got shot, or before Halford put you in the position he did."

"To kill him, you mean? To kill my own brother."

"Yeah, I guess that's what I mean. However you want to word it, before what happened, happened. Halford was, I don't know, not handling things very well. He'd always been paranoid, a gift from your father, but toward the end there, with Hal, it was something more than that. He was acting bizarre. Sometimes I couldn't understand the point behind some of the things he did."

"Well, no shit."

"Clayton, please, just hear me out."

"Fine. What do you mean bizarre?"

"He—he just got weird on us sometimes."

"Weird how?"

Mike conjured up an example. "Like a couple times he called us all out to the compound—to the table—in the middle of the night, or early morning sometimes, before sun up, just to count rounds of ammunition, or go over financials that everyone seemed to understand but him. He was talking to himself a lot. Sometimes right in front of us. It started right after your father died, and over time it just got worse. It got some folks doubting his ability to lead, and if he caught the smell of that doubt on any of 'em..."

"He'd kill them. He'd kill his own people. You're not telling me anything new here."

Mike suddenly looked tired and a bit ashamed as he spoke. "On that day, the day he attacked that girl in your office, the day you shot him, he killed a boy right in front of us, not even an hour earlier, right on his front porch. He shot the kid in the belly point blank with a shotgun. He told me to clean it up. I knew that kid. His name was Rabbit. He was a sketchy little shit, but he was loyal—stupid, but loyal. More importantly, that boy was born and raised not twenty minutes up the road from where we're sitting right now."

"Jesus," Kate said. "You and this boy were close?"

Mike looked confused. "Well, no. Not really, but that

ain't the point. The point is, he was a good kid. Born on Bull Mountain. We being square or not don't matter. He was one of ours, and Hal cut him in half, and then told me to clean up the mess like he was just a spilt beer or a turned-over shit-bucket. That's when I knew it was all going to end. I just didn't know at the time how badly."

Kate leaned back and crossed her arms. "And you wonder why in God's name I question why you followed that psychopath?"

"Because I loved that psychopath." Mike's voice hardened to match Kate's. "He was my brother. Just like Buckley was. Just like Clayton is. You fight for your family. You don't turn your back on them even when they get lost. You know that as well as I do. Halford was lost. It was my job to help him find his way back." Mike picked up his hat and slapped it back on his head, pulling it down low over his brow. "But I failed. I failed him, and I'm living with that. I don't want to fail you now, Clayton. I know you did what you had to do with Hal, and it's over and done, but now we're here."

"And where is that? And what does any of this have to do with that kid at the pond?"

"Hal kept us liquid. We did everything with cash, but he never kept it in the same place. Something else he learned from his father. He had stashes all over this mountain, a lot of them, and I knew them all. At least I thought so. Back then, I was the only one other than Hal himself who knew exactly where and how much money we actually had. When the raids started I figured the Feds would turn up most of it, but I was wrong. They only found what Hal left lying around. After the dust settled, the Feds stopped looking, and I was finally cleared of everything. So I checked all the stashes and they were all cleaned out—every one of them."

"How much?" Clayton asked.

"A little over three and a half million, by my records."

"Jesus Christ. You're here about money. I should've known."

"Just listen. Even the emergency cash that hadn't been touched since your deddy's day in the chair was gone. I just assumed Hal brokered something with Bracken and his boys, or had stepped up to using offshore banks because he didn't even trust me anymore, but the Feds would have found something by now, and they haven't. I think they just stopped looking. The million or so that they did find was a big win for them, so I think they've cashed out."

"Halford could've been burning it the last few years he was alive, if his mind was slipping like you say it was."

"I thought about that for a while, too, and the truth is, I wouldn't have put it past him."

"But now you don't believe that?"

"Now I have new information."

"Tell me."

"Mark came to me shortly after he got here with something his grandfather, Ernest, told him."

"So he was already here?" Kate shot a confused look at Mike, and Clayton shot a confused look at her.

He thought about the lie she told him about where she was the other night, but opted to stay silent.

"You didn't bring him here to help you find the money?"

"No, Kate. He was already here, but I did bring him in on it after the fact. That's the truth, ma'am."

Clayton moved them past the awkwardness of the moment. "So what did Ernest say?"

"He said about three months before he died, Halford reached out to Ernest in the middle of the night—I told you he did that a lot—and had him clear out every stash on the mountain. Every dime. Asked him to bring it all to the compound. He told him it had to be done that night, and before sun up."

"Why?" Clayton asked.

"Ernest didn't know. He didn't ask. He was one of your father's old guard. He came up in rank by not asking questions. Minding too much of a Burroughs' business is how you caught a bullet. He just did what he was told."

Kate got up and got three beers from the fridge. "And he didn't think to tell anyone after Hal died?"

"Like I said, he was old guard. That meant not runnin' your mouth—period—about anything. Besides, money never mattered no how to any of those old-timers. I doubt he even would have told Mark if he wasn't his grandson and hadn't gotten him all liquored up after a night of spades, shortly after he got here."

Clayton took the open beer from Kate. "So why didn't you tell me all this when you found out?"

"Because money makes people crazy. It makes people do crazy shit, and we have enough crazy shit going on. Imagine the trouble we'd have on us if every hillbilly this side of Floyd County thought there was a payday at the end of the Bull Mountain rainbow. Coot Viner and his boys would be the least of our worries."

"And you were worried I'd get crazy, too?"

"No, Clayton, never. I was never worried about you. It was just... well... you and Kate have been in a bad place lately. With the new baby, and all, I figured between me and Mark, we could find it on our own."

"You thought you'd have that payday all to yourselves."

"No. I thought I was protecting you, protecting your wife—and Eben. Like I said, I failed your brother. I didn't want to make that mistake again. I was going to bring you into the fold once Mark sniffed it out. It was a bad decision, and I'm sorry. But I've never lied to you, Clayton. Not once since we were kids."

Clayton said nothing. To his knowledge, that was true.

Kate ran her hands through her hair and exhaled long and weary. "And not once did you think if Clayton found it, he would turn the money over to the police and not you."

"Of course we considered that, but it would be Clayton's decision to make. It still is."

"Mike, there is no money," Clayton said. "I think you're right. I think he burned it just because he could. My brother was crazy."

"No, Halford wasn't crazy. He was smart. You all are. That's why the Burroughs have been on top of the food chain for so long. The only problem is he was too smart for his own good, and sometimes that can be dangerous, as you well know."

"And you think this cash is what these Viners set out to rob Tuten to find?"

"I think they acted on a piece of the puzzle, but if that's the case then already too many people are looking, and that's bad news for anyone living up here."

Clayton slid back into his chair and laid the knobby walking stick across the flat surface. He felt the world swirling around him. "I can't believe this is happening." He looked at his wife. He really looked at her this time. Her brown hair was pulled back in a ponytail, her eyes so big and green and inviting, he wanted to just dive into them. "So what makes you think I can find something the Feds or a professional tracker like Mark can't?"

"Because I think Halford would have left it for you, and only you to find."

"You give me too much credit, Mike. My brother hated me."

"That's where you're wrong. Halford didn't hate you. He was scared of you."

Clayton laughed out loud. "Now that is a line of shit, if I ever heard one."

Mike took a swig from his beer. "You remember the story you told about the flood? The one you told Bracken at the compound?"

"About the first time he tried to kill me? What about it?"

"I was there that day at the creek. I saw him standing

there watching you in the water. I yelled to him to help you. Do you know what he said?"

"Fuck you, Mike. Let him drown?"

"No. He said he couldn't. He said if he saved you, then when the day came that your deddy gave you Bull Mountain, then it would be his own fault."

"Bullshit."

"I told you, Clayton. I've never lied to you."

Kate stood up. "Jesus, Mike. That doesn't make Halford afraid of anything. That just proves he was a selfish prick who only cared about himself even back then."

"That's one way of looking at it, but it definitely lends a little perspective. Doesn't it, Clayton?"

Clayton said nothing. He killed his beer.

The three of them sat in silence for a long time before Mike told Clayton about the attack on the compound. "This son of a bitch, Coot, said he was claiming three of us. He's already killed two of my men. I believe he's coming after you next. I won't allow that to happen. That's why Nipper and Lo-Fat are outside."

Clayton still said nothing. He got up, grabbed another beer out of the fridge, and sat back down. He rolled the length of hickory slowly back and forth on the tabletop and then stopped.

"I think I know what needs to happen next."

"I met a woman today who claims to be kin to that boy I..." Clayton got lost in his admission.

Mike brought him back. "The boy at the pond?"

"Yeah. Her name's Vanessa. Vanessa Viner. She was the boy's aunt."

Kate started to interrupt, but Clayton raised a hand and she stayed silent. "She claims to be working with Bracken. She says she's his connection to the dope they want to run through here. She also says she's the one that inadvertently planted the seed that led her nephew and his buddies to try and pull off that robbery. She feels like it's her fault, and his demise is on her. She told me her family has no intention of exacting any retaliation."

"And so the other night?"

"She said her brother is acting on his own. She knows what that animal did out at Deddy's and claims that she had no part in it. The way she says it, she's the black sheep of this Viner family. She says she turned her back on all of them years ago for a new life. She even changed her name to put distance between her and them, but she's still the only one that her mama, Twyla, the woman in charge of the whole bunch, will trust. That apparently don't sit well with her brother already, so when Twyla gave the final word on this situation, Coot headed this way on his own, despite them both."

"It was his son," Kate said, almost in Coot's defense.

Mike ignored her. "So do you trust this woman?"

"I don't know yet, but it was a ballsy move just coming here to talk to me. Even if she's not telling the truth, I do believe her deal with Bracken is more important to her than what happened to her nephew."

"So what does she want?"

Clayton sat back in his chair, and scratched at his beard. "The same thing Bracken wanted. To be cut in."

"And what do we gain by allowing that?" Kate said.

"Other than what Bracken laid out already? She says she'll put a leash on her big brother, and the war we started ends—now."

"And we are just supposed to take her word for it?"

"Kate, I'm not sure I can believe anyone about anything right now, but I do know that in the brief amount of time I spent with this woman, I can tell you that she's nobody's fool. She's smart and she cares more about money than anything else."

"Who does that sound like?" Kate said directly to Mike.

"C'mon, Kate. That's not fair."

Clayton felt a buzzing on his leg, and ignored it. "Who's working your left hand, Mike?"

"Tuley."

Clayton noticed his wife's unease at the mention of Tuley's name for the second time.

"What have you got him on right now?"

"You. He's watching this place."

"Take him off."

"Clayton, you're not safe. We need this place protected."

"I'm capable of protecting my own home, Mike. But if it makes you feel better, keep those two outside, but keep them in the woods. I don't want to see them. I need Tuley somewhere else."

"Where?"

"He's a tracker. Have him track this Cooter, or whatever his name is, but no contact. Tell him just to observe and report. As long as we know where that asshole is, there shouldn't be a problem here."

"Why don't we just have Mark take him out?"

"Because, Michael," Kate said, "it runs the risk of this Vanessa woman coming unglued, and if Clayton thinks she's the more formidable opponent, then it becomes a bigger problem."

"How about because I'm the goddamn sheriff of McFalls County, and I just don't give orders to have people killed. That's why." Clayton locked eyes with his wife. He didn't know why he was so surprised at the way she thought. Kate had always been the strongest woman he'd ever known. It was what made her so attractive to him all those years ago in the first place. It was why he married her. Mike stood up, leaving the rest of his beer to sweat on the table.

"I'll contact Mark right now."

"Good, and then find out if Bracken Leek is still in Georgia. If it's possible, set up another meeting at Deddy's house. I want to know his take on Vanessa and what he knows about this supposed stash of money."

"Oh, it's possible," Mike said, a little too eagerly.

Clayton and Kate both stared at him.

"What?" Mike held his hands up.

"hing," Clayton said. "Make the call." He was that not only had Mike kept Bracken in the state, he was most likely still in McFalls County. Mike pulled a walkie from his coat, proving Clayton right, and disappeared from the room. Clayton and Kate both sat silent and listened to the front door close as he left. They sat there like that for a long time. Finally, Kate got up and cleared the table. She poured Mike's beer down the sink and tossed away the empty bottle. "I'm going to take a shower."

"Okay."

"Are you coming?"

He wanted to, but that's not what he said. "No, Kate, I'm not taking a shower. This thing—all this—I'm not okay. I'm not okay at all. What I did to that boy has got me twisted up."

"I understand."

"No. I don't think you do. You just found out your husband is a murderer. No self-defense call to make this time. No lives in the balance. Just a straight-up murderer."

"No, you're not. You put down a rabid animal that threatened to come after your family. It's different."

"Keep telling me that, maybe someday I'll believe you."

Kate didn't argue. She poured her own beer down the sink and tossed her empty bottle away, too. "Don't take too long." She walked to the table and placed her hand on his. "I need you."

"I'm not so sure that's true."

She turned to leave.

"Kate."

"Yes."

"You were with Mark the other night. Not Charmaine. Right?"

"Yes."

"He wanted your help convincing me to join this treasure hunt, didn't he?"

"Yes."

Clayton sat in the chair with his back to her. "But you didn't know that when you agreed to see him, did you?"

She hesitated but finally said "No" and left the room. After a quick stop to check on the baby, she quietly closed her bedroom door. When Clayton heard the shower start, he stood up and got himself another beer. He twisted the top and drank most of it in front of the open fridge. He grabbed another one and walked into the den. He sat the bottles on the coffee table and sank down on the couch. He looked at his phone to see a missed call from Charles—his home number. After a long while he pulled a medicine bottle and a small folded-up piece of paper from his pocket. He opened the bottle and shook out two white ovals. He chewed the pills dry, washed them down with the rest of his second beer, and unfolded the slip of paper. He read the numbers he'd written on it to himself. It was the plate number of the black BMW he'd seen parked on Main Street outside of Lucky's after he left Vanessa sitting at the bar. The last two digits were E and D. They matched the car used in the Fannin County murder that Charles Finnegan had asked him about earlier. The drunk who saw the car thought it was a peach on the tag but it wasn't. It was an orange. Vanessa Viner was a killer.

"You can take the girl out of Boneville," Clayton said to himself, and tossed the paper on the table. He opened his third beer and just held it. Beer wasn't going to cut it, tonight. He laid his back deep in the plush sofa and waited for the hydrocodone to work its magic.

Clayton wasn't sure how long he'd been asleep when he came to. The pills had caused him to doze off sitting up. He'd spilled his beer into his lap while he slept, and had a wet stain in his crotch that made it look like he'd pissed himself. "Goddammit." He put the bottle on the table and started to stand when he saw the black man standing next to the couch with the hickory cane he'd left on the table.

"Howdy, Sheriff." Tate swung the length of wood and caught Clayton across the right side of his face. He fell backwards into the couch and went back into the deep sleep he'd just come out of. Tate poked the cane into Clayton's chest and arms until he was satisfied that he wouldn't be getting back up and then turned his attention to the other side of the house and the real purpose of his visit.

21

Mark already had eyes on Coot Viner when Mike pulled him off babysitting Clayton Burroughs, so it didn't take much time at all to swap out designations. This post was much more suited to his skill set anyway. He shifted his weight from his left hip and leg to his pelvis. He'd already cleared the dander and debris from underneath his perch in the soft earth, so the motion was nearly silent. Silence and the ability to blend in were paramount in his occupation. So was patience. He'd been watching the movements of the Viner clan for the past two hours and had already put Coot and Donnie in his crosshairs a dozen times as they sat around an old fishing shed by Little Finger Rapids. The other one, Tate, wasn't with them, and he reported that back to Mike. Coot Viner was a speed freak and Mark watched both him and Donnie shovel that shit up their noses the whole time he was there. The more Coot did, the louder he got. He was already beginning to fancy himself as the heir apparent to the North Georgia drug trade. Mark had dealt with people like that his whole life. He knew ego would be his downfall. It always was.

Pride will kill you faster than a bullet.

He wanted to cap both these pricks right now. It would be fun. It would be easy.

Or maybe not.

Mark's own ego kept him from hearing the man with a scar circling his left ear come up behind him until it was too late. All he saw next were stars.

When Mark woke up he was hogtied with his face pressed into the moist dirt of the creek bank. "You feel that, Tuley?" Coot said. "That's the steel trap pinching down on your tail."

Mark remained still, belly down, and cursed himself for being so arrogant. He'd assumed his man had swept the area before he got there.

"Whatcha' think, Big Sexy? I guess us Viners ain't the bunch'a dumbasses you took us for after all. Whatcha' think he had this big fancy gun for, Donnie?"

"I reckon he was thinkin' of shootin' somebody, Coot."

"Maybe so, Donnie. Maybe so."

Mark slowed his panic as his mind cycled through possible escape scenarios. Coot and his buddy were talking. That was a good thing. He needed to encourage that.

"Was that your plan, Tuley? Were you thinkin' of shootin' me and my cousin here, from fifty yards away like a bitch?"

"I was just watching, Coot. Doing a little recon, is all."

"Oh, recon—with a fuckin' .50 caliber? You must really think I'm stupid." Coot kicked Mark in the side. The steel-toed boot cracked three ribs.

"Did you honestly think we weren't waiting for some half-ass nonsense like this from you people? Did you really think we are that dumb?"

"Well, actually..."

Donnie swung the next boot, and caught Mark right under his exposed armpit. This time he nearly passed out from the pain. He could taste the stomach acid in his mouth as the nausea hit. He held back the sick and struggled to control his clarity, like he'd been taught.

"We ain't dumb, Tuley. We knew that Burroughs clown would make this play. We also knew Mike would send you since you're his pet *big-city assassin* and all, so Tank waited right where he said you'd set up shop. He's been out here watching you watch us. We showed you exactly what we wanted you to see." Coot smiled wide. "You got played, Big Sexy. How's that feel?"

Mark didn't answer. He couldn't. Coot was right. He'd been cocky and took his opponent for granted. He was sloppy. This was his fault.

Tank? Goddamn. They had someone on the inside the whole time. Or they flipped him. How could I be so stupid?

"You know what your problem is, Tuley?"

That's it, keep talking, you little shit. Keep talking until I find my in.

"Why don't you tell me, Coot, since you got it all figured out?"

"I do, don't I?" Coot smiled again, and puffed the lion on his chest out a bit. "Your problem is you think you're better than everybody else who comes from around here. But guess what? You ain't. You were born the same white-trash folk we were. That means you and me, Tuley, are one and the same. Fuckin' peas in a pod. Only there's one major difference. You know what that is, Tuley?"

"You got a tiny pecker?"

Coot and Donnie both looked at each other and chuckled. "The man's got jokes, Donnie."

"He's a real funny fella, Coot."

"He sure is, but no, Tuley, the difference is I accept who I am. I *love* who I am. How 'bout you, Donnie—you love you?"

"Sure do, Coot."

"But you?" Coot pointed Mark's long-distance weapon at him with one hand. "You must have a self-esteem issue. You think the country life is below you somehow. You think you can just put on some fancy clothes, spend a couple of years in the big city, then come back here and act all high and mighty. You look down your nose at a fella like me like you got something over me. But here's the news, dickhead. You *are* me. And the sad truth of it is, if you'd have just stayed up here and thrown a few dirt clods with the rest of us hillbillies, maybe I could've used you right now. Maybe you'd be batting for the winning team."

"Why don't you spare me your bullshit preaching, Cooter, and just get on with it?" Mark knew without proper training, the rifle Coot was holding would rip his arm off if he tried to fire it. It also kicked to the left, and that would give Mark his shot at grabbing what he needed from his ankle.

Coot smiled again. "Get on with what, Tuley? Killing you? Oh, I'm gonna kill you. Don't worry on that none. We'll get to that soon enough. But first we're gonna make you watch."

"Watch what? Watch you and the retard here get it on *Deliverance*-style?"

"See, Donnie, I told you the man's got jokes." Coot squatted down, laid that sniper rifle across his lap, and grabbed a handful of Mark's hair. Donnie shoved his rifle in closer to keep him from resisting, and Coot leaned deep into his face. "No, we ain't fuckin' each other, Tuley. I don't swing that way. I'm all about pussy—and speaking of pussy—right now, as we have this little chat, fate would have it that my cousin, Tate, is on his way to see that sweet piece of ass you were out romancin' the other night, and after he torches that shit-trap she lives in, he's gonna bring her out here for a little party."

Mark struggled against Coot's grip, but Donnie pressed the barrel down hard into Mark's left eye socket.

"Then you're gonna watch me and my boys give her something she is in desperate need of." Coot leaned in a little closer. "Now, I don't normally share my ladies, but it ain't really sharing if you think about it. My cousin there is pretty straightforward, you know? But me? I'm more of a backdoor man, if you catch my meaning."

Mark twisted and bucked under Coot's grip and hair came ripped from the root. The pain was fierce, like an army of fire ants attacking his scalp, but it was for nothing. Donnie bashed the stock of his gun down on Mark's head. There was no more containing it. There was no more fending it off. They beat on him for a while longer, well after he blacked out.

22

It wasn't the smoke that woke Kate up, or the stink of kerosene, or the smell of burning wood. It was Eben. He was screaming. Kate bolted upright, the first and most often fatal mistake of anyone who's died of smoke inhalation in a house fire, but she took in only a short breath of the blue-black haze that had begun to bank down from the rafters of her bedroom. She gagged and immediately began to hack the poisonous gas back out. She instantly went blind. Her eyes swelled like twin bee stings. Panic seized her muscles stiff. She fell back down to her side and wiped at her eyes while she coughed. Out of instinct, she reached across to Clayton's side of the bed. He wasn't there. She tried to yell his name, but nothing came out but a thick wheeze. Her mind was frantic. She gauged the distance. Eben was still in his crib by the sound of his crying. It was still black—still night. Where was Clayton? Heat. Smoke.

Oh, my God—fire.

"Eben!" she wheezed again into the blackness, her voice a stifled croak, her lungs still struggling to expel the smoke. Her throat turned to sandpaper. That second attempt to speak brought on another coughing fit. She reached out and covered her mouth with the bed sheet. Still coughing, she spilled off the bed to the hardwood floor, landing on her shoulder. The sheet, still clutched to her face, pulled from the bed as she fell. The air was better down low and she was able to see just barely through one eye. It was like trying to stare through molasses as it was being poured onto her face. The coughing settled down. Blackened drool filled the section of sheet. She pressed her cheek directly on the cool wood of the floor and through the cotton sheet she took in as deep a breath as she could, then held it. Eben was still screaming. It was coming from every direction. Too many things were happening at once. She felt like she was losing her mind. Everything was spinning. Her heart thundered in her chest, and she was lost on her own bedroom floor. Eben's screaming made her want to scream as well. The wood of the floor on her face wasn't cool anymore. She had to get up. Her son needed her to get up. The monitor. It was the monitor making her son's voice come from both sides. She focused on the further voice—his real voice. She reached out across the floor trying to remember where the door was. How could she not know the direction of her own door? Where were the windows? Where were the goddamn windows? A soft orange glow was coming from her left, or her right. She couldn't tell exactly where.

Her eyes were watering but she was able to see a little more now through both. She had to find the door. She began to crawl, sliding her belly across the floor, pulling herself along. If she could just find the wall.

Eben. Think of Eben.

She pulled herself to a wall and rubbed her hand along the baseboard. She followed it until she felt the molding of the doorframe. Her instincts told her to stand up, but she only lifted herself onto all fours and stopped.

Stay low, Kate. Stay low and get to your son.

The bed sheet caught on something as she inched through the open door, forcing her to let go. She lifted the collar of her T-shirt up over her nose and mouth, wetting it with saliva, and kept going until she was completely out into the hallway. The orange glow was everywhere now. In some places, she could make out the actual flames licking the walls of the hall toward the den and kitchen.

The den. Clayton. She yelled for her husband again, this time her voice ringing out.

"Clayton!"

The thick blanket of smoke was swelling down closer to the floor. It looked alive. If the devil was a living, breathing thing, then this was what it looked like, and it was moving toward her—toward her baby. She pulled herself down the hallway opposite the branching fire and knocked over a small table that held a lamp and a few family photos. It toppled onto her and one of the picture frames cut a gash across her scalp. The pain only sharpened her. It made her angry and she focused.

"Eben," she yelled. Her throat was still coarse and burning but her voice was louder now. It hurt to yell, but she didn't care. "I'm coming, baby. Mama's coming." She shoved the broken table out of her way and slid a few more feet toward Eben's room, staying as low to the floor as she could. When she felt the baseboard of the hallway give way to the doorjamb, she pulled herself in front of it with every bit of her strength and pushed. The door didn't move. It was closed—and cool. She reached for the doorknob, careful to keep her face covered with the over-sized T-shirt. The brass knob was cool to the touch.

Hope flooded her brain. The smoke might not have reached Eben's room yet. She turned the knob and pushed the door open. The cool air that rushed her face was like waking from a dream. She slid into the room, cutting her hip on the brass threshold, and swung the door closed behind her, kicking it shut with her bare feet. The air in the room was cool and normal. Moonlight shone in from the window. She lay flat on her back on the floor and took a deep breath of the clean air. She allowed herself only a second to let the sweet oxygen rush through her. The feeling of relief spread through her body until she could feel the tingle of it in her fingertips. She rubbed at her eyes and scrambled to her knees. Eben was still crying like crazy, but she could see him now standing there, holding onto the edge of his crib for support and knew he was okay. He'd be okay. She'd be okay. He had saved her life with his screaming. She could snatch him up and slip out that window to the safety of the night outside.

Clayton would be waiting right outside—right outside that window. She knew he'd be coming for Eben, too. "I'm here, baby boy," she said. "I'm here. Everything is going to be all right."

"I wouldn't bet on that, bitch."

Kate twisted on her knees to see Tate Viner blending into the darkness at the foot of Eben's crib. Without thinking, she lunged at the shadow figure. She surprised Tate but only managed to wind him a little, before she fell back to the floor. Once he got his weight on top of her, there was no contest. Her lungs had nothing. Her strength was gone. His hands covered the entirety of her neck as she uselessly picked at his calloused fingers to pry them loose. They only tightened. She tried to turn her head, to see her son—just once—but she couldn't. If she could just motion to the window, Clayton would be there. He had to be there. He was always there.

He wasn't.

I'm sorry, baby boy. I'm so sorry.

She repeated those words over and over in her head until a blackness settled down on her deeper and more absolute than the smoke filling her home.

Clayton woke up sweating. The light and haze surrounding him threw off his senses, but the fire spreading from the fireplace and swiftly moving its way across the carpet and up the walls sharpened him and brought him quickly into the moment. He was on the floor between the couch and the coffee table. The heavy oak table was slow to burn and was serving as a barrier between him and the flames. That table had most likely been what kept the flames off him and kept him alive. He was suddenly aware of the throbbing pain and the knot on the side of his head. He had been hit. A man was in his house. How long had he been there? How long had Clayton been passed out? Where was... "Kate!" he shouted, and pulled himself out of the crevice he was in. He knew fire. He'd been around enough firemen to know he had to stay low. He looked toward the hallway leading back to the bedrooms. It was engulfed. "Kate!" he yelled again. No answer, nothing but the crackle of the red-and-orange beast chewing away at his home. His hip and leg were killing him, but the pain only made him move faster. He crawled his way into the kitchen, which was the path of least resistance and pushed the chairs and kitchen table out of his way from underneath. Huge flames rolling over the door and licking at the ceiling blocked the entrance to the house. It was so hot. The air was thinning and the acrid taste of phosphorous was making his mouth fill with spit. He looked up at the window above the sink. He wasn't sure he could get through it, but it was the only way out. He had to make it work. If he could get outside, he could move around the house to the bedroom windows. "Kate!" he screamed a final time; still no response. He crawled to the cabinets under the sink and opened them. He pulled out a red-and-white checkered tablecloth Kate kept under there for when company came over. He carefully pulled himself upright and grabbed a blender off the counter. With as much force as he could muster, he took the heavy steel base of the blender and smashed the window, knocking out the frame and most of the glass. The cool night air rushed at his face but it also fed the flames that had followed him into the kitchen and were now covering the archway. The heat on his back was unbearable. He wrapped his fist with the tablecloth and ran a padded hand around the edges of the window, clearing the rest of the glass. He ignored the pain in his leg as he awkwardly got a foothold on the counter and pulled his entire weight through the hole he'd made. For the second time in twenty-four hours Clayton fell to his knees, this time after tumbling through a massive thicket of red-tipped azaleas. The small branches cut his face and tore at his clothes, but he quickly dropped flat and rolled several feet out into the cool, dew-covered grass. He didn't allow himself to rest in the comfortable safety outside, as he scrambled to his feet and made for the back of the house. The pain in his leg and side was practically unbearable. "Kate!" he yelled over and over as he ran. The windows to the bedroom were dark and still locked. That meant no one had come through them. He banged on both of them with the fist he still had wrapped in the tablecloth. He knew that if the fire hadn't pushed its way in there already, busting the windows open would only pull it in, so he held his bare hand up to the glass. It was hot on his palm, but not enough to burn him. He looked in and could make out the shape of the bed. More importantly, he could see that Kate wasn't in it. "Where are you?" he said out loud, but immediately knew the answer to that question. He knew exactly where she'd be if she were able to get out of the room. He continued around the house to Eben's window. It was wide open. A tidal wave of relief rushed over him.

She got out. She got to Eben and they got out.

He was panting, and leaned down on his knees as he screamed her name again. He still got no response from her, but this time he could hear something. He could hear Eben crying. The boy was still in the house. Clayton pulled the collar of his shirt up to cover his nose and mouth and stuck his head into Eben's window. His son was on his back still lying in his crib. The baby's screams chilled Clayton's blood. He'd never heard anything like it.

"Hold on, buddy, I'm coming." He shook the tablecloth free of any shards of glass, balanced himself on the window ledge and tossed the red-and-white material into the crib. Clayton stretched his arm into the room as far as he could, grabbed hold of the crib's railing and pulled. Once it was where he could reach down into it, he covered the baby with the tablecloth and pulled his son out of the window and into the safety of his arms.

Then he collapsed.

He fell on his back into the grass with his eyes closed, and held his son close to his chest. Eben kept screaming but he was safe. They were safe. His eyes popped open.

Kate.

He struggled to make it to his knees. He needed to set Eben down somewhere safe and go back in, but before he could stand, he noticed something that took him a few seconds to process. Kate's Jeep—it wasn't there. Kate wasn't there. Where would she go? She would never leave Eben in the middle of the night without letting Clayton know. She would never just leave. Another tidal wave washed over Clayton as the reality of the situation made his head spin.

Jesus Christ. No—

He carried Eben and limped to the Bronco parked next to where Kate's Jeep should've been, and nestled the hysterical baby into the safety-seat in the back. He swung open the driver's door and snatched the handset from the radio. His first call was 911, and then he switched it over to the channel he knew only one person would be listening to.

"Mike! Come in. Mike!"

"Clayton?"

"Mike! I wasn't the target. They didn't come for me."

"What are you talking about, Clayton?"

"Mike, they have Kate."

23

LITTLE FINGER RAPIDS

Coot Viner laid his Smith & Wesson .357 on a particleboard shelf inside the shack he'd found out by the small rapids. The inside of the four-by-six shed was covered in Freddy Tuten's dried blood and it stank like hell. Tate was effective in extracting information, but his methods were sloppy. Coot stepped to the entrance and took a piss directly out the front door. It made a puddle in the dirt and mud. He zipped his jeans, and cupped his fingerless gloved hands together over his mouth and breathed heavily into his palms to try and keep his face warm. The mountain wind had turned cold and cut through the trees and off the water like a thunderstorm of razor blades. He pulled his baseball cap down tight over his brow and rubbed his hands together for the friction as he stood on the rickety front stoop of the shack. His wind-chapped cheeks were a brighter shade of pink, and the weather shift made him eager to get home, but that changed when he saw the headlights appear from the main road above him.

He called out to Donnie who had been down at the water's edge, drinking whiskey straight from the bottle.

"Heads up, cousin. It's game time."

Donnie had done enough amphetamines to make him immune to the biting weather and was trying to even himself out with the liquor. He screwed the cap on his bottle, joined Coot at the shack, and pulled out a fat baggie of a yellowish caked-up powder. He huffed a bump off one of his overgrown pinky nails. Coot felt at his own dwindling supply in his jacket pocket. He looked at Donnie's baggie with envy.

"You've had enough, Donnie. Save the rest for the drive home."

Donnie didn't argue, but snorted another bump anyway. He held the open baggie out. Coot snatched it and huffed a bump off his key to the Tracker. The fire and rush of adrenaline from the dope instantly warmed him up. They both watched through watery, bloodshot eyes, as their cousin maneuvered Kate's canary-yellow Jeep Wrangler through the trees until it came to a stop in the clearing next to Coot's Tracker. Tate got out of the Jeep, cupped a lighter, and lit a smoke.

Coot wiped his sore nose with the back of his hand. "You burn the house?"

"Yeah."

"The sheriff, too?"

"Yeah."

"You watch him fry?"

"No."

"So how do you know he's dead?"

"He's dead, Coot. I promise you."

"You promise me." Coot mocked his cousin's choice of words.

Tate lifted his hands in the air. "I brained him, and I set him and the place on fire. What else you want?"

"Nothing. How about the kid?"

Tate hesitated for just a second and pulled in a chest full of warm smoke. "Coot, Twyla said not to hurt anybody in the family. We shouldn't even be out here."

Coot grabbed him by a handful of his coat. "I don't give a damn what Mama said. I asked you a question. Did you handle the kid?"

Tate yanked himself free of Coot's grip. "Yeah, I handled the kid, but when all this is said and done, that shit is on you. You're the one who's gonna tell Twyla what happened, and you can leave me out of it. I'm not going to answer to her for you going off the reservation on this."

"I'll handle Mama."

"You better."

"You threatening me, Tate?" Coot sniffed at the meth stuck in his nostrils that was making his nose run.

"Calm down, Coot. I'm just sayin'. I did what you asked, like I always do without question. I just don't want that woman pissed at me—and she's gonna be pissed."

"She's gonna be fine," Donnie said.

"Shut the fuck up, Donnie," both Tate and Coot said in unison. Donnie did.

Coot wiped his nose on his sleeve, and banged his fist

on the hood of the Jeep. "Whatever. Let's pop the hatch on this piece of shit and get this party started."

Tate tossed Coot the keys. "Y'all have fun."

"What, you ain't stickin' around for a taste?"

"Ain't my style, Coot. Y'all do whatever you want, but violating bony white women ain't on my bucket list. I'm going to find me a warm motel somewhere and relax. If I get my pecker wet, it'll be by somebody willing."

Coot shook the keys in Tate's face. "Your loss, amigo." He moved to the back of the Jeep. Donnie watched Tate stomp out his smoke and climb the steep path back up to the road. The truth was, he wasn't much down for this idea either, but he wasn't about to have Coot get crazy on him, and he knew he would. He'd rather have Twyla mad at him, than to suffer Coot's cranked-out wrath. He set his whiskey bottle in the dirt, and joined his cousin at the back of the Jeep.

Coot held the keys to the Jeep up to the moonlight and found the small silver one that unlocked the tailgate. He twisted the latch, pulled back the crossbar holding the spare tire, and swung the gate open wide.

"Here." He tossed the keys to Donnie. "Chuck those in the creek."

"Why?"

"Because I said so. I don't want this pretty lady getting any ideas about leaving the party early." Kate was in one of Clayton's T-shirts and a pair of light-blue cotton pajama bottoms that were more brown now than blue after pulling herself through a burning house and then being dragged through her front yard. Her bare feet were scraped-up and filthy, and her ankles were bound with a large black zip-tie. A similar strip of black plastic bound her wrists up tight, and a red bandana wrapped her mouth, cutting into her cheeks. It was tied so tight it stretched the corners of her mouth in a horrible grin. She'd been crying and her nose was clogged, making it a struggle for her to breathe. She looked helpless and pathetic, and Coot couldn't have been more pleased.

"Well, lookie here, cousin. The queen of Bull Mountain all wrapped up like a birthday present and scared as a shit-house rat." Coot adjusted his crotch as he spoke, and stuck his head in under the ragtop. "Well, ain't this a fuckin' pickle? You know who I am, sugar?"

Kate just glared at him, trying to control her tears. She was bunched up as close to the rough lining of the backseats as she could be.

"My name is Coot Viner." He pointed back at Donnie. "That there is my dumb-ass cousin, Donnie. Our names ring any bells? They should. I'm sure your husband or that scar-faced fuck told you a little about me."

Kate didn't move. She couldn't.

"Killing my boy was the dumbest move your hubby could've made, and this here is his reckoning. Part of me hopes he lives through what Tate did to your house so he can get the full effect of knowing that what I'm about to do to you is all his fault." Coot reached into the Jeep and grabbed hold of the zip-tie binding Kate's feet. She kicked at him, but once he had a firm hold on her ankles, he pulled hard, and Kate slipped out easily, falling to the ground. She landed on her hip and shoulder with no way to break the fall. She struggled to ignore the pain of the impact, and immediately tried to scoot away from the two men.

Coot watched her and laughed, knowing there was nowhere she could go. That's when she saw Mark. He'd been beaten and hogtied. One eye was swollen shut, and his nose was obviously broken, smashed flat and fleshy like a dull-purple silver dollar. If he were still alive, he'd never look the same again. She was flooded with guilt. Mark was covered in mud from the creek bank, most of it dried in flakey chunks that hung off his skin like tar-paper shingles. His immaculately white T-shirt was now as brown and slick as the sludge he was embedded in. For a brief moment, the pain faded, and anger flooded her brain. She inched toward him, and Coot walked alongside her. He watched her reaction with immense pleasure, and smiled wide like a kid at Christmas. This was better than Christmas.

"Oh, yeah. That's your boy, right? We worked him over real good, but don't worry. He's still alive. We thought you might want a witness to this. Don't close your good eye, there, Big Sexy. I promise you ain't gonna wanna miss this."

Mark didn't move.

Coot reached down to grab Kate's shirt, but she shifted

in the dirt and swung both feet into his crotch. Coot fell back and cussed, hopping around like he'd stepped on an anthill. Kate took advantage of the precious few seconds and struggled against her restraints. Donnie kicked her in the stomach, ending her struggle. She buckled and saw a flash of white, but she didn't pass out. Coot recovered and got a handful of her T-shirt and pajamas. He flipped her over roughly on her belly. He grabbed a fistful of thick brown hair, and twisted his hand into it tight, pressing her face into the marsh.

"You're gonna pay for that, too, bitch." He wrapped her hair tighter around his fist and pulled Kate a few feet through the mud to the shallow edge of Little Finger Creek. Her face rubbed across rocks and grime. An exposed root caught the gag, pulling it free to hang around her neck. She kept her eyes closed and her mouth pressed shut to keep the slime and mud from blinding or choking her as she listened to Coot babble on about what he was going to do to her. Once she could lift her neck high enough to clear the mud she screamed. Coot turned her head like a puppet and slapped her with an open palm.

"None of that shit, girl. There'll be plenty of time for that in a minute." He twisted his fist again until some of her hair started to separate from her scalp, and then used his free hand to grab the back of her waistband. He hoisted her entire weight onto a huge, smooth chunk of limestone that hung out over the rapids, and called back to Donnie to help hold her down. Donnie lumbered over, unsure about any of it, but did as he was told, like he always did. He didn't have to strain to keep her down. Kate's second wind after seeing Mark was gone. It wouldn't have mattered anyway. They were too strong. She caught a sudden whiff of Coot's body odor. The sour stench came on her fast and twisted her stomach into a fist. Panic poured over her neck and down her back like a pitcher of ice water. She closed her eyes and retreated into one thought until it became a mantra that pumped through her brain as surely as the blood in her veins.

Find a way. Stay alive and find a way.

She repeated it over and over until her entire body fell into sync with the words, slowing and shutting down all her other senses. She repeated it until it was all that remained of her.

Find a way. Stay alive and find a way.

"Pull her goddamn arms down, Donnie."

The big man pulled at Kate's bound wrists stretching her arms out in front of her, down over the creek side of the huge rock. He had to stand ankle deep in the shallow rapids to do it, and it just made him all the more ready to be done with all this. Coot jumped up on top of her and straddled Kate's thighs right above the soft crooks of her knees. When she did find temporary bursts of strength to buck at him, Coot just pressed down harder. She found her voice and screamed again, but it wasn't fear—the sound was more feral, like an animal.

Coot produced a sharp, thin-bladed knife he'd found in the shed. It was the kind of knife normally used to scale and gut fish, and it was caked with Freddie Tuten's dried blood. He held the razor-sharp blade to her throat. "You scream anything other than my name from this point on and I'll slice your neck open from ear to ear. You'll bleed out like a strung-up whitetail, and then you know what? I'll do you anyway."

Kate was lost inside her head.

Find a way. Stay alive and find a way.

"You ain't shit, woman. I know you really thought you were, being married to that clown sheriff an' all, but you ain't. You never were. I'm the king of the jungle now. I'm the lion on top of the mountain, not you. You see this?" He whipped her head to the side and pulled open the front of his shirt. The jailhouse lion tattoo roared underneath. "That's who I am. You're just a gazelle—a rabbit maybe. That's it. You're a walking, talking Happy Meal."

Kate didn't scream, but she spoke with a cold tone from a place beyond fear. She was defeated and helpless but she had moved past being frightened and into a rich hatred that thickened her skin as well as the air around her. She spoke the only words that mattered, with a voice she didn't even recognize as her own. "My name is Katelyn Burroughs, and you can't hurt me."

Coot laughed and looked at his cousin. Donnie forced up a chuckle, but didn't think any of this was funny.

"I'm done talkin'. Donnie, you got her?"

"Yeah."

Coot used the scaling knife to cut at the fabric of Kate's pajamas, right at where it bunched up between her legs. He carefully sliced up the seam until he reached the elastic waistband, and easily hacked it in half. The dirty blue material slid right off her, falling to the sides of her hips, leaving her exposed and bare.

"Look at that, Donnie. No squirrel covers. I was hoping for a nice thong or something to hang from the rearview of the Tracker. That's too bad."

Kate's pink skin was the only clean thing for miles. Maybe the only clean thing left on the mountain. Donnie looked away. He stared down into the shallow rapids and tried to think of something else. He wondered where Tate had gone. He wished he'd gone with him.

"Just get it done, Coot. My feet are cold."

Coot smiled and set the knife down on the rock. He used both hands to rip the pajamas further down Kate's legs, and then propped himself up to unbuckle his pants. Mark shuffled violently in the mud onto his side and bellowed underneath his gag. Coot smiled at him and mocked the sound he made as he slung his belt into the grass by Tuley's face and lowered his jeans. Mark twisted in the mud again, flipping himself over to his other side to face away from the creek. Kate watched him turn away. She understood.

Coot took off his gloves with his teeth, and spat into his hand. He rubbed at himself and cussed at the cold. After a moment he spat again onto Kate's naked backside. The cold bite of the wind and all the crank in his system was causing him some difficulty. Donnie looked up in disgust while Coot shifted and shook his right leg frantically to push the tangled mess of denim down past his knee.

Once his leg was free, he reached down to get a better grip on himself. He pushed himself up closer onto Kate, and then a shot rang out. The bullet whizzed past his head close enough to skin his cheek.

The gunshot sounded like a cannon echoing over the mountain. It missed its intended target, but took Donnie in the shoulder. The bullet stung like a snake bite and the impact caused him to slip backwards into the creek. He just sat there in the rushing water, confused, as blood started to ooze out from the tiny hole in his jacket. Coot immediately slid off Kate into an awkward barrel roll, and covered his face with both hands. Once he hit the ground he jammed himself close to the side of the limestone for cover. His jeans still hung off one leg in a tangled knot, and he patted at himself all over to make sure he hadn't been hit. He stayed still and waited for a second shot, or a voice from the shooter, but heard nothing but the churning rapids of the creek. He tried to hike his pants up, but couldn't, his hands were shaking too bad. He cautiously looked out and around the big rock, squinting his eyes to see through the trees. A lantern on the stoop lit the area well enough, but he couldn't see anyone. He yelled out, making empty threats, but heard only the echo of his own voice. He spun himself and peeked out from the creek side of the rock. Donnie was still there, sitting in the water looking at his bloody shoulder. He'd been hit, and was out in the open.

Why wouldn't they hit him again? Coot thought. *He's a sitting duck.*

He looked up at Kate, who had shifted only slightly on the rock and still appeared to be lost in her mind. He peered out a little further to see Mark, still hogtied, and still lying on his side facing the other way. It took Coot another careful scan of the area before he saw it—a small silver glint in the mud next to Mark. He stared at it for a long time before he finally stood up and shook his head.

"Son of a bitch." Coot stepped out from behind the rock, shook his pants off his leg, and walked over to get a better look at the hunk of metal in the mud. It was just a few inches or so from Mark Tuley's fingers. "You sneaky bastard. A purse gun?" Coot bent over and picked up the weapon. He held the small gun up to the moonlight, and stood in the cold, naked from the waist down, and studied the tiny gun. It was a single-shot .45 caliber pistol. The thing was as small as a Dillinger but with a bigger boom, easily concealable in a purse—or in a pocket—or a boot. "Jesus Christ," he said. "Tank didn't think to search your boots? I swear to God, Tuley, I'm surrounded by retards. I'm going to shoot his ugly ass with this thing the minute I see him. You had this mini-cannon on you the whole time? Hey, Donnie, come take a look at this thing. This asshole could've shot my pecker off."

Mark grunted through the gag. He was obviously laughing. Coot squatted and pulled back the tape. "What's so funny, motherfucker?"

Mark sucked in twin lungfuls of cold mountain air that caused him to cough, but through the hacking his laughter only got louder.

"You missed, Tuley."

Mark just kept laughing.

"I mean, you gotta know I'm gonna kill you now, right? I'm gonna cut your goddamn throat, so I fail to see what's so funny."

Mark took in some more cool night air and tamed his laughter down to a breathy giggle. "Yeah, Coot, I know, but that shit you said was pretty funny, you gotta admit?"

"What did I say, Tuley?"

"You know. What you said a minute ago."

Coot drew a blank.

"That thing about your pecker."

Coot stayed a blank.

Mark did his best to smile even through the pain of a busted lip and all the broken teeth. The fear fell away from his face as he looked directly into Viner's bright blue eyes. "I appreciate the confidence in my abilities and all." Mark spat out a wad of blood and snot that stayed connected to his tongue and stuck to his cheek. "But there ain't a sharp shooter on the planet that could've shot something that tiny. I mean, holy shit, Scooter, that thing is like a toddler's. I bet you ain't even grown any hair around it yet."

Coot stood up.

"C'mon, Scooter, let's be honest here. Man to man.

Is that the real reason they call you 'Cooter'? Is it because that little package of yours looks more like a clit than a dick?" Mark cracked himself up and the laughing made him cough out more blood and snot. "It's more like a *Jolene* than a *Johnson*. Not even half a stack of dimes. Jesus, man, I'm the one staring death in the face and *I* feel sorry for *you*." Mark spat one last time and but never once closed his eyes. Coot reached for the scaling knife in his jacket.

He found nothing.

Mark laughed again. He was almost hysterical.

"Keep laughing, Tuley. I'll be right back."

Coot turned back to the rock and for the first time since he'd arrived on the mountain he saw something that scared him. The rock was still there, but Kate was gone. He frantically shook out his pants, and hustled toward the stone.

"You lose, Scooter," Mark said. "She's going to kill you."

"I doubt that shit. She won't get that far." He looked out at the creek. "Hey, Donnie, it looks like we're just gonna have to shoot these two and call it a night." He pulled up his pants and zipped the fly. "Donnie?" He strained his eyes to see his cousin lying on his back now in the shallow water of the rapids. Small spurts of black blood were arching from the several puncture wounds that crossed his chest. His face glowed a pale white.

"Son of a bitch."

Coot ran for the shed and made a quick grab for his shoes and the .357. "I'm coming to get you, Kate." He knew she couldn't go far. She was beaten, half-naked, and barefoot. He'd find her. He had to. He could let this go sideways. He grabbed the lantern from the stoop and held the light up to shine on the creek bank. He ignored his cousin and found what he was looking for. The indentations in the soft dirt from Kate's footprints were clear as day. He smiled as he put on his shoes. "Here I come, baby girl. Here comes Deddy." He followed the tracks in the mud up from the bank and into the trees. Kate's pajama bottoms were tossed into the brush and Coot studied the trail. Snapped branches and fresh tracks led up to a cluster of pine trees beyond a steep trench. He set the lantern down in the thick dander of the forest floor and whistled. "Come on out, sweetheart. You don't want to keep ol' Coot waiting." He cocked the heavy pistol and moved through the trench and toward the trees. "I'm sorry about our date night, but killing my cousin like you did means we need to skip over the romance and get right down to the nitty-gritty. Come on out here and let's finish this up clean." He took a wide step up to clear the ditch when he felt something rustle by his foot. Kate reached out from underneath the layers of matted leaves and pine straw and sliced across the back of Coot's ankle with the scaling knife. He screamed. Before he could fall, she stuck him again in the calf and the blade went right through. He toppled to his knees, and slid down into the trench. Kate emerged from where she'd buried herself and pounced onto him, knocking him down flat onto his chest. He screamed again and again as she brought the knife down over and over and into Coot's back until he stopped making any sounds at all. Her entire arm was slick with blood, and it shone a glossy black in the lantern light. She slid off him and rolled him over. She let the knife fall into the darkness before letting out a scream that echoed through the foothills. She grabbed a hold of his jacket and stared directly into his chalky face. "You still in there, Coot?"

He burped out a black bubble of blood. It popped and it oozed down his lip and chin.

"Good," she said. "Because I want my face to be the last thing you see in this world. I want you to know that you were right. You *are* just like this." She banged her fist down on his chest. He was too far gone to even flinch. She brought another fist down on the lion tattoo, now slick and painted red with the blood from her hands. Coot's pale-blue eyes were wide and shone like crystal in the moonlight. She slapped him to keep his attention. "That's a male lion." She pushed down on the tattoo. "Lazy—arrogant—weak. Anyone who knows how to read knows it's the female lions that do all the killing. Remember that wherever you're going, Coot Viner. Remember that, and remember who sent you there." She spat in his face. "I told you. My name is Katelyn Burroughs and you can't hurt me."

That was the last thing Coot Viner heard before his

eyes glazed over for the last time and what was left of him faded from existence.

Kate stared at his face, and held onto his jacket for a long time until finally she rolled off him and lay on her back in the crust of leaves she'd used as cover. She stayed like that until her breathing slowed and the chill of the night began to set in on her bare legs and sticky, wet arms. She willed herself to sit up, and looked toward the road. All she could think about was Clayton and her son, and whether what Tate had said about what happened to them was true. She prayed it wasn't as she stripped Coot's shirt off his body, and pulled off his shoes.

24

"I can't raise a soul on the radio."

"I thought you had people on the house, Mike."

"I did. Three of my best men. They're either flipped or dead. I think Tank was bought."

"What about Tuley?"

"I can't raise him either."

"He would never flip on us."

Static.

"I know. I don't want to think about what's happened to him."

"Mike, focus. Mark can take care of himself, but before he went dark, did he report back at all about the Viners?"

"Yes. Earlier. He radioed in to tell me one of them was missing. The black one, the one named Tate."

"That's the one that hit me." Clayton probed at the wound that cut across his temple. "He's got to be the one that took her, Mike. Where did he say the other two were?"

"An old fishing shack off Little Finger, but there's a hundred of them."

"No, there's not. There's four, and there's only one secluded enough to…"

Static.

"Clayton?"

"Pine Camp Road. Mile marker 31."

"I'm on my way now."

"Where are you?"

"The compound—your deddy's place."

"Clear it. Take every man you've got. Do you hear me? Take every living soul in that house and get to that shanty. I can hear the ambulance and the fire trucks now. As soon as I know Eben is okay, I'm headed there, too."

"Clayton, stay with the boy. I'll bring Kate back."

Clayton looked at his son in the rearview mirror. "The summit is almost a half hour away from Pine Camp. I can make it there faster."

"Okay, boss."

"Take every man, Mike. Every man."

"Okay."

"And Mike?" Clayton cranked up the Bronco to meet the ambulance at the main road.

"Yeah?"

Static.

"If you make it there before I do, I want this bastard, Coot, alive until I get there."

"Of course."

"Now go."

"Already moving."

Clayton slammed the handset down in the cradle and hard shifted the Bronco into gear. The sound of sirens was loud. They'd be there any second. He headed up the drive to cut them off. He didn't even look at the fire that had now consumed his entire home. He didn't care. Everything he cared about was in the woods. Alone. Counting on him.

Hang on, Kate. I'm coming.

Kate had slipped on Coot's tennis shoes and tied his shirt around her waist like a long skirt. She felt disgusted by the idea of it but she had no choice. Once she was covered she searched through the dead man's pockets for a phone or the keys to the Tracker. No luck. She did a blind search for Coot's gun but found nothing again. The night air was rancid with the smell of copper and shit. A strong whiff of the vile smell caused her to dry heave into the tall grass. She wanted to pass out. She suddenly thought about Mark and turned to look back up at the limestone casting rock. It was nothing but darkness, but she couldn't go back. He wouldn't want her to. She needed to make for the road. There was a better chance at being seen by someone there, and the black one—the one that kidnapped her and brought her out here might come back.

"Mark," she screamed in a hoarse voice that left her throat raw. There was no response. She started to cry and felt the temperature drop a few degrees. She was shivering. She yelled his name again, but this time her voice was barely audible. A night bird sang out and the crickets got louder and louder as she strained to hear something, anything from the man who had helped her survive the night, but there was nothing. He gave her a gift—a gift of time. She wouldn't be doing either of them any good by going back. She needed to climb the ravine to Pine Camp Road. After she wiped her eyes dry and settled her breathing, she started up the hill. She could barely move her legs. She was so tired. She'd never felt this tired, or dirty, or alone. The road was only fifteen yards up the hill, but it might as well have been fifteen miles. She was exhausted, but she didn't stop clawing at the cold dirt and knobby roots until she managed to make the distance to the road. Her knees caught every briar and sharpened stone in her path, but her mind was so far removed from pain, she didn't think it was possible to feel it anymore. She knew by now that if Clayton were still alive he'd be out looking for her. She knew he'd know how to find her. She didn't know how he'd know, but she knew he would all the same.

What if he didn't survive the fire? What if my husband and son are dead?

She caught a chill in her bones for thinking that and dismissed it. That just wasn't true. She wouldn't allow it to be true. He was coming for her. Michael would be, too. They would have every single man loyal to her family scouring the mountain. She needed to make it easier for them.

The road.

The moonlight reflected off the broken line of yellow paint, but she stayed back from the asphalt, taking cover in the shallow ditch that ran the length of the road. She propped herself up behind a thick pine tree, and looked through the branches up at the moon. She thought about her magnolia tree. She thought about the day she cut it down, how each branch fell to the ground. Within seconds, the exhaustion took her, and she passed out.

It could have been a few minutes or a few hours before the first set of headlights appeared and slowly crept toward her over the road. A flashlight hung out of the passenger-side window and swept back and forth across the trees. When it shone into the branches above Kate's head, she awoke, but just barely. The waxy leaves of the magnolia were dark and thin. She thought she might be dead, and the lights coming through the trees were angels coming to claim her—to save her—but angels never saved anyone. They were just for retrieval—always after the damage was done. She could hear her name.

"Kate!"

They were calling her name.

"Kate! Is that you? Kate?" She was drained and bordering on delirium, so she answered the angels and rolled out from behind the tree. She lifted her arm the best she could into the twin streams of light. She heard her name again, and this time it was clear that the voice did belong to an angel. The voice calling her name belonged to a woman.

*

It was almost another twenty minutes before Clayton arrived at the ditch. He'd left the Bronco running by the side of the road, high above the fishing shack. He jammed the shifter into park and jumped from the truck, leaving the door wide open. That's when he spotted Kate's Jeep down by the water. He nearly killed himself in a half run, half tumble he took down the hill, but he didn't let up until he got to the bottom and found Mark Tuley in the mud and the body of Donnie Viner in the creek. He slid to his knees beside Mark and instinctively pulled a folding knife from his sheriff's coat. He cut the binds on Mark's wrists and ankles, and Tuley grunted as all four limbs sprawled out into the mud.

"Mark, where is she?"

Mark groaned. Clayton lifted him by his shirt almost completely off the ground. "Where is Kate?"

Mark groaned again. Except this time Clayton saw that he was pointing toward a dim light in the distance. And he wasn't grunting. He was saying "Go."

"I'll send help."

"Go," Mark said a third time and wilted back into the ground. Clayton was already on his feet, headed down the overgrown trail toward the overturned lantern, calling his wife's name.

"Kate!" He held tight to the hope of seeing her alive, and that light fueled it. He reached for his Colt as he ran toward the light, not realizing that he was already holding it. He slowed when he saw the shirtless and cut-up corpse of Coot Viner covered in blood and pine straw, but that was all he saw. Hope could deal the hardest blows.

"Kate!" he yelled again. Clayton's eyes began to tear. He picked up the lantern, swung it around frantically to find anything remotely resembling a trail. When he found it, he hustled up the hill, following the tracks Kate had made in the dirt. Ignoring the pain and the permanent damage he was doing to his leg, he went faster and faster as he got closer to the road. He saw the ditch and the drag marks made in the clay before he got halfway up, and his mind went haywire. He screamed for her. He screamed for anyone. He ran his hands over the width of cleared dirt made by someone's body. The red clay and moist leaves trailed onto the blacktop and stopped right on the side of the road—right where a car would have been parked. There was no way Mike could've beaten him here. He would've radioed Clayton if he had. Someone else had her. Clayton's eyes went from gray to black as they sank back deep in his head, but his anger broke as quickly as it came. The tears came full force. He screamed for her again, but there was nothing—nothing but his own voice bouncing back at him. This wasn't happening. The world was spinning. He'd failed her. He screamed again and again, and tried to pull himself out of the ditch, but his injured leg had become a useless piece of elastic. He dug his Colt into the ground to anchor himself but the pain of standing was too much to take. He fell backwards into the soft earth. He pointed the dirt-covered revolver straight up as if he could put a bullet into the moon itself and right everything that had gone wrong. That's when he saw the angels, too. Only these weren't angels. They were headlights. Then he heard the truck. It was louder now, the engine knocking and grinding. He listened as doors opened and slammed shut. He lowered the gun and aimed it toward the approaching footfalls. He thumbed the hammer, his finger already squeezing the trigger. He fired.

"Whoa, shit! Clayton. It's me, Mike."

Clayton's gun hand dropped limp, and he fell back again into the ditch. His hat twisted and fell off, tumbling down into the debris.

"Did you find her? Clayton? Oh, my God, where is she?"

"I don't know..." he said, barely able to breathe. "I don't know." Clayton looked up at Mike and the several other men silhouetted by the truck's headlights.

"Please, help me. Help me find her."

"Get him out of there."

Two men Clayton didn't know shimmied into the ditch and pulled him out. He wasn't able to stand on his own, so they walked over to the truck and propped him against the grill.

"Here, Mr. Burroughs," one of the men said, and held out Clayton's hat. He took it and laid it on the hood. He was still holding his gun with white knuckles, and used it to steady himself against the rusty metal. No one said a word while he wiped his eyes clean.

"Tuley is down there by the shack. He's in bad shape but he's alive."

Mike whistled and pointed, and two more men bolted into the woods.

"He needs medical attention. But you need to move fast. There are two other bodies down there that need to disappear," Clayton said. His voice became more his own. "Coot and Donnie Viner are dead. I think Kate took them both out."

Mike took off his ball cap and crushed it in his grip. "Then what the hell happened to her, Clayton?"

"I don't know. I followed her trail to here, but it ends cold right there." He pointed to the side of the road just ahead of where they were standing.

"Where do we start, Clayton? Tell me, man. What do I do?"

Clayton shifted all his weight on his good leg and nearly fell over, but Mike and the others sprang forward and steadied him. "There are only two more players I'm aware of that aren't accounted for. The one who broke into my house, Tate, and the sister, Vanessa."

"I thought you said she wasn't involved in all this."

"*She* said she wasn't involved. I said I didn't know what to believe. All I know for sure is that Kate is still missing, and those two are the only lead I've got left, so take some of these men, and find them. I'll take two of them with me and we'll—"

The squawk of a radio and a burst of static broke over Clayton's words. "Sheriff Burroughs? Do you copy?" The man standing next to Mike was monitoring the police channel. When Clayton looked at him, he quickly grabbed the scanner from his belt, and handed it over.

"Cricket? It's me. Talk to me."

"Sheriff. It's about Kate."

"What about Kate? Do you know where she is?"

Static.

"Clayton, she's at McFalls Memorial. A woman just brought her in. She's in bad shape. You need to get over there ASAP."

"She's at the hospital in Waymore?"

"Yessir."

Clayton closed his eyes and fell back on the truck. "And she's okay?"

"No, Sheriff, she's not okay. Debbie Payne, the nurse that just called here said she looks like she's been through hell and back, but she's alive. What the hell happened out there?"

"She'll live," Clayton said to himself, and a wave of relief rippled through him. "No time. I'll fill you in later. Call Debbie back. Tell her I'm on my way—and tell her to send an ambulance to Pine Camp Road. Mile marker 31. There's a man down that needs immediate attention. High-flow diesel."

"Yessir. I'm on it."

"Cricket?"

"Yessir?"

"Who was the woman that brought her in?"

"I don't know. Debbie said she didn't know her. She only got a last name. Viner, I think?"

Clayton and Mike exchanged looks and Clayton tossed the radio back to its owner. Cricket came over the speaker again asking about what was going on but Clayton ignored her. "Turn it off," he said to the kid with the scanner. The boy turned the knob until it clicked. "Mike, we need to get rid of those bodies. They need to disappear right now."

"Say no more, Clayton. We'll handle this. You go."

Clayton began to limp off toward the Bronco without asking for any help. Mike nodded to the kid with scanner, and he hurried up the road after the sheriff to keep him steady.

"Clayton?"

"Yeah?" He didn't stop walking.

"You think Vanessa knew this was going to happen? Do you think she planned it?"

"I don't know yet."

"Clayton, could she have let this happen only so she could step in and gain your trust?"

"Maybe, but if I were you, I'd dig a third hole."

25

Clayton sat in the cold white hospital room and held Kate's hand as she slept. He rubbed his thumb over the tape holding the IV in place on the top of his wife's hand and felt an ache he'd never felt before. After everything he'd been through—the shooting that left him crippled, the constant pain that lived in his bones as a result, and even the heat and flames of the fire that consumed his home and nearly killed both him and his son—none of it compared to the hollow throbbing that kept him glued to that uncomfortable steel chair beside the bed Kate was lying in. She'd nearly died. He knew that part of her had. What she'd been through, and what she'd done to survive, meant the person she was twelve hours ago was long gone. He ran a finger lightly through her hair. It felt like wheat straw. She will hate that people saw her this undone—this vulnerable. Now he understood what she felt like for all those months when he lay in a similar bed in Atlanta after being gunned down. Now he understood how lonely it must have been for her wondering if he would ever wake up, or if she was going to have to face her life without him. How could he have been so selfish? How could he have let this happen? He'd promised her he would always keep her safe and she had believed him. He believed it every time he said it, but when the wolves finally came, she had to face them alone. He squeezed her hand softly and the tears came again. They were coming in waves every few minutes. He watched her and refused to let himself sleep. A machine on the other side of the bed would beep every few minutes as well, and it startled him every time. It spat out a ribbon of paper that meant nothing to him—just a scribble of ink that he wasn't able to understand—but her chest rising and falling to the same rhythm as his own he understood well. She was alive. He flinched again when the door to the room opened and the nurse, Debbie, came in wearing scrubs and holding a steel clipboard. She smiled at him as he wiped at his eyes.

"How's she doing?"

"No different," he said. "She still hasn't woken up."

Debbie quietly ripped the paper ribbon from the machine and recorded the EKG reading on the clipboard. "That's good, Clayton. She needs to rest. No different is a good thing."

Clayton crossed his arms on the bed railing, and rested his forehead on them. Debbie pulled another chair from beside the door over to his. "Listen," she said, as she sat down, "I know you want to be here when she wakes up, but that may not be for a long time. She needs to sleep. We've given her something to encourage that, and by the look of you, I'd say you could use a little rest yourself. Why don't you let one of the nurses take a look at that cut on your face and then maybe try to get some sleep yourself?"

"I'm fine," Clayton said. He didn't move.

Debbie sighed. "Well, then, at least let me sit with her for a little while so you can go clean yourself up."

Clayton looked down at his boots and for the first time since he'd been there he noticed the smears of red clay on the floor that he'd tracked in when came into the room. It only cemented the feeling that he dirtied up everything clean he encountered, just by being present. Still, he made no attempt to get up.

"She's in the best place she could possibly be right now, Sheriff, and I won't let her be alone. I promise. Go see Eben. He needs you, too. Kate is going to be okay." Debbie put her hand on his shoulder. "You both are."

Clayton stayed still for another minute before looking at the woman in scrubs making promises she couldn't keep, and picked up his hat from the floor. "The woman that brought her in."

"What about her?"

"Where is she?"

Clayton found Darby Ellis standing in front of the room Mark Tuley had been brought to. Darby had only that day been released from the same hospital and should've been at home in bed. Instead he was dressed in his tan pressed uniform and waiting to hear from Clayton.

"How's he doing?" Clayton asked.

"Not good. He should be dead. He's got massive contusions on his head, chest, and back. His nose was smashed. He'll need reconstructive surgery if he ever gets out of the woods. Both his legs were broken, and a hairline skull fracture."

"Jesus."

"The big problem was all the internal bleeding. The docs say they got it under control, but right now, I suppose it's in God's hands."

"He'll pull through."

"I hope so, boss." Darby removed his hat and rubbed at the thick bush of sandy-blond hair. "What the hell happened, boss? Who did all this?"

Clayton tucked his hands in his pockets and looked through the window into Tuley's room. "I don't know."

Two things Darby knew about the man standing in front of him was one, he wasn't much of a liar, and two, if he did lie, he never looked you in your eye, and always tucked his hands in his pockets.

"Clayton. I'm here to help, man. Tell me what you need, and I'm on it."

"I know, Darby, but you're already doing it. You're not cleared for duty yet, and that man in there needs someone like you looking out for him. Stay here. If I find out anything, you'll be my first call."

Darby didn't press it.

"Has anyone else been here?"

"Scabby Mike and Nails McKenna, of all people, tried to come up earlier, but Jim, the security guard didn't let them. Family only."

"Is he okay?"

"Who? Mike or Nails?"

Clayton looked at Darby. "Jim."

"Oh, yeah. They left without incident."

"That's good." Clayton turned to leave.

"Sir, about Kate. I—"

"I know, son. I know. I'll tell her you were asking about her when she wakes up."

"Yessir."

Clayton left Darby in the hallway and made his way to the elevator. He found the small waiting room Debbie told him about on the first floor. The woman who brought Kate in said she'd be waiting down there in case the police or anyone else needed to speak to her. Clayton knew that meant Vanessa was waiting for him. She was waiting to pull him deeper into the web of false security she'd been spinning since he met her at the diner. He could feel it in his bones that she was a snake, but he needed to look in her eyes. He needed to know for sure if she was involved— if it was all her to begin with. His heart was pounding out of his chest as he pushed open the door and steeled himself to face this Viner woman again, but she wasn't there. No one was. Just an old lady crocheting something blue in her lap, who looked as tired as he was. The woman set the needles and whatever she'd been making on a purse at her feet when Clayton entered the room. He didn't sit down, and she didn't stand up.

"Hello, Sheriff. Are you here for me?"

He looked down at the insignia on his jacket. "I'm sorry. No," he said. "I was looking for someone else."

The old woman looked around the small room. "No one here but me."

"Can you tell me when the other woman left?"

"I'm sorry, son. There hasn't been anyone else in here since I sat down."

"How long have you been here?"

"Goodness. For several hours, I suppose."

Clayton looked confused. "A young woman. Blue eyes. Blonde hair. Very tall? No one fitting that description has been in here?"

"I'm sorry, Sheriff, but no."

"I'm sorry to disturb you, then." Clayton turned to go.

"Don't be," the woman said, and shifted a long length of plastic tubing connected to the small portable oxygen bottle next to her. She picked the knitting needles back up. "Her hair is black."

Clayton turned back around. "Excuse me?"

"Vanessa. Her hair is black. I don't understand why she wears that silly wig."

Clayton stood confused.

"I believe you are looking for my daughter, Sheriff."

Clayton stared hard at the woman and saw the resemblance. "You're Twyla Viner."

"I am," she said, and stood up slowly.

"You're the one that brought my wife here?"

"Yes, I am."

Clayton felt off balance. He wasn't expecting this. He was carrying a sledgehammer of pain and rage with nowhere to swing it.

"Did you do this?"

"To your wife?"

"All of it, woman. Don't play ignorant with me. Did you spearhead what those bastards did to us tonight?"

"No, Sheriff. I did not. My stepson, Daniel, brought all this here on his own. In fact, I begged him to stay off this mountain, but Daniel has always walked his own path."

Clayton stepped closer to her, still feeling the weight of that hammer. He spoke in a soft growl. "That path ended abruptly tonight. He won't be walking anything ever again. I hope you know that."

Twyla closed her eyes briefly and exhaled. "I'm sure you're right, son, and I feel responsible for that—for all of it. That's why I'm here."

"Where is Vanessa?"

"I don't know."

"I don't believe you. Was she involved?"

"No. I rarely deal in certainties anymore, Sheriff, but I can tell you this. I know my daughter, and what happened here tonight is not something Bessie May— I mean, Vanessa—would be a part of."

"Well, I need to hear that from her, so if you know where she is, I suggest you tell me."

"And what do you plan to do if you find her?"

"I'm not going to ask you again, Twyla. If you know where she is, then tell me."

Twyla motioned to the long couch she'd been sitting on. "Do you mind if I sit? My knees aren't in the best shape."

"I don't care what you do. Where is she?"

"Clayton, please, just sit a minute. Listen to what I have to say, and then I'll tell you what you want to know."

Clayton stared at the old woman and tried to get a fix on her. It was easy to see where Vanessa got it from. They were both impossible to read.

"Talk," he said. "And be quick about it. I'm running out of patience. And I promise you, if I find out that you had anything to do with what happened here tonight, you and me will get back around to this conversation real soon."

"I understand."

The old woman sat herself carefully back down on the couch and attached the nasal cannula across her upper lip. Once she was situated as best she could, she sat in silence for a moment and breathed the oxygen in deep through the tube. Clayton sat and listened as the old woman wheezed and apologized for the time it took her to catch her breath. Clayton said nothing. He didn't care.

"I never imagined my life would ever end up the way it has. An old woman who can't even walk to the mailbox without getting winded. I wanted so much more. For myself and for my children. But here I am, and I have to try to make the best of what I have left."

Clayton watched her breathe in broken half-breaths as she spoke. Her face was worn and chiseled away by age, stress, and cigarettes, but Clayton could tell from her eyes that there used to be beauty there. She'd been stripped of it the same way coal is stripped from the earth, leaving nothing but a dried-out and hollow crust where nothing ever grows again. The thought of that happening to Kate in that cold room above him made his hammer that much heavier. He shut down the small talk.

"Skip to the part of the story I care about, Twyla. I don't know you and I don't care about your life."

The woman shifted in her chair to lean in closer to the sheriff. "We have a lot in common, you know. There are stories I could tell you about the people that come from this place that would have us chatting for hours."

"All right. This is over." Clayton gripped the edge of the couch to push himself up.

"I knew your father."

Clayton stopped himself, and glared at her. The woman glanced around the room as if she was worried about being overheard, although she knew she wasn't. She really didn't care if she was. Her interest in having secrets diminished a long time ago. "I was the one who killed him."

"What?"

"Well, not me exactly. I sent my husband Joseph and his son, Daniel, to burn down your father's barn. I thought if

I destroyed all their machinery I could keep your brothers out of this wicked business, before they even started, but all I accomplished was getting your father killed. I think that's when it all started for Daniel, too. He was just a boy back then, but after that night, something had changed in him. I never saw him the same after that. Looking back on it, I've recently come to believe that the fumes from that chemical fire are what caused my Joseph's cancer as well. I think because of what I asked him to do that night, I killed him, too." Twyla spoke casually, as if she hadn't just confessed to killing Clayton's father, and Clayton was so baffled by it, that he took off his hat and settled into her story as if it wasn't *his* father she'd just confessed to killing.

"I'm responsible for the death of almost everyone I've ever loved," Twyla said. She looked directly and deep into Clayton, and it made him uncomfortable. "I don't expect forgiveness and I don't expect you to understand how sorry I am for everything."

He said nothing. He was suddenly acutely aware of how crazy this woman might be. His father's death by fire was public knowledge, anyone could claim to have done it, but what she said stunned him enough to keep listening. Twyla saw the bewildered look in his eyes and took another shallow breath. "I can only imagine how I must sound to you, right now, Sheriff. I don't know how that information makes you feel, or if you believe me or not either, but that's not the point. The past isn't why I'm here. I've lived in fear of the past nearly my entire life. I don't want to be ruled by fear anymore. That was your father's way—your brother's way. I've done that long enough and look where it has got me—where it has got us both. Your wife and son are in hospital beds. My husband is dead. I have dead children. My grandson is dead, but not me. I'm still alive to bear witness to it all and I just can't—won't—do it anymore. I want to spend the time I have left on this earth living without fear, fear of dying, or the fear of more people being killed. That's why I'm here. I've reached a point in my life that I've come to accept that the bad blood that has been the curse of my family must have something to do with me. I used to believe that I was the one that protected them from it, but the truth is, I fueled it. I failed them. I failed them all. All but one, and I'm here to plead for her life."

Another shallow breath.

"Are you done?" Clayton was through listening to this fairytale. He stood and put on his hat. "Tell me where I can find Vanessa."

"You know you look just like him—your father."

"Cut the shit, lady, and tell me where she is."

"I told you, I don't know."

"So this was all some bullshit tactic to keep me here? What, you were supposed to keep me listening to your bullshit long enough for her to make her getaway? Do you really think there is anywhere on this earth she can hide from me after what she's done?"

"Please, Clayton. You're wrong. I'm familiar with the anger you're feeling right now, but please don't do this. Don't be like the rest of them."

"Where—is—she? Last chance."

Twyla pulled in as much oxygen as her frail lungs could allow, and reached down to pick up her purse. She took out a small slip of paper and handed it to Clayton. He opened it. It was an address.

"Is this where she's going?"

"No, but it's where you can find what you're looking for to end this. You'll find what you need there."

Clayton studied the slip of paper and then looked at the old woman. She wasn't going to say anything else. He left the room without another word, and once the door clicked shut, Twyla Viner collected her things. It took her several minutes to get the rolling cart that toted the oxygen bottle over the threshold of the waiting-room door, but she managed, and walked slowly out into the hospital's small reception area. She rolled the cart to the counter where a friendly looking black man in a gray security guard's uniform sat tapping at a computer.

"Can I help you, ma'am?"

"Yes," she said as she read his name tag. "I was wondering if you could do me a favor, Jim."

Jim stood. "Yes, ma'am, what's that?"

"Do you think you could get this to one of the patients here?" Twyla laid the navy-blue wool blanket she'd made on the counter.

"Certainly, ma'am. Who's the patient?"

"Burroughs. Eben Burroughs."

26

Tate Viner slipped the key card into the slot on the door, and dropped his duffle bag on the chair next to the bed. He slid the light switch on the wall to the on position and nothing happened. He slid it up and down a few times in the dark before giving up. "Goddammit. Ain't nothing does what it's supposed to anymore. Fuckin' cheap-ass hotel." The room was still a mess from the past few days he'd spent there, but he sure as hell wasn't going home until he got word from Coot. He wasn't going to be the one to explain to Twyla all the ways Coot decided to screw the pooch in North Georgia. He'd expected to get a call by now, but for two goddamn days, still nothing. He was tired of Coot's shit. Maybe he did need to be the one that told Twyla. Maybe she'd finally see that he was the one worth turning the business over to, and not that psycho, Coot, who was probably off on an amphetamine bender right now with that dip-shit, Donnie. Tate walked into the bathroom and hit the switch. The light in there worked, and he washed his face in the sink. Tate showered, dried himself and wrapped the wet towel around his waist. He didn't bother trying the main light switch again. Instead he fumbled through his duffle for the bottle of gin he'd bought while he was out, twisted off the top, and sat down on the bed. He reached over to the nightstand and pushed a button on the base of the lamp, filling the small room with a low orange light.

"Howdy, Tate."

Tate shot back across the bed, dropping the open bottle of gin to the floor. With one hand instinctively holding the towel in place, he pushed his back against the headboard and made a grab for his duffle bag.

"There ain't nothing you need in that bag, Tate. I took the knife out while you were in the shower." Clayton shifted on the small sofa and opened his coat to show Tate the tactical knife in the inside pocket. He also gave him a good look at the silver Colt a few inches below it. "I like it. I think I'll keep it."

Tate swung his head from side to side taking in the whole room, his eyes wide and frantic.

"I gotta be honest, son, I'm kinda surprised that you don't have a gun in here somewhere, but I guess I shouldn't be." Clayton lifted the slightly charred hickory walking stick from his lap. "Seeing that suckering folks in their sleep is more your style."

"Hey, now, look, Mr. Burroughs, I know what you're thinkin' but you got it wrong. I swear."

Clayton crossed his legs and ran his hand down the length of lightly charred wood propped against his leg. "Can you believe that out of everything you destroyed that night, this old stick, of all things, made it?"

"Mr. Burroughs, please, just listen."

"Hickory is a stubborn wood."

"Please, man."

"Okay, Tate. I've got a minute. What have I got wrong? What about you taking my head off with this stick and setting fire to my home isn't what it seems? What about leaving me and my son to burn alive, and then kidnapping my wife, and delivering her to those animals am I not understanding? Please, go ahead, tell me what I'm missing."

Tate slid down to the edge of the bed, but Clayton put a hand on the grip of his revolver. "Tell me from right there."

Tate put his hands out to his sides. "Okay, okay. I'm chill. Look, I ain't sayin' I didn't do some terrible shit, but I swear I'm the one that saved y'all."

"Do tell."

"I ain't lyin', man. Coot wanted all y'all dead. He told me to light y'all up and watch it happen. He wanted you to burn, not me. He's the one that went off the reservation. I gave you a fightin' chance."

"Is that right?"

"Yeah, I lit the fire, but I gave you time to get out. I swear I wouldn't have let anything happen to that little baby. That's not what Twyla wanted. I didn't want to do it, either. It was all Coot. He's the one who needs to pay. Go find him."

"Coot's dead." Clayton let that sink in before adding, "Donnie is, too. Kate killed them both just a few hours after you left her there with them."

Tate inched forward on the bed, still holding onto the towel at his waist. "Well, hell, man, you done already got your revenge. What's the point in killing me? I was just trying to get my family through all this without all the killing. Please, man. I was trying to do what's right."

Clayton's eyes went cold and gray. "Leaving my wife to be raped and tortured is what you consider what's right?"

"Please, Mr. Burroughs. I tried to stop it. I did."

"Well, don't worry. Kate stopped it. She drove a scaling knife through both of them, about twenty times each so's I could tell. We threw their worthless bodies in a hole. It felt good doing it. There ain't but one loose end left to tie up." Clayton moved his cane to set the end on the carpet.

"So now you gonna kill me? Throw me in a hole, too, after I broke rank and showed you mercy?"

Clayton stood up. "No, Tate, I didn't come here to kill you. I came here to tell you that your cousins are dead and thought you'd like to know who led me to you. Your own blood that sold you to me."

Tate inched forward a little more, but Clayton looked unfazed.

"That bitch, Bessie May."

"Oh, no. I haven't seen Vanessa yet. It was Twyla.

I guess she knew where you'd be. She wrote it all down pretty for me. After she helped get Kate to a hospital, she was more than happy to help me get to you. I guess you ain't the favorite, after all." Clayton crossed the room and set his hat down low on his brow. He twisted the knob on the door. He cracked it open and then stopped and turned around. Tate was standing now.

"You know what?" Clayton said. "I don't want you thinkin' I didn't listen to what you said. You called it mercy, right? Well, one good turn deserves another, so here—" He opened his coat and removed the tactical knife he'd taken from Tate's duffle. "Here's your fighting chance." He dropped the fixed-blade knife to the floor. "Goodbye, Tate. Best of luck to you."

"I don't understand."

"I know you don't, but you will." Clayton opened the door and stepped out into the night, but before the door closed, Nails McKenna leaned his head down and stepped in.

"I know you're the one who done it."

"What the fuck?" Tate made a quick move for the knife, but Nails kicked it under the bed and wrapped a massive arm around Tate's neck. He pulled back on his deformed fist and squeezed the muscular black man with every bit of his strength. He lifted the six-foot Viner at least four inches off the floor and squeezed tighter and tighter. He pulled on his forearm until the veins in it bulged. Tate's eyes went red as capillaries burst. His face turned a bright eggplant color as he tried to dig his fingers into the airtight gap between his neck and Nails' arm. He flailed his legs, knocking over the lamp and side-table, but Nails didn't give. Tate pushed both feet off the edge of the bed but only moved the big man back a few feet to the wall. Nails braced himself, and squeezed harder.

"I know you're the one that done it," he said again. Tate gurgled and tapped frantically on Nails' arm for mercy—for just one more breath so he could explain. There was no mercy to be had. Tate finally stopped moving, but Nails held him suspended and limp. He waited out all the twitches, before dropping the dead weight to the floor.

"He was my friend." Nails reached into his pocket and pulled out a photograph. It was the photograph Freddy Tuten had kept in his bar by the safe ever since he'd known the man. That picture of Freddy and his brother, Jacob, taken while they were both stationed in Korea, was the only thing Freddy cared about in this world. Freddy had told Nails all about the day that picture was taken one night at The Chute after everyone else had left and gone home. Freddy said he'd never talked to anyone about it before. It was the last time Nails could remember feeling human. That night meant everything to him. He laid the photograph on Tate's body, and stood over it, replaying that single conversation in his mind between him and the only person in the world he considered his friend—a friend who was killed and dismembered for no reason. Nails stood in a trance over Tate's body for nearly ten minutes before he used his good hand to unzip his fly and pissed all over him.

Clayton drove north for two hours without stopping. For the first time in a long time he didn't find any comfort in being alone. He wanted to be with his family. He ran his hand down the length of the hickory walking stick lying across the passenger side seat of the Bronco. He'd gotten pretty attached to it over the past few days. For over a year now he'd had too much pride to use it. He didn't care about pride much anymore. Pride had always let him down, or gotten people killed. He was done courting pride. It was time to be the man he wanted to be and not the man everyone expected him to be. That man was needed at McFalls Memorial with his wife and son, only there was one more thing to handle. He placed a call to Scabby Mike. By the time he reached McFalls County, it was all set up.

27

BURNT HICKORY POND

The sun was just beginning to come up over the water, and Clayton stood by the headstones that marked the final resting places of his father and both his brothers. This place was the most polarizing spot on the mountain for the youngest and only surviving member of the Burroughs clan. The pond was a battleground for his ghosts. Those from his childhood—of him and his brothers swinging out into the emerald water on a length of rope and old tractor tire—and those from the most recent years, and the men those children became. The ghosts of his past and present were in a constant struggle that had rooted him in shame and guilt for most of his adult life.

That was going to end today.

The pond was also a riddle. One he never thought much about until recently. It never made sense to him why Halford had buried their father there—but it did now. As Clayton watched Mike's pick-up pull into the clearing, he moved to the back of the Bronco and popped the back latch. He removed two shovels and laid them against the truck. He pulled out a soft pack of smokes and held a crooked one in his hand for a long time without lighting it. He finally stuck it back in the pack and tossed them into the open window of the truck. He was done with that shit, too. Mike cut the engine and got out.

"Okay, man. I'm here. You want to tell me why you wanted me to meet you here? I thought we were going to finish this at the compound."

"We are, but there's something I want to show you first." He grabbed one of the shovels and tossed it to Mike. He took the other one for himself. "C'mon."

The pond rippled in the morning breeze, and the trees began to brighten in the sun. Clayton stopped in the saw grass that covered his deddy's grave.

"Hey, Clayton, hold up." Mike had stopped just shy of the patch of grass. "You ain't thinking of digging someone up, are you?"

"Not someone, Mike, but something."

Mike still didn't come any closer.

"What's the matter, Mike? You ain't spooked about digging a hole, are you? You've dug more than anyone I know. You should be over that by now."

"I just don't understand, Clayton. Tell me what's going on."

Clayton read his deddy's name out loud to the familiar tree line for maybe the last time. "Don't worry, Mike. He's not in there."

"What makes you think that?"

"I just know."

"Well, for whatever reason you're thinking about doing this, maybe me being here to help ain't such a good idea."

Clayton sat his hat on the slab of granite. "And why's that?"

"Because you're the man's son. You can do whatever you want to his grave, but I ain't your kin. I can't be known as the guy that dug up and defiled the bones of Gareth Burroughs. That kind of mojo can get me killed around here."

Clayton jammed the shovel deep into the moist earth and grinned. "And *that right there* is exactly why I know there's no bones in this box."

"What right where?"

"Fear."

"I don't follow."

"Yes, you do, Mike. You were right. Halford wasn't crazy. He was just our father's son. Deddy learned early on that this whole house of cards—this whole mountain—is built on fear. It was the most valuable tool in the woodshed. I'm not tellin' you something you don't already know, Mike. Fear is the currency of kings out here, and whoever collected enough of it was able to keep shit flowing downhill in a straight line—away from them. Deddy was a master at it, and Halford was even better. If you convince everyone to be afraid of you long enough, it begins to get confused with respect. All the cogs in the Burroughs machine stayed oiled and running smooth for decades and the people here called it leadership, but the truth is everyone was just scared shitless of bucking them. After enough time passed, and enough stories got rewritten, it became legend."

Mike wiped the first of the day's sweat from his face. "I don't know, Clayton. I didn't stand by your brother because I was scared of him. I stood with him because I loved him."

Clayton tossed a shovel full of dirt and grass to the side of the grave. "Do you remember the time Hal thought you had a thing for Michelle Wallen way back in the day? He held you by your shirt collar over the quarry by Pumpkin Center. What's that drop? About seventy-five feet?"

Mike either didn't know or he wouldn't say. He just stood there holding the shovel.

Clayton pushed his red hair back out of his face. "You see what I mean about time getting things confused? He would have dropped you that day in front of everyone if you'd told him the truth."

Mike thought on that a few beats. "Hey, hold on now, how do you know what happened between Michelle and me?"

Clayton curled his lip in a smirk. "I grew up to be a detective, Mike, remember?" He shoved the spade into the ground a second time. "It makes sense Hal would use that same fear to keep everyone away from his money, too. I mean, if you were to go digging for treasure, where's the one place you wouldn't dream of digging up without suffering the wrath of every man on this mountain?"

Mike nodded. "Gareth Burroughs' grave."

"Right—because that kind of mojo can get a man killed around here."

"You're a pretty smart fucker, Clayton. You get that big brain from that old man in there whether you wanna admit it or not."

"I told you, Mike. There ain't no old man here. My father is buried out in Cooper's Field where he belongs. Only Halford would know exactly where, and he'll never tell. That was a last *fuck you* from him to me." He tossed more dirt.

"Now that, I believe." Mike walked over and began to dig.

"You want to know something else?" Clayton asked.

"What's that?"

"I think Hal wanted *me* to find it, too."

Mike laughed. His ability to believe that one was sketchy at best. "Oh, yeah? And what in the world makes you think that?"

Clayton looked at Halford's headstone just to the left of his father's, and he kept looking at it while he spoke. "Because he buried him here. Why? It never made any sense to me. I think he knew it would bother me. He knew I'd never leave something alone if I couldn't get my head around it. I think he knew eventually I'd figure it out. And like you said, I am the man's son, right?"

Mike thought on that and hoisted the shovel. They dug for a while until they hit something solid. Mike felt the steel point of the spade hit wood hard enough to reverberate through the handle. It was a tight, muffled sound, not hollow like a coffin. With the side of the spade he scraped back enough dirt to see the plywood underneath him.

"Are you ready?" Clayton said.

Mike nodded and they both dropped to their knees. Clayton scraped his shovel along an entire edge of the crate until it was clear. Once he unearthed a corner, he stood back up and Mike used his shovel as a lever. He put everything he had into it, but it didn't take much to crack the rotted wood. A corner of the board splintered and gave way. He set the shovel to the side, squatted back down and helped Clayton brush away more of the dirt. No odor of death. No stink of rotten meat. They pulled at the broken chunk of wood until it snapped off in their hands.

The cash inside was banded and wrapped in cellophane. Mike reached in and pulled out one of the dense bricks of mixed bills. "Well, fuck me runnin'."

28

Clayton was still filthy from the dig at the pond as he sat
on the front porch of his deddy's house and looked out at
the land he grew up on. It was nothing like the house he'd
lived in as a child, but even though the house was now
more of a fortress than a home, he couldn't help but feel
like a kid again, sitting in the sun, wishing he could be his
big brother, and knowing that he never would be. It was
strange now, seeing the place vacant and quiet like this. It
filled Clayton with a longing he didn't know he still had.
A longing to belong to something that was never his to
begin with. The slab of concrete that used to be the floor
of the family barn—the place where his father died—
was still there. He thought about Twyla Viner and the
story she told. It made sense. More sense than believing
his father did it to himself. The slab was covered in oil
stains and dried mud from when Halford used it as a
place to fix up old junkers and midnight-run cars, but
Clayton thought he could still see the char marks on the

concrete where his father burned to death over ten years ago. It was probably his imagination, but the thought of it still unnerved him. Clayton missed his father, as mean and spiteful as he might have been, and even though everyone on the mountain had come to know this place as The Burroughs Compound, to Clayton, it would always just be Deddy's house. He took out his phone and dialed the hospital.

"Can you connect me to Room 1108, please?"

"Please hold."

Clayton held the line and listened to a series of beeps until Charmaine Squire's voice answered. "Clayton?"

"Hey, Charmaine, how's she doing?"

Charmaine's voice was hushed, but Clayton could tell she was excited. "Oh, my gosh, Clayton. She's awake. She's whacked out of her gourd, but she's awake."

Clayton stood up and grabbed his cane. "Is she talking?"

"The doctors said she's not supposed to, but she's been asking for you ever since she opened her eyes. You need to get your butt down here right now—wait a minute—hold on."

Clayton heard muffled voices as Charmaine held the phone to her chest. "Clayton, you there?"

"Of course."

"The doctor said just for a second—here."

He waited.

"Clayton?" Kate's voice was dry and rough.

"It's me, baby. I'm here."

"Where?"

"I was just wrapping up a few things at Deddy's. I'm on my way."

"Don't be long."

"I won't."

"Okay."

"Kate? Kate, I love you."

"I'll tell her you said that, Clayton. She's still in and out, but I'm sure she'll be awake again by the time you get here. Will you be long?"

Clayton heard the car coming and sat back down on the steps. "No. Not at all."

The BMW pulled through the open chain-link gate and circled around the gravel lot until it came to a stop in front of the porch. Vanessa cut the engine, and Clayton watched her as she inspected her make-up in the rearview mirror, and folded her sunglasses into a case she put in her purse. Without looking like she was in a hurry at all, she finally opened the door, and stepped out. She was taller than Clayton remembered, and this time her hair was jet black, and not the golden-blonde wig she wore at Lucky's. With her hair dark like that she looked familiar to him, but the anger spiking his blood wouldn't allow for more questions. Clayton hadn't even noticed anything about her before. He noticed everything now.

"Clayton."

"Vanessa."

"Am I early?"

"Nope."

"Um…" Vanessa looked around the property and held her hands up. "Did they walk here? Is Leek inside?"

Clayton scratched at his beard. "Nope."

"Are we playing games here, Sheriff?"

Clayton squinted his eyes at her. "Nope."

"I thought we were supposed to meet here and discuss our new partnership."

"Is that what Mike told you?" Clayton tipped his hat and scratched at his head now. Vanessa was losing her patience.

"Yes. It is."

"Well, I reckon we must've got our lines crossed somewhere. Bracken is back in Florida by now, I'm sure. It seems my family has come into a small windfall. One that will be enough to hold this place together without it becoming the opiate highway you were looking to turn it into."

Vanessa glared at him. "Is that right?"

"Yes. That's right. It makes one wonder if it was all worth it, doesn't it? Killing our people, attacking my family, burning our home." If there was any looseness in the way Clayton was handling this conversation, it fell away as he counted off the events of the past few days.

Vanessa let her hands lower. "Okay. I'm not sure what you're implying, but I'm out of here."

Clayton picked up his Colt from behind the railing and stood up. "Stop right there, and step away from the car, Vanessa."

She kept her back to him, facing the BMW, and

considered her options, and then she did exactly what Clayton thought she'd do. She went coy. She turned to him. "Oh, c'mon, Sheriff, do you still not trust me?" She had already unbuttoned her jacket almost as a reflex. "It's like I told Mike, and now I'm telling you, I had nothing to do with what my brother and the others did. I'm just here to do business."

Clayton aimed the gun. All the tremble he might've had in his hands just days ago had fallen away and he held the gun as steady as he ever had. "Get on your knees, Vanessa." He took the two brick steps and walked forward.

"You're kidding me, right?"

"Does anything about this .45 caliber look like a joke to you?"

"So, what? You're going to kill me now? You're going to kill the one person capable of making you the wealthiest man in McFalls County?"

"I told you, money isn't an issue anymore. I found my brother's money, so that game is over. Your drug deal with the bikers isn't happening. That only means I needed you here for one reason." Clayton clicked back the hammer.

"You're making a mistake."

The gun didn't drop an inch. He took another step toward her. "I said get on your knees."

"I will do no such thing," she said and then as if she was talking to the trees, quietly she said, "Take him, Chon."

Clayton took another step and grinned. That was all the proof he needed.

Vanessa spoke louder the second time. "I said take him, Chon. It's gone south. Take him, now." Still nothing happened. The knocking of an old Ford engine caused Vanessa to turn and look behind her. Scabby Mike's pick-up was coming up the dirt road toward the compound. She turned back to Clayton but was beginning to look desperate. Mike pulled through the gate and cut the engine to the truck. He reached over the seat and opened the passenger door. Vanessa and Clayton both watched as Mike kicked Chon's lifeless body out into the gravel—a single, bloodless bullet hole above his left eye.

Clayton lifted his hands slightly and looked at Mike disappointed.

"What?" Mike said. "I didn't do it on purpose." Mike circled in front of his truck. "The little fucker just didn't want to cooperate."

Vanessa turned to Clayton and cold fire burned in her pale blue eyes. Her demeanor switched for a third time.

There she is. Clayton thought. *That's the real Vanessa. Finally.*

"You didn't have to kill him. He did nothing to you."

"Please. He would've killed me sure as day if Mike hadn't got to him first."

"You're a sheriff, Clayton. Not a murderer. You don't have to do this."

Clayton looked down at his shirt and then unpinned the silver star from above the left pocket. He tossed it in the dirt. "Not anymore," he said. "Not as of right now." He took a final step forward, putting the barrel of the Colt just inches from Vanessa's pale face. "Now get on your fucking knees before I blow them off you."

Vanessa's hands began to shake as she stood her ground and stared into Clayton's gray eyes, searching for an angle—for mercy. She found nothing. After a few seconds of silence, Scabby Mike produced his own gun and racked the slide. Finally, Clayton watched as Vanessa vanished and Bessie May Viner took her place. She looked humbled and weak, on the verge of tears, and then she did the one thing she had vowed never to do again since the day she left Boneville. She obeyed and dropped to her knees.

"Do it, then, you fuckin' hillbilly. Go ahead and do it, but don't think I'm going to beg you for anything."

Clayton got close enough to her to see the sweat on her forehead caking up her make-up. She looked down at the gravel. "I told my mother you were no different than the rest of them."

"You were right, and the only reason your mother is still breathing is because of what she did for Kate. Her last-ditch effort to make right all the things you did wrong."

Vanessa looked up at him, cocked her head and stared directly down the barrel of the .45. "You met my mother, right?"

"I did. She begged me to spare you. Why would she do that if she didn't think you were guilty?"

Vanessa didn't drop her stare. "Well then, let me ask you a question, detective. After spending time in the same room with my mother, do you really think she could've driven those back roads and found Kate, much less lift her unconscious into her car? She can barely lift herself out of a chair. Did it ever occur to you that she might've had help?" She cut her eyes at Chon's dead body as Mike dragged him across the gravel lot. She looked back down at the dirt and Clayton held his gun on her long enough for Mike to put Chon's body in the trunk of the BMW. Vanessa flinched when Mike slammed the hatch.

Clayton holstered the gun. "Go home, Vanessa."

She looked up at him. More resentful then relieved.

"It's over. Go home."

Vanessa didn't waste any time getting to her feet. "Just like that?"

"Just like that."

"And I don't have to worry about that one?" She pointed at Mike. "Or the big, ugly one that killed Tate coming after me once I leave?"

"No, but I want you to leave my county and don't ever come back."

Vanessa didn't need to be told again. She scrambled to the car, and turned the engine over before she even had the door closed. Mike moved to stand next to Clayton and they watched her circle the lot. Within seconds she was gone, leaving nothing but a cloud of dust.

Mike tucked his gun back into his pants. "You sure about this, Clayton?"

"I am."

"Even after what she did?"

"I am."

"She didn't hesitate calling her little buddy to kill you."

"I know."

Clayton walked back to the porch and picked up his cane. "What did you do with the gun you shot the little guy with?"

"It's with him in the trunk of her car."

"Is it traceable?"

"To him, maybe. It was his."

Clayton laughed a little and took a seat on the front steps.

"What?" Mike said.

"Nothing, man. Give me a minute." He laid his gun down on the porch next to him and took out his phone. He tapped in a number and it only rang once.

"Special Agent Finnegan."

"Hey, Charles."

"Well, hello there, Hayseed. I must've hit the white-boy lottery, getting to talk to you twice inside of a week. What's up?"

"I can't talk long. I just wanted to let you know I've got a line on your Fannin County murder."

"Do tell."

"The car you asked me about. I got a call from a buddy who said he just saw it up by Burroughs Summit."

"What buddy?"

"Does it matter?"

"I suppose not. You sure it's the same car?"

"Pretty sure."

"How long ago?"

"Just now. There are only three main arteries that head off Bull Mountain. If you can get your people in place, it'll be like shooting fish in a barrel. You can sew up Sheriff Kirby's murder"—Clayton smiled at Mike—"and who knows what else you'll find."

"I love it when you talk all cryptic like that, Hayseed."

"Well, just be quick about it or you're gonna miss the boat on this."

"Okay, I'm on it, right now."

"Wait, Charles, one more thing."

"Shoot."

"The job you mentioned last time we spoke—with the Atlanta office. Is that still on the table?"

"You're damn right it is."

"Are you free to talk about it anytime next week?"

"Clayton, I work for the GBI. I'm always free."

"Then it's a plan."

"What about your current gig? Do you think the fine, upstanding citizens of McFalls County can do without their fearless sheriff?"

Clayton looked over at the glint of silver in the gravel. "Well, seeing as I just quit, I reckon they'll have to."

"Well, hot damn, Hayseed. Dinner, then?"

"Only if you're buying."

"That's a deal."

"We'll talk again soon. Right now, you need to go clear a murder."

Clayton ended the call. Mike sat down on the steps next to him. "You were never going to kill her, were you?"

"No, Mike. I'm not a murderer, and believe me, life in prison will be worse than death for a woman like that."

Mike shook his head. "See? Halford was right to be afraid of you."

Mike made his way off the summit and Clayton watched him go. Once the old truck had disappeared from view, he walked to the Bronco and opened the back latch. He leaned his walking stick on the bumper and pushed the McFalls County-issued duffle bag full of plastic-wrapped wads of cash to the side. He lifted out two five-gallon jerry cans of gasoline and carried them one at a time to the porch. It took him about ten minutes to soak both the inside and outside of the house. It took less time than that for the Zippo he'd bought a few days ago at Pollard's to light up the trail he made out into the lot. There was no one around for miles, and he'd made sure that Mike would be busy enough with his share of the money to not have to come back. The house was far enough away from the wood line for it not to be a risk for a forest fire so there was no reason to even call County Fire when he was done. The parts of the old house that were still made of wood went up instantly and oddly, Clayton felt no remorse. He watched it burn long enough to make sure the job was thorough, and then tossed his cane into the back seat, cranked the Bronco and pointed it south toward McFalls Memorial. His whole life he'd been pulled in two directions. Would he be the man at the top of the mountain or the one crushed underneath it? Clayton had made the decision to be neither. He never even looked in the rearview mirror as he cleared the gate. He turned on the radio in the Bronco and let the sound of Waylon Jennings fill the inside of the truck as the highest point of Bull Mountain burned away.

EPILOGUE

Annette rifled through what was left of the cash she had, and separated out the eleven dollars she needed to pay her check. That left her with eighty-nine dollars and sixty cents. She felt like the money should've lasted more than two weeks. She also thought that, after two weeks, she'd be out of the state, but there she was. At least she was out of McFalls County. That thought thrilled her. She'd never even seen flat land before, but every time she began to feel good about herself she stopped it cold by thinking about her children. She nearly burst out crying again. She'd already done it twice since walking into the truck stop, and people had begun to stare. Although, maybe it was because of the way she looked. She hadn't taken a shower since those nice people who gave her a ride in Habersham bought her a room at the Motel-6. After the shower in that place, with those cute little bottles of fancy soap, she'd felt the cleanest she'd felt in years, but that was over a week ago, and now she felt like a filthy hippie. She was only a few days away from standing at an intersection holding a cardboard sign. Her hair was so greasy she had to pull it back in a bun to keep from scaring herself in the mirrors of gas-station bathrooms that had become her new method of hygiene.

"Should I take that?" the waitress said as she passed, pointing at the check and the cash on the table.

"Oh, yes, ma'am. Thank you."

"No problem, honey. I'll be right back with your change."

"Oh, no, that's okay. You can keep it."

The waitress, a large woman with blue eye shadow and the prettiest shade of bubblegum lipstick rested a hand on the money and gave Annette a sweet smile. "Are you sure, honey?" She leaned in a little. "Don't take this the wrong way, or nothing, I'm not trying to get into your business, but it looks like you could really use the extra money more than me. I don't mind you not leaving a tip. You weren't any trouble at all."

"Oh," Annette said. "Thank you. It has been a little rough lately. I haven't quite found the right path yet, if you know what I mean."

"Honey, some of us never do."

"I really like your lipstick," she blurted out without thinking. God, she missed wearing lipstick.

"Well, thank you, sugar." The waitress smiled. It was a kind smile. "I'll be right back." She picked up the cash and the check for Annette's breakfast, and started off, but

Annette reached out and stopped her. She kept her voice down. "I hate to ask, ma'am, but are those showers over there open for just anybody?" She pointed to the doors leading to the stalls.

"No, honey. I'm sorry. Those are just for our long-haulers. If they caught a pretty young thing like you in there, there ain't no tellin' what kinda Hades would break loose."

Annette suddenly felt embarrassed like she'd pressed her luck. "Oh. Okay. I was just wondering."

The big woman offered up another smile but this time it was weak and sad. The kind Annette was used to. The waitress walked off toward the register. After a few minutes she came back with a dollar and some loose change and set it on the table with her receipt. She leaned in and kept her voice down, too. "Listen," she said. "I told Hector to close off the showers for cleaning, so no one would go in there. So if you're quick about it, you can go clean yourself up if you want, but don't dilly-dally. I don't want Hector sniffing around and getting either of us in trouble."

"Oh, my god, thank you." Annette was quick about gathering her things.

"If you want to leave your stuff right there, I can watch it for you. Just make sure you take your cash with you. I can't be responsible for that. There's already some soap and shampoo and fresh towels in there, so you should be good to go."

"I don't know what to say, ma'am. Thank you."

"I suppose that'll be good enough."

Annette showered quickly and redressed in the same

clothes she'd been wearing. She slipped back out from behind the big yellow sign that said *closed for cleaning*, and only a few people pointed and whispered. She didn't care. She felt good. She went back to the booth, and collected the rest of her things; there wasn't much. A Dollar General bag with some clothes she'd found, a pair of flip-flops, a thin blanket, and the Gideon Bible she'd taken from the motel in Habersham. When she picked up the yellow plastic bag she saw something inside it she didn't recognize. She reached in and pulled out a tube of lipstick. It was the prettiest shade of bubblegum. She looked over at her waitress. The big woman winked at her, and Annette mouthed another thank you at her from across the diner. She scooped up the money and the receipt, and headed out the door. She hadn't made it a quarter of the way across the asphalt parking lot before a man's voice hollered out. "Hey, good lookin', where you headed?"

The kindness of the waitress inside had Annette feeling good about herself for the first time in two weeks, so she let herself answer. It felt strange talking to another man other than her husband without the fear of consequences, but she welcomed the feeling. She walked up to the side of the burgundy Peterbilt, where a handsome, middle-aged man with blue eyes and shaggy blond hair sat behind the wheel.

"I'm not quite sure where I'm going yet, mister. Why you asking?"

"Well, because wherever it is you're headed is a place I'd like to be headed myself."

"Is that right?"

"Yes, ma'am, it is."

"You promise to be nice to me?"

"I got no choice. That's the way my mama raised me."

Annette smiled. The blond man did, too. She liked his smile. The trucker motioned to the other side of the cab and she climbed in. She looked at herself in the huge side mirror, and pulled the lipstick out of her bag. She covered her chapped lips with pink bubblegum and blotted it on the receipt from the diner. She felt pretty again.

"So what's your name?" the man said, and stuck his hand out for her to shake. Annette suddenly felt that rush of sadness again. She didn't want to tell him her name. It would be like invoking a ghost, or maybe this man would know her husband. He might even try to take her back. She'd rather die than go back. The trucker sat there with his hand out and waited, but Annette didn't want to answer him. She didn't want to be Annette anymore. She felt ill and looked down at the receipt in her hands that was now covered with pink kisses. The waitress had written something on the back.

Good luck out there, honey.

—Twyla.

Annette felt renewed. She smiled at her new friend and shook his hand. "I'm Twyla," she said. "It's nice to meet you."

"The pleasure is all mine, Miss Twyla. I'm Joseph. Joseph Viner. How about we just start driving and see where the road takes us?"

ACKNOWLEDGEMENTS

My friend and fellow writer, Jordan Harper, wrote in the back of his extraordinary debut, *She Rides Shotgun*, that writing novels is hard. I think he was half right. Writing and revising and rewriting my own debut, *Bull Mountain* was a sheer and utter joy. Writing that book, without the slightest bit of expectation as to what would become of it, was probably the most fun I've ever had standing up. The part of me that agrees with Mr. Harper would want to amend his statement to "Writing a *second* novel is hard."

Because it was.

There's a huge difference between writing a story in the dark, creating a world all your own, word by word and page by page that no one may ever be a part of—and then trying to do it again in the bright light of day. The expectation and amount of people counting on you, from your publisher and editor, to your family and friends, all the way down to the readers you owe everything to, is similar to living inside a pressure cooker set to eleven. The transition from being a firefighter and part-time short story writer to published novelist being ushered around Italy and compared to master writers like Steinbeck and

Mario Puzo can be, to put it lightly, pretty damn jarring. I got lost in the dark quite a few times during that journey and I owe a massive debt of gratitude to Nat Sobel and Judith Weber, for turning on the light, never giving up, and talking me off the ledge a lot more than once. I love you both, and I always will.

The following people also helped me believe that not only could I do this job, but I could also continue to have fun doing it; *The Southern Independent Booksellers Association*, and all the wonderful bookshop owners, that hand sold my first novel and made my career possible. The independent bookstore is one of the last magical places on earth and I'm blessed to have met so many. Go and find one out in your hometown and see what I'm talking about—you'll never want to leave. *The International Thriller Writers Association* for taking me in and making me one of their own. There is no elite club, folks. These people love what they do and make me love it even more just by being around them. Matt Blackwell from Barnes & Noble—AKA Thunder Smoke Mandando— my friend and easily one of the kindest people on earth. Reba Brown, Kat McCall and Steven Uhles—for forming such an unlikely and beautiful alliance. David Hutchison at the Book Tavern, Chuck Box—for taking the time to help me figure out the road map to where I really wanted to be. Reed Farrel Coleman—just for being Reed. Damn, you're cool. Zach Steele of the Broadleaf Writer's Association and Joe Davich at Georgia Center For The Book for bringing Georgia into the light. Chuck Reece and The Bitter Southerner. Ellen and Gary at The Foxtale Bookshoppe and Nic Cheetham, for the polish—you were right, the last line fucking sings.

And finally, for all the women in my life that I wrote and dedicated this book to. My mother, Doreen—my wife, Neicy—and my daughters, Talia, Ivy, and Olivia. You are my pride, and I'm *Lucky* to have you.

I can't wait to see all you out there on the road.

BRIAN PANOWICH
East Georgia
10/2017